HE'S
WITH
THE
BAND

HE'S
WITH
THE
BAND

JULIE STONE

Entangled Publishing, LLC
10940 S Parker Rd
Suite 327
Parker, CO 80134
rights@entangledpublishing.com

August is an imprint of Entangled Publishing, LLC.

Edited by Stacy Abrams
Cover design by Elizabeth Turner Stokes
Cover photography by conrado, Viorel Sima, and Tsuguliev/
Shutterstock

Manufactured in the United States of America

First Edition January 2022

This book is dedicated to anyone out there working towards their dream. It isn't too late. You aren't too old. There is no expiration date on your happily ever after.

The lights were bright and flashing to the point I couldn't see past the first row, not that I would have tried to look if it was possible. All I could think to see was the man dancing with me. The man who had pulled me up on stage, who held my hand to his lips as the driving beat sent me tumbling back to the girl I'd been the last time I'd seen him. Though, back then I'd never captured his attention.

It was a rush, more than I was prepared for. And it had my mind spinning with what-ifs and could-have-beens. Of the choices I'd made, and the life that might have been mine.

But I'm getting ahead of myself...

Chapter One

It was hard for me to believe we were finally here. D-Day.

Divorce.

Jack, as usual, was way overdressed in his gray wool suit and French cuffed shirt. Beads of sweat had started to gather on his forehead and he twisted at his cufflinks as we sat on a bench outside the courthouse waiting on my lawyer. I was actually shocked he was willing to sit here, on the same bench, and wait with me. All three of those things went against everything Jack, my soon-to-be ex-husband, stood for.

He didn't sit. Or wait. Or, lately, acknowledge my existence. I represented failure, another thing Jack did not do. If he was being honest, he was as shocked as I was we were here, but for different reasons.

We had been married for just shy of twenty-two years. He'd swooped into my life full of pretty words and promises and the ability to kiss all my sense away. Unfortunately, the only thing real about the guy were those kissing skills. For all his promises of a beautiful life, what he delivered was a man incapable of taking care of himself.

Turns out, while my twenty-year-old self was marrying for stability, he was marrying to replace his mother. And her housekeeping, and her cooking, and her general way of always being put together and doing as she was told. I was none of those things, no matter how hard I'd tried to be.

"We're due in court in ten minutes," Jack said, checking his watch for the hundredth time. His voice was terse, as it so often was with me. Letting me know that whatever I was doing was inconveniencing him. This wasn't new—in fact, it had been part of our relationship from the start. I just chose to ignore it.

"He said he was close," I offered brightly. I refused to get drawn into some sort of tit for tat. His lawyer, who had been on time, was waiting outside the courtroom to make our excuses in case mine really didn't show. Unlike Jack, who had connections and found the best, most competent lawyer, I'd found mine on the internet. Taking family portraits at a franchise studio didn't lend itself to rubbing elbows with the best and the brightest legal minds.

Jack turned to me and for a second I thought he was going to put his hand on my knee. "Maybe it's a sign, Campbell. Him not showing up. Maybe it's the universe trying to give you one last chance to come to your senses." He leaned forward just a hair, but enough that I pulled back slightly. The thought of it made my blood pressure spike and I pursed my lips together so as not to blurt out that there wasn't a snowman's chance in hell.

Also, since when did Jack believe in signs?

"I'm here! Sorry I'm late!"

I had to squelch my cry of relief. I'd never been so glad to see anyone in my whole life. I stood to shake Steve's hand, and Jack shifted away from me.

Steve, my lawyer, ignored my outstretched hand and pulled me into a completely inappropriate hug.

"Are you drunk?" I asked as I pulled back. He smelled like the floor of a dive bar—stale beer and cigarettes.

"Maybe? Had quite a night. Slept in my suit, but new tie!" He held it out and waved it a bit like a flag. For sure he was drunk.

Jack sighed dramatically in disgust. "It didn't take you long to fall right back to your old life, a lawyer like that," he muttered just loud enough for me to hear.

And there it was.

My *old life*. The one I'd left in the dust when Jack proposed, thinking myself saved from the uncertainty, saved from my worst instincts, saved from people like Steve.

But Steve, with his rumpled suit and apologetic smile, had been nothing but kind to me. I looked from him to Jack and all I could think was that Steve had probably had more fun on his epic Tuesday night than Jack had allowed himself to have in fifteen years.

I shot Jack a look and then looped my hand through Steve's arm. "Plenty of time," I said and let him lead the way toward the courthouse and the start of my new life.

"Your honor, as you can plainly see, I have been the primary breadwinner over the duration of our marriage—my wife's hobby job was but a small contribution. As she is the one who has brought these proceedings, I must ask that I be released from the obligation of supporting her further."

The sound of his voice, this particular tone, made me reflexively sit up taller, check to see that only the top two buttons of my blouse were undone, to smooth back my hair and make sure nothing was out of place. It was that last part that reminded me I didn't have to do as I was told anymore. My hair was down and untamed. My red waves hung unrestrained down my back and I went from anxious to angry in a hot second.

I leaned in and whispered in Steve's ear. "Hobby job? Does he mean the one he insisted I take instead of pursuing my career as a photojournalist?" I was seething.

Steve patted my hand to calm me and switched his angle to reply. "He also shouldn't be speaking at all, that's what his lawyer is for."

Yeah. There was little to no chance Jack wasn't going to speak. That would be ceding control to someone else. Even if he was paying that someone else and that someone else was an expert in his field. No one knew better than Jack.

Except, apparently, this judge.

"Mr. Spencer, there is no need for your personal pleas in my courtroom. Unless you're called upon, your voice in these proceedings belongs to your lawyer. Do you understand?"

"But your honor"—Jack flashed what I knew to be his most charming smile—"I just wanted to make sure you understood my perspective."

The judge, unlike most people, was not moved by Jack. "A court of law is not the place for individual perspective. If the court wishes to hear from you, we will let you know."

It was almost worth the drama I'd gone through during arbitration to see that smile disappear and hear someone have authority over Jack. The funny part about all of this was he had no reason to be pleading his case anyway—we'd already negotiated down to the last fork in our drawer (which, by the way, he'd gotten).

I'd already agreed to take no spousal support in exchange for keeping the house. Though, I didn't really want that either. Too many memories of a life controlled entirely by the man who sat at the opposing table. I'd come to realize in the months we'd been separated that I felt lonelier sitting next to him than I did when I was actually alone.

Steve had argued against my concessions, telling me by law I was entitled to more, but I didn't want more. I just wanted out. When I'd married Jack, that control had seemed like stability and love to a girl who grew up with neither. Structure was a comfort. But over the years, from our friends, to my job, to the clothes I wore, Jack decided it all. And comfort changed to control.

"Your honor, I appreciate your candor. I just want to say one last thing…" What that might have been, we'd never know, as the judge pounded his gavel to quiet the courtroom. He declared us divorced upon signature of the papers before him. And then he turned to exit the courtroom, but not before giving me a sympathetic look as if to say he didn't blame me one bit.

"That's it?" I asked Steve.

"That's it. You're officially divorced! Uh…congrats?"

Chapter Two

In the end, I walked out of that courtroom feeling pretty much the same as when I'd walked in, with the added bonus of a sense of relief. I didn't even have time to dig into it, though: I had to hurry off to an appointment at my so-called "hobby job" at the Portrait Hut, which was now my only source of income.

It was my least favorite kind of appointment—toddler holiday photos. For one, it was summer, so that kid would way rather be splashing in his kiddie pool than putting on an argyle vest and corduroys (the standard outfit for his demographic) and two, the neurotic Pinterest mother would hang over my shoulder suggesting better ways for me to get the shot that would fulfill her "vision."

But at least it was a distraction.

I unlocked the door of my studio, which was a pretty generous description of the space. It was little more than a remodeled office in a strip mall...and it wasn't even mine and it was certainly not a hut. I was just the staff photographer. I rarely saw the owner, who cared way less about photography than about the bottom line.

My backdrops and props were all limited to what the company sent each season. So Mama Pinterest could press all she wanted about having a "unique look"—that wasn't going to happen here. Most days it reminded me of that sad little photo studio tucked away in the back of Sears in the eighties. That magical place where families in matching outfits gathered too close together in front of a tan backdrop—a color that flattered no one—all for the sake of posterity.

I had never sat for one, since marking any sort of occasion wasn't really my mom's style. But I do recall my best friend in eighth grade bemoaning the chambray shirt and khaki pant combo that her mother had chosen for theirs. It might have been the first time in my life I was thankful that my family wasn't picture perfect.

After all, who rolls their pants up and goes barefoot in a Sears?

As much as I loathed the work, it still put a camera in my hand for money. That's what I told myself on the days the soulless work really got to me.

I flipped on the lights and pulled the Christmas backdrop to the front of the ones I had hanging on rings in the tiny space. Then I pulled out the winter/holiday props. Those were the only spots of flexibility. I'd broken the rules and not sent back last year's, so at least there was some variety. It was the most rebellious thing I'd done in years.

If my younger self could have weighed in on what I counted as rebellion now, she would have rolled her eyes and probably taken a can of spray paint to it.

Mama Bear was late. Par for the course, really. Once upon a time, I wouldn't have even thought this counted as photography. Would have looked down my nose at any photographer who sold out to do cookie-cutter portraits. Once upon a time, I actually considered myself an artist.

I glanced at the gingerbread house backdrop and shook

my head.

This was not art.

A sense of melancholy washed over me. Not for my marriage, but for the person I'd let get swallowed up by Jack and his ideas of what a perfect life should look like. A real artist didn't want perfect. And yet I'd let myself be gaslit into a belief that perfect was the only measure of success. Why had I given up on myself so easily?

Before I could answer, my appointment stormed in, screaming toddler in her arms.

"I'm so sorry, Beckham is a bit upset about this whole thing," she said breathlessly. "But I just know you'll work your magic and get him smiling in no time!"

I had to force myself not to roll my eyes at this.

My "toddler magic" was essentially bribing with food that wouldn't stain. And I was fresh out of organic non-gluten GMO-free, so this should go well.

"Why don't you set him down there in front of the backdrop and see which of the props seem to engage him, and we'll go from there," I said as brightly as I possibly could. My portrait voice, I called it.

She scowled slightly, waving her hands at the setup. "I'm not sure this goes with my vision."

And there it was. The V-word. If I had a dollar for every time I heard the word "vision" in my line of work, I wouldn't have to work, or so the saying goes.

I turned and walked toward where my camera was already on its tripod. "As we discussed, the company dictates what backdrops are used this time of year. They like uniformity, branding. Your holiday card is our best advertising!" Portrait voice again.

She sighed heavily but did as she was told. Young Beckham quieted down as he looked wide-eyed at his new surroundings. And then let out a squeal as he reached for the oversize stuffed candy canes that littered the floor.

Snap. Snap. Snap.

I looked through the viewfinder. Pure delight on that baby's face, even stuffed into his ridiculous old-man-looking outfit. Yeah, I was that good. After twenty-odd years at this, I should be. The mom even offered a coo of appreciation.

Thirty minutes later, he had made his way through the props, eaten his body weight in Goldfish, and just as his mother was insisting I try a more "sophisticated" shot of him sitting on a miniature bench (seriously, did she think he was actually seventy-five?), he filled his diaper.

"Well, I think we have some really great shots, and I believe Beckham has moved on to other things."

She leaned over my shoulder to look through the viewfinder. "I just really wanted some portraits of him on the bench."

And so we sat Beckham on the bench.

Which he obviously did not like. A full diaper does not make for comfortable seating. He stood, his toothy smile replaced by one of discomfort. Years of doing this told me that we weren't going to get anything close to a usable photo. But the customer was always right, or so I told myself. I snapped a few more as the baby's face went from discomfort to pure frown. The mom started clapping and saying his name, trying to, what? Distract him? Make him smile? Scare the shit out of him? Too late, that had already happened.

Pun intended.

I glanced at the spectacle she was making, and that's why I missed young Beckham sticking his hands down the back of his diaper and coming out full. He shrieked. His mom shrieked. I looked over just in time to see him start wiping his fingers on my bench, and then when that didn't clean them off, down the front of his argyle vest.

"Oh my GOD!" his mother said, scrambling for the wipes

she'd used to disinfect every inch of that bench before she'd let Beckham get anywhere near it.

That outfit was not coming back from this. Our photo shoot was over.

She scooped him up, holding him away from her, and raced to the changing table I had long ago set up in the far corner of the room. It must have been bad, because she let out another "Oh my God!"

I busied myself spraying down the bench, thanking the good Lord myself that Beckham hadn't cleaned his hands on the gingerbread backdrop. Disinfecting *that* would have cleared my books for at least a week's worth of appointments. Though, when I thought about it, that didn't seem all that bad.

"I'll send you the proofs once I get them edited. There will be a link with your discount code in the email, so you should be all set." I had to yell at this point because young Beckham was not enjoying his cleanup.

"And what's the policy if there isn't one that's usable?" she asked, the baby, naked but for his fresh diaper, on her hip as she walked toward the front door.

It was a standard question that I got often, but it still made me so sad. Her baby was adorable. I'd love to sit his naked self in front of that backdrop and hand him a plate of cookies, showing off his delightful chubby thighs. But that wasn't what Pinterest was pushing this year. I sighed.

"We'll have to book another session."

She started to argue the price, but Beckham took it up a notch, now swatting at her with his tiny fists, his cries forming the word "home," over and over. So she just nodded and walked out.

The dirty diaper was sitting in a ball on the changing table.

Apparently her "vision" didn't include cleaning up after herself.

Chapter Three

Just as I was slipping off the rubber gloves, the diaper taken care of, my phone rang.

"Campbell! I got wine! I got champagne! What else do we need for tonight?" Marissa, my dearest friend, singsonged.

I glanced at my calendar. Wednesday. On Wednesdays Jack and I had pork chops and watched *Antiques Roadshow* on PBS. Jack loved that show for the people who thought they had forgotten treasure and found it was worth next to nothing.

"I can't. It's a weeknight. Jack and I…"

"What the actual hell are you talking about? There is no Jack and you anymore, unless he pulled a fast one and got the date moved?" She sounded panicked.

Oh my God. She was right.

I was no longer beholden to Jack and his routines and schedules. I could do anything I wanted on a Wednesday now.

"Holy shit. I'm just so used to the schedule, *his* schedule. Holy shit."

"You scared the crap out of me! Are we going out?

Staying in? How are we celebrating the first night of the rest of your life?"

"What if...we didn't make a plan," I ventured, feeling a new lightness in my chest. "Come over and let's just see where the night takes us?"

Marissa literally gasped through the phone. "Campbell Spencer without a plan? Do I even know you anymore?"

"Cavett," I corrected. "It's Campbell Cavett again."

"GAH! You took your name back? I didn't know that was happening. Campbell Cavett sounds like a wild child!"

Wild child. I like the sound of that. The memory of that.

"Seven o'clock, my place," I said.

"See you then!" Marissa replied like she was taking a direct order and then hung up decisively.

This day was officially over, so I locked up and headed for my car, a gray four-door sedan with beige interior. High safety ratings but zero sex appeal. This car was as boring as the NPR station that Jack had programmed first on the radio.

I unlocked the door and climbed inside, remembering the last car I'd picked out for myself: a used VW Bug, sky blue. I'd paid cash, babysitting money—my life savings at the time. It had been old and unreliable. The passenger window sometimes just fell straight down for no reason, and it didn't always start. But it was effortlessly, undeniably cool. And it started when I'd needed it to, when I'd hit the road and left my dysfunctional, fighting parents in their dirty falling-down house.

I'd loved that car and what it had done for me. It had gotten me on the open road. I wondered how many miles I'd traveled in it, my eyes trained on the tour bus taillights in front of me. The corners of my mouth lifted at the memory.

Inside the sedan, I flipped down the visor and looked at myself hard in the tiny mirror, trying to recognize any part of myself. The past twenty-odd years were literally one boring blur. And even though I felt unrecognizable from the inside, the outside was vaguely familiar. Same red hair, same ice blue eyes, a few extra lines around my eyes and mouth. Forty-two. How was that possible? I sighed. Maybe, just maybe, Campbell Cavett could bring back the spark Campbell Spencer had let be snuffed out?

I turned the ignition and reached for the radio. Once, a long time ago, music was the thing that mattered most to me. A place to put everything I felt: happiness, sadness. Confusion, anger. There was a song for all of it. It was my therapy.

It directed my emotions like nothing before or since, and had always been there, giving me just what I needed, when I needed it. I punched the scan button and left it up to the universe to decide just what song would play me home. And when it landed on a driving beat and a scorching guitar, the tension of the day melted away.

Campbell Cavett sounds like a wild child.

Oh, Marissa. You have no idea.

There was cake. Chocolate with some sort of malted buttercream icing. "*Straight outta Marriage!*" it said in a gothic-looking yellow font.

"A celebration should always have cake," Marissa had declared and handed it to me when she walked in. "I know we're seeing how the night plays out, but cake is never the wrong call."

Marissa was the best, the most thoughtful human being on the planet. She was single, too, though not by choice. Her husband had passed away almost thirteen years ago, leaving her with a daughter to raise. That and the high bar he'd set in the romance department had kept her single and down to earth.

I was happy to see her, happier still to see the cake, and to not be alone with my thoughts anymore. She was right, this was worthy of a celebration. I needed to focus my energy there, and not on the fact that it took me so many years to figure out I missed myself. There was wine, too. Pinot grigio.

It was so ridiculously stereotypical middle-aged woman, but let's be honest…it didn't stop this forty-two-year-old woman from throwing it down.

"To new beginnings!" Marissa exclaimed.

White wine and cliché toasts. This was officially the opposite of wild.

I lifted my glass to receive her well wishes. Marissa was my best friend, and always well intentioned, so her heart was in the right place. I took a healthy swallow of my wine and closed my eyes tight.

Marissa laid her hand on my arm. "Are you okay? Would you rather this was more of a wake than a celebration?"

"Hardly," I replied. "I'm ecstatic. Over the moon, all the usual things one says when they are recently divorced from a man who loved the idea of who he turned them into, and not the person they ever actually were."

Marissa raised her eyebrows. "Man, that's deep."

"I just can't stop wondering where I'd be if I hadn't fallen for Jack's particular brand of bullshit," I said.

"I think it's normal for you to feel like that."

"I let so much of my life fly by without paying attention. So many New Year's resolutions that this was the year I took control and then did nothing to change a bit of it. This isn't where I wanted to be, or what I wanted to be doing! No little girl is out there dreaming of this job, these clothes, this house. I mean, look at this place! It's so…so…*beige*!" I was practically yelling while I waved my arms around to include my entire living space in my outrage.

Actually, the room was a very nice shade of beige—"Rice Cracker" it was called. But beige was a metaphor for what I was trying to get across. This life had no excitement, no color. I was an artist, a photographer, I saw things in color and lines and shapes and shadows. But there was none of that here. And I had to wonder if there was not much left in me either.

Marissa shrugged. "I think you were just trying to be in love."

"A person shouldn't have to *try* to be in love. Not with a person or with their life. That's something that should just be." I took a drink of my wine.

"Don't beat yourself up. Jack is an ass. But he's attractive in an uptight way and he can be very charming. So you were fooled. But you're not anymore. You signed at the 'X' and now you can move on to better things."

She was right. What was the point in looking back? Unless it was way back…

I stood, ignoring the way both my knees cracked when they extended, and crossed the family room to my newly acquired record player. Jack, of course, had taken his state-of-the-art sound system, but I'd been happy to replace it. Vinyl was so much better. How had I forgotten? I grabbed the album on top of the stack and put it on.

The song started, and the crackle of the needle only made it a more authentic trip down memory lane.

One. Two. A one, two, three, four.

"Oh my Gawd! Is this Golden Tiger?" Marissa crossed the room, grabbing hold of my shoulders and spinning me around. Her ability to recognize the song from just the count-in cemented her place in my heart.

"I *loved* them!" She threw her arms up in the air, swaying with the beat.

I was never very good at hello, but baby, you make me want to try.

The voice that launched pretty much every fantasy of my youth—Davis Scott. I let myself succumb to the song. Singing along, remembering. That summer, my Golden Tiger summer.

My heart squeezed.

I crossed the room to where Jack had left his liquor (which was only for show and guests anyway), pulled out a bottle of whiskey, and poured two shots. I handed one to Marissa, who took it skeptically. White wine and margarita Mondays were as crazy as she got.

"Cheers to the good years!" I said and threw back the whiskey.

It burned, like whiskey always does, but this time it felt good. Like a cleansing.

I poured another.

"I thought I'd feel different when the divorce was final. Like I had a new life. But the thing is, it's all still the same. Same ridiculous beige house, same uninspiring job I hate. Just no Jack."

Marissa did her shot, throwing her head of jet-black curls back in dramatic fashion.

"No offense, but your job *is* pretty terrible. All those annoying parents and screaming kids."

I nodded. My ears felt warm. "Don't forget about the sulky teenagers. They might be worse, yours excluded of course."

"Of course. Sasha is never sulky." She rolled her eyes.

"You know, once upon a time, I wanted to be an actual photographer. I had talent, too. Or so I was told."

"You should quit your job," Marissa said, a slight whiskey slur to her words, but to my fuzzy brain, it sounded like a good idea.

I nodded in agreement. "I totally should."

The song switched to a pounding beat. The bass coming

in low and hard, and then the guitar. I turned the volume up so loud the pictures on the walls shook.

By the time the vocals started, Marissa and I were shout-singing along and dancing. Jesus, how long had it been since I danced? We made it the whole song, collapsing on the couch as it transitioned into a ballad. My heart was pounding.

"I cannot believe I still know all the words!" she said breathlessly.

"I don't think I could ever forget them."

I poured us another shot, the booze spilling out onto the cream carpet I despised.

"If I sold this crappy house, I could quit my job and live off the money until I figured out what's next!" I exclaimed. "Clean slate."

Marissa nodded her encouragement. "Now you're talking. Take control of your own destiny!" We upended our shots, slamming the glasses down on the Pottery Barn coffee table in—you guessed it—beige as though it were a water-stained bar top.

I let my head fall back on the couch, embracing the way the whiskey was somehow able to make all the harsh edges of my life smooth. I hummed along to the song, grasping at the fine threads of that perfect summer. I turned the album over in my hands, so familiar but so out of context in these uniform walls. Destiny, that was a word I hadn't thought about in a long, long time.

"I think I read somewhere that they're launching a reunion tour, to celebrate the twentieth anniversary of their first tour," Marissa mumbled.

My head rolled in her direction. "Who?"

She blinked. Slowly and then again.

"Golden Tiger. Something about going back to their roots. Before the stadium tours. To reconnect with their fans."

The burn in my throat caught fire in my cheeks. Their first tour was the one I followed.

When I was someone else.

She fumbled for her phone, typing with her thumbs and then holding it directly in front of my face.

My eyes struggled to focus. I reached for her hand to steady it and bring it closer.

There he was, Davis Scott. His mouth pulled to one side in his infamous smile. They were all there. Tony. Rex. Alex. Slightly older, but no less attractive, their arms slung around each other's shoulders in that casual cool way. I felt my insides go weak. The headline screamed at me from the screen.

GOLDEN TIGER IS COMING BACK TO THE STAGE

The band that showed the world how to rock and roll is headed back on the road. They all but disappeared without so much as a smoke machine send-off. But they're back. Gone are the giant stadium tours— instead, they're bringing it back to the venues where they got their start. Playing the small clubs and bars that made them famous for their intimate but raucous shows. Do they still have that magic that set them apart, and can they measure up to the bands they inspired? Time will tell, but shows are already selling out, so clearly their fans are thrilled by the news.

Marissa pulled her hand away and poured us another drink.

"If they have a show anywhere near us, we should totally go," she slurred, handing me my glass.

I wasn't the sort of person who believed in signs, at least Jack and I had had that in common, but as I stared at those familiar faces, the taste of whiskey in my mouth, a new song began.

If you can't love yourself, at least come let me love you.

Baby, don't you know? I can love your life right, when you've done it all so wrong.

I picked up her phone, still open to the article. The first show was in Chicago, only a short five hours from our quaint little Iowa existence.

"Yes. Yes, we should!" I replied and threw down my shot.

Chapter Four

The rest of the night was a blur of more whiskey, more music, and poor food choices. Or at least that's the story I put together when I woke up in my bed, wearing an oversize T-shirt and my leopard-print pajama pants (my first post-Jack purchase. He never would have allowed such a wild thing). The whiskey bottle was on its side and empty next to a bag of Doritos on my bedside table, bright orange crumbs ground into the carpet.

I laid my pounding head back onto the pillow and tried to piece it all together.

Golden Tiger. Reunion Tour.

Had we bought tickets? How much had I told Marissa about that summer? It was murky, but even as drunk as I had been, I couldn't imagine sharing every last detail.

Or had I?

Something big lingered in the back of my hungover brain, hiding behind the fog, but I couldn't pull it through. Maybe I'd confessed it all, but it didn't feel like I had.

From across the room I could hear my phone ringing and

ringing before mercifully stopping. The ding of a voicemail, and then the pinging of a text. I was used to this. Jack was always relentless in his need to talk to me. The ringing started again.

"For the love of all that is holy, please make that stop!" I heard a voice say.

I hadn't noticed that Marissa was next to me in my king-size bed. I got up and stumbled across the room, kicking an empty wineglass as I went. I reached the phone, sending whoever was calling to voicemail before checking the texts.

It seems clear from your previous texts that it is in our best interests to part ways at this time.

Shit.

Shit. Shit. Shit.

"Marissa. Did I text my boss last night?"

She gave a bit of a moan. "So much whiskey."

Not the answer I was looking for.

I thumbed back through the texts, and holy shit, there was my answer. A very short and to the point text saying that I was bidding adieu to anything I considered soul crushing.

Starting, apparently, with my job.

"Shit," I said, this time out loud, panic starting to rise. I didn't disagree with the sentiment, but it seemed rash. I was newly single. I had a mortgage to pay.

My phone dinged with another voicemail. Slightly terrified, I hit the button for it to play on speaker and was pleasantly surprised to hear my friend Sam's voice.

"Campbell! I am so excited that you're going to unload that house! I already have a buyer in mind! A newly married couple looking to get into that area! Hoping to show it this afternoon! Squeal! I am so thrilled for you! The market is hot!"

"Way too much enthusiasm," Marissa groaned, then

rolled over and grabbed her own phone, no doubt checking to make sure *she* hadn't made any life-altering texts or calls herself last night.

Oh my God. What had I done?

"We bought tickets for opening night of the Golden Tiger tour. It's tomorrow night. In Chicago?" Marissa sounded confused, but to me, it was the one thing in all of this that made any sense.

No job. No mortgage. No responsibility.

Taking it back to where it all began...

• • •

Marissa thought that I was having a bit of an emotional breakdown, and maybe I was. After all, I was forty-two, childless, newly divorced, unemployed, and potentially homeless. Truly the opposite of where societal norms told me I should be in my life at this point.

But I'd never felt better.

She kept repeating how illogical and irresponsible it was to go to the concert. Yet she was standing in my driveway, surrounded by suitcases and coolers, surveying my trunk as we packed it.

Sure, I should probably be looking for a new job, or begging for my old one back. And yes, looking for another place to live or calling off the listing of my house was the responsible thing to do. But all I could think about was getting to Chicago for opening night of the Golden Tiger tour. I felt untethered from who I'd been all these years—and it wasn't just because of my hangover.

I needed an escape, or at the very least a break from the person I'd been living as for the past twenty-two years. I needed some damn perspective. Responsibility could wait a few days.

Marissa, on the other hand, needed some convincing.

"You aren't the one who imploded your life in one drunken night," I argued. "What do you have to lose?"

"I'm just torn about what sort of friend I'm supposed to be in this situation. Do I point out how insane this all is and encourage you to rethink your choices? Or do I jump in the car and cheer you on for living your life to the fullest?"

I shrugged. Even in running away to a rock concert, Marissa had shown some responsibility—finding a place for her daughter, Sasha, to spend the night and asking her friend Drew to run her coffee shop for the weekend. I, on the other hand, was jazzed about kicking my responsibilities to the curb. Clearly. And frankly, where had being responsible really gotten me for the past two decades?

"What if I let you try and talk some sense into me while we drive to Chicago? Come on. You love Golden Tiger. You want to go! This mess will still be here when I get back, and besides, you already bought the *nonrefundable* tickets."

I don't know which argument worked, but I was guessing it was the nonrefundable part. She closed the trunk and climbed into my car.

"Hold on! I have to grab something," I yelled, running back into the house. My camera bag, which held both my newest digital camera and my old film camera, was sitting on the floor of the hall closet.

If I was going to try and capture even a bit of the person I'd been, I was going to need them.

Back at the car, I climbed behind the wheel and tossed the bag into the back seat. Then I threw the sedan into reverse before Marissa could change her mind. She didn't say one more negative word, just cranked up the radio, and we sang and laughed all the way to Chicago.

Chapter Five

And now here we were.

At the opening night of the Golden Tiger Reunion Tour.

Never in my wildest dreams could I have imagined I'd be doing this again. Memory lane was not really something I'd let myself wander down when I was married. But hearing that album the other night had opened the floodgates, and now those memories dominated my thoughts. Even with the stage set in front of me, the huge, stalking Golden Tiger emblem placed prominently above the drum set, the smell of cheap booze and old cigarettes hanging like a memory in the air, I still had a hard time believing it was really happening.

I'd pinch myself, but I didn't think the Spanx I was wearing would give me the inch I'd need.

I raised my camera and took a shot of the setup. And then one of the crowds. Frankly I was shocked no one had stopped me from bringing my equipment in. But the security team seemed a bit distracted by the throngs of women streaming through the gates. Maybe with cell phone cameras, nobody cared anymore? Man, back in the day, having a camera at a concert was enough to get you bounced right out, no matter how short your skirt was. Unless, of course, you had a press pass.

"To Golden Tiger!" Marissa exclaimed, holding up her red Solo cup, then draining it and crushing it in her hand. I did the same, laughing almost deliriously from the rush of alcohol and pure adrenaline.

We were at Kingston's Mines, a club on the Northside of Chicago. The energy was palpable, and my body hummed with it. This was the same cheap beer this place had served for generations. No fancy microbrews here, and I was glad. Authenticity was important, especially when you were trying to forget your present life by way of revisiting your past.

Guilty.

"I cannot believe we paid this much, and we aren't even on the floor!" Marissa yelled over the whistles and claps.

I shrugged. "Who's saying we aren't going to make it to the floor?" She raised an eyebrow at me. The Campbell she knew would never suggest such a thing. But that Campbell wasn't who she'd come to the concert with—not by a long shot.

Marissa and I had met when she'd opened up her coffee shop. At the time, I was doing a bit of freelance work and needed some promotional pictures for my portfolio. We clicked almost immediately, a friendship based on caffeine and sarcasm and telling the other one exactly what we thought. Except about my past.

Not that it was a secret, really. It just didn't fit into who I was trying to make myself be, for Jack. Most days, those memories felt like they belonged to someone else anyway. And so they stayed mine and mine alone.

I glanced around. The crowd was a mix of nostalgia seekers and hard-core fans. I didn't know where I fell on that scale, but I did match the majority-female demographic.

The band always had a strong female following. Though now they all looked a little older, more haggard, their thick black eyeliner smudged but not intentionally. A few decades will do that to anyone.

Wait. Was that how I looked?

I tugged at my distressed miniskirt and shifted my black T-shirt off my shoulder a bit self-consciously. I'd felt edgy when I put it on, but now it felt a little desperate. Like I was trying too hard to be someone I wasn't or push myself back in time to someone I used to be. And if I was being honest, I had to push a little more than I remembered to even get this skirt on.

A smidge of the excitement for the night drained out of me. I leaned over to tell Marissa I was going to run to the car and grab a jacket, but then the lights went out.

The reaction from the crowd was deafening. Marissa grabbed my hand and screamed.

It was as if that beat was somehow connected to my pulse. I felt it as much as heard it. And I was gone.

Lost in the rush that is hearing live music.

The bass guitar joined in, pounding deep in my chest, then the lead guitar commanded me to sway and stomp my feet. The music took control of every part of me. The lights flashed to the beat, swirling in an uptick, gaining energy. And then at the center of it all, Davis Scott appeared at his mic stand.

His voice was as crystal clear as ever and in perfect harmony with the guys singing backup. His opening line barely out, he strutted his way back and forth at the front of the stage. My heart ached at the sound of his voice as it sucked me back in time, filling me with what I now knew was longing.

And I wasn't alone. There wasn't a person in the club who wasn't under his spell. How had I forgotten how this felt? To be part of a crowd but having my own intimate experience.

It was magic.

As the opening song came to a close, the video screens on either side of the stage filled with Davis, his sly half smile on his face as he took a drink from a beer he had sitting on the ground by his mic stand.

"Thank you! It's nice to know you remember us after all this time. We sure remember you. Especially all you ladies!"

The way he held that last word, well, I am in no way proud to admit it did something to me, but it sure as hell did. Like an electric charge to my core.

I screamed. Marissa screamed. Every woman in that club screamed.

And I wasn't shocked to see a few bras fly through the first rows and land on the stage.

Sadly, they looked more Playtex Eighteen Hour than Victoria's Secret. Was it the thought that counted when it came to undergarment flinging? Davis didn't seem to notice, or mind. He had us all right where he wanted us.

The slow beat of a power ballad started.

I remember the you of yesterday, but will you remember me tomorrow?

The screen changed from Davis to old photos of the band. The exact sort of nostalgia a reunion tour called for, so kudos to the marketing department. There were photos of giant crowds and lines outside of venues. Their glory days, and, I would venture, the glory days of everyone in this club. Women in Golden Tiger shirts and ripped jeans, giant hair and too much eye shadow. I recognized some of their faces. A lot of their faces, actually.

I held my breath, terrified and hopeful. Wondering.

And then there I was, my red hair like flames around my face. A sultry pout on my lips, standing with a group of girls in similar poses. It was gone before I could process it.

The memory of that photo came rushing back to me. For one amazing summer, I had been a Golden Tiger groupie. Or, at least, she had been. I wasn't even close to being that badass girl anymore. But it was proof she had existed.

I hadn't conjured her as I slugged through my adult life, trying to fold myself into something I wasn't. Too stubborn to admit, even to myself, that I'd made a mistake. It was good to see her; until now, I hadn't acknowledged how much I missed her. Any smidgeon of self-doubt about being here, about how much we'd spent or how I felt in my outfit, was gone.

I glanced at Marissa. Had she picked me out in that picture? It didn't seem like she had, which wasn't a surprise. Nothing about the Campbell she knew would suggest that sort of past, and that was disheartening. How could my best friend not know one of the biggest things about me?

Jack, that's how. Jack and his ideas about what was proper and what wasn't.

The music built to its cheesy yet poignant chorus. "Love yourself, baby, cause I'm no good at loving you!" Marissa sang along, throwing her arm around my shoulders and dragging me into the present. We swayed and sang our guts out to the inevitable conclusion of the song.

"I have to pee!" she shouted in my ear. I nodded, still a bit lost in the fog of the music. I followed her as the unmistakable sounds of a drum solo began. We had time; this would go on for a bit.

The lines were long, but no one was messing around. Once we'd made it through, we found our way to the bar for a refill.

"Sorry I bitched about the seats," Marissa said, sipping the foam from her beer.

I shook my head. "Totally fine, they were expensive tickets."

"It's just that I wanted the full experience, you know?

Front row, being sung to, eyes locking. The whole rock and roll fantasy."

"Oh, I get it—more than you know."

She raised an eyebrow. "Do you now? Please elaborate."

I smiled wickedly. I wasn't embarrassed of my days following this band, so why had I acted like I was?

I opened my mouth to share the story, but then the drum solo started winding into a guitar solo, and I turned back toward the stage.

It was calling to me like a siren song. I glanced back at the bouncer who stood guarding the floor area, his nose buried in his phone. This was our one chance. I reached back to grab hold of Marissa's hand and stepped down toward the stage, one foot in front of the other, fully expecting to be stopped at some point...but nothing. Not when we reached the back of the crowd, not when we approached the velvet rope of the floor seats, and not even when we reached the opening to the VIP section.

"Oh my *God*!" Marissa screamed so loudly my eardrums vibrated, and I squeezed her hand in response.

Much like riding a bike, the art of making my way to the front row came back to me. I stepped forward, paused, then sideways, then forward again. Slow but steady, Marissa in tow, with each step I felt like I was shedding some part of the person I'd become. We were making progress, and then the guitar stopped, and the lights went out. Around us the crowd seemed to relax, so I took the opportunity to rush forward, dragging Marissa behind me.

"Don't let go of my hand!" I yelled over my shoulder, but there was no way to know if she heard. And then, as I knew it would, the beat dropped, the lights went up, and the crowd surged forward, carrying us with it until I felt my hipbones collide with the metal barrier.

We'd done it. Front row. Not that this small venue was

much of a challenge. I'd done it before in a ten-thousand-person arena. You just needed to know how.

Beside me, Marissa raised her hands in the air and let out a scream, or at least I think she did. The sound was lost in the guitars that joined the drums and that was that. If the opener and the slideshow had opened the door, this front row vantage point had done the rest. For the next four songs I sang and pounded the barrier to the beat.

It was everything I needed it to be. I closed my eyes and swayed as the tempo slowed, wishing I had a cigarette lighter. Could you still buy those? All I owned were the long ones that I used to light my vanilla scented candles.

The irony was not lost on me.

After all, I wasn't some free-spirited teenager. Not anymore, no matter how much my whole heart was longing to be tonight. But if I kept my eyes closed, I could let the nostalgia keep me adrift from my reality.

This was a particularly cheesy ballad, with promises of giving up the road for true love, if only it could be found by a man in a denim vest without a shirt and a woman in a ripped-up miniskirt.

"DAVIS! DAVIS! DAVIS!" came the screams from behind me, and I opened my eyes to see that he was crouched right in front of me, giving the song all he had, straight to me.

And yes, I was spat on. And yes, his sweat flew dangerously close as he stood and pounded his fists on his chest with the beat. My eyes widened as he stared directly into them. It was ridiculous how alive this made me feel. I was just a face in the crowd to him.

But, damn, I wanted to be the girl I'd been when he sang to me last.

The laws of the universe say that your entire life path can be altered by just one decision, even if it's a small one. Life is a series of choices, really, when you boiled it down.

The ones I'd made then made no sense to the person I was at this concert tonight. Maybe I was letting the nostalgia get the better of me, but the way I felt in this moment with Davis Scott singing straight to me, I wanted to go back, make all different ones, and see just where life would have sent me.

Or maybe I could make a different choice *now*. The idea of joining the tour, following the band, doing it all over again…it made me feel…what? I couldn't put my finger on it. Alive? Myself? Whatever that unnamed feeling was, it made my heart pound in my chest.

I shook my head. It was an absolutely ridiculous thought. I was too old to entertain ideas of directions of the universe and different choices. I had responsibilities. Adult responsibilities. But then Davis shook his head, too, as though he was responding to me.

He winked, and I felt faint.

He was holding out his hand, and I was taking it. He was pulling me up on the stage. I felt like I couldn't breathe. Then, all of who I was seemed to slip away.

Davis Scott was dancing and so was I.

Together. He put a hand on my hip, and we rocked back and forth, inches apart. Another sly smile. Another wink, and then he put the mic back up to his mouth.

"You and me, we don't know slow. There's nowhere else to go, so stay. Tomorrow, tomorrow is another day." He sang, head tilted forward, eyes closed.

As the rest of the band came in on the chorus, he stepped away from me and toward them and I had the presence of mind to pull out my camera and start snapping. Caught in the moment, I didn't hesitate as they did their thing. And when Davis saw me, he turned the full force of his charm in my direction.

Suddenly I didn't feel too old for anything.

Chapter Six

I was escorted offstage when the song ended, my heart still pounding as I gulped air like I'd run a 5K. Sure, part of it was that I hadn't worked out since Jazzercise was a thing, but it was also everything else: the wink, being on stage, dancing with Davis. The feel of my camera solid in my hands taking actual photos. It was more than a little overwhelming.

I reached out and put my hand on a post to steady myself, and the young man who'd seen me off looked suddenly alarmed.

"You okay, lady?"

I nodded, sucking in as deep a breath as I could manage in my Spanx. Granted, it wasn't much, but it helped.

"You can just stay back here and watch the rest of the show if you want. Only a couple songs left." He looked relieved that he wasn't going to have to deal with an old lady puking over her interactions with a rock band.

That wasn't what this was. I was overcome, but not like that. What I was feeling had more to do with myself. I had discovered that the girl I'd been—even if she'd been buried under years of bullshit, suburbia, and control—still existed. She was still in there.

Not snuffed out by a life that consisted of daily commutes to an uninspiring job, a needy husband who insisted on routine, and a house of beige walls.

I smiled.

On stage, the music continued. It was surreal, and I edged closer to the wings to get a better look. From there, just outside the lights, I could see everything: the interactions of the guys with each other, the way the crowd was reacting to them, and how they seemed to take that energy and put it back into the songs.

It was a sight to see, especially from this angle. I held up my camera. The lights, Davis, a hint of a smile on his face. It was the shot of the night—I was sure of that even as I pushed the button—and the thought thrilled me. Something else that hadn't happened in too many years to count.

I took a deep, calming inhale and caught a trace of a scent, something familiar. It was musky, like aged whiskey, and it made me feel instantly at peace. I glanced around, trying to place the scent, the memory, but came up empty.

"Thank you, Chicago! We couldn't have done this without you!" Davis's voice boomed through the speakers.

The room went pitch black as the lights went out. The applause from the crowd was thunderous, even back here. I was suddenly very aware that I wasn't where I needed to be. Surely there would be an encore. I needed to get back out on the floor and find Marissa.

To my relief, the lights came back on and they launched into their biggest hit, "The Road Back Always Leads to You." And though I knew I needed to move, I was frozen in my spot. I'd find Marissa one way or another. She wouldn't want me to miss this moment. She was that kind of friend.

The stage was a whirl of energy. Rex the guitarist and

Alex the bass player were standing side by side and swaying to their own beat as they played. Alex's ebony skin glistened with sweat from the effort. Rex's mouth was set in a serious line as his fingers flew across the strings, their speed living up to his nickname of White Lightning. Davis joined them, then he was up by Tony, the drummer, his Puerto Rican flag bandana tied around his forehead in his signature look. Then Davis was back down in front. They were not missing a beat, though maybe the beat was just a titch slower than it had been back in their heyday. I could see just the hint of age on them all, less hair, more laugh lines. Somehow that made them even more attractive to me.

Then it was over, and as they came off stage, punching one another in the shoulders, letting loose yells of celebration, Davis paused where I stood.

"Make sure I see you at the after-party." His mouth pulled into that smile. Having it aimed right at me left me speechless. I could only nod. This was it. I was going to Golden Tiger's after-party.

It wasn't until after they'd all disappeared that I realized I had no idea where the after-party was.

My phone buzzed in my pocket. Marissa.

"Hey!" I answered, stretching my neck, trying to find anyone who could tell me anything about the after-party.

"OH MY GOD! I cannot believe you got on stage! Where are you?"

"Backstage still." I glanced out at the stage where the roadies had begun cleaning up the equipment.

"You danced with Davis Scott!" she shrieked, so loudly I swear I heard her through my phone and also through the now emptying theater. I couldn't fault her for her enthusiasm. It was how I felt too.

"It seemed like it was happening to someone else. Like I was just watching it."

"Girl, it happened. I got a video."

Of course she did. I'd kiss her if she was standing next to me. "You're the best. Seriously."

"I know. I can't wait to show it to you!"

"Also, get this: Davis invited me to the after-party. But I have no idea where it is."

"Wait. What? You have to find out." She said this like it was some sort of epiphany.

"I'm trying. Wait for me out in the lobby. As soon as I know, I'll come get you."

I hung up before she could respond and walked in the direction the band had gone, thinking maybe the party was happening somewhere back here. But the more I looked around, the more I realized the dressing rooms of this place weren't nearly big enough for a Golden Tiger after-party.

I should know. I'd been to a few, though never by invitation.

I found my way to the backstage door, hoping to find their limos, but no luck. The only people out there looked more desperate than I felt.

I turned and went back inside.

How had they all gotten out of here so quickly?

And then he appeared, like a mirage in the desert—the kid with the earpiece who'd brought me off stage.

"Excuse me!"

He turned. "You can't be back here. The show's over."

"Yes, I know. Davis Scott invited me to the after-party, but I don't know where it is. I was trying to find the guys, but they're already gone. Help?"

I hoped this came across as a question and not a desperate plea.

He shrugged. "I just work at the theater. I don't have anything to do with the band."

My shoulders drooped. My one chance.

I thanked him and then turned to go find Marissa and break the news that we would not be going to the Golden Tiger after-party after all.

"I know they're staying at the Gwen," he offered, and I stutter-stepped. That's where we were staying.

I picked up my pace, calling over my shoulder, "Thank you!" It was at least something.

A destination. Somewhere to start, but more than that, I had a mission. I had a plan. I was going to get my old self back.

Chapter Seven

An hour later, I decidedly did not have my old self back.

After searching every inch of the hotel, Marissa and I sat defeated in the bar.

"Whatever. Who needs a fancy rock and roll after-party when we can drink right in the very exclusive lobby bar of the Gwen?" Marissa said, holding her double margarita in my direction. She was well on her way to a good time. She'd already done a shot of tequila while we waited for the blender to mix up her drink. I held up the whiskey on the rocks that I was sipping, and we clinked glasses.

After the month I'd had, a rock and roll after-party was exactly what I wanted. Dare I say, needed? But I was trying to stay positive for Marissa's sake.

"Definitely a perk, not having to figure out how we're getting home."

She nodded in agreement, draining her margarita. "And you never know, they may just show up here for a drink after their party!"

I did know. They weren't going to do that.

No, once the party was truly raging, they would sneak out with whatever groupie or girlfriend caught their eye or move on to an even more exclusive after-after-party. I shook my head loose of the idea that it could have finally been me.

"Tell me everything about Davis inviting you to the party!"

It was a short story, but I dragged it out, sharing all the details of being pulled on stage, and my dance, and finally my brief interaction backstage. How he'd smiled, winked. Working myself all up again as I told it.

"Show me the video."

Marissa fished her phone out of her purse and pulled it up. "I'm going to go get us another round while you watch it."

She handed it to me and then disappeared through the expanding crowd. I was glad we'd gotten here in time to snag an out of the way booth. If I couldn't be with the band, I didn't want to be with their other fans. I watched the video, amazed by the woman in it. She was laughing, dancing, flirting. I hit replay when it was over, then sent it to myself before setting the phone down. I sipped the last of my whiskey and fought against a growing ache inside.

I glanced up to the bar. Where the hell was Marissa? Though I was leery to lose our booth, it seemed wrong to not go in search of her.

On the bar sat what had to be our drinks, but Marissa was nowhere to be found. I motioned to the bartender. "Any idea where the woman who ordered these is?"

He shook his head. "She did a shot while I made them, but she was gone when I got back." I sighed and pulled out my wallet to settle our bill. It was one thing to want the wildest night of your life. It was another to attempt it when you weren't much of a drinker.

Bottom line: Marissa could not hang.

I went in pursuit. First the bathroom, but there was no

sign of her. I crossed my arms to try and hold my shit together as I rode the elevator up to check our room. If she wasn't there, I didn't really know what my next step was.

My search was short and sweet. Marissa had, in fact, made it back to our room. The clue? She'd slid the chain lock in place, rendering my key useless. And she had for sure passed out, because no matter how loudly I pounded, she didn't get up to unchain it.

"Marissa! Let me in!" I shook the door against the chain. So much for an epic night. No Davis. No after-party. And now, it would seem, no bed.

"Everything okay out here?"

The voice startled me, and I whirled around, embarrassed that I'd been loud enough to wake another guest, my apology at the ready.

"God! I'm so sorry, my friend passed out, and the chain is on our door…" But then my heart chugged into my throat, stopping me mid-apology.

My eyes widened. His hair was shorter, some silver at the temples, a few wrinkles on his white skin, but I could never forget his face.

His soft gray eyes were a striking contrast to his square jaw, always a faint smile on his lips. Like he'd either told a joke or was in on one. He towered over me in a way that used to intimidate the shit out of me if I was being honest. Rugged, and more handsome than I recalled. The past twenty-odd years had treated him well.

He was talking, clearly having no clue who I was, but I was crossing the distance between us, pulled by rote memory. And then he said my name, and he was hugging me, and a sense of calm and comfort washed over me. I couldn't believe I hadn't been able to place the scent earlier.

Musk with a trace of whiskey.

Vince Caparelli.

I stepped back and gave him the brightest smile I could muster. "Well, this is just like old times!"

As the Golden Tiger stage manager, Vince Caparelli had been the gatekeeper of the tour. The one who decided who was cool enough to hang with the band and who wasn't. And I almost always fell into the latter category, though I'd tried to always be nonchalant about it, hoping that eventually Vince would see me in a different light and let me inside.

Our "friendship" was based on that dynamic, with a generous amount of trash talk to go with it. There were times he made me furious, and times he made me laugh. But he'd always been there. A constant in that wild summer. I had forgotten any of the bad when I'd thrown myself into that hug. My nostalgia pulled at me from all sides, just happy to see another familiar face.

"If this was old times, I'd be out in some alley loading equipment and trying to keep the girls at bay." His voice was still low and slow. Like gravel, but not the kind you worry is going to ruin the paint on your car. More like the kind you drive at sunset, windows down, music low.

It took me right back to that alley, and smoky bars and velvet ropes—the ones I always managed to find myself on the outside of.

"And I would have been trying my best to sneak around you and onto the waiting tour bus."

He gave a slight chuckle at that.

"I much prefer this. In my old age, I imagine myself more of a lover than a fighter."

"Old age? Um, speak for yourself. I prefer the term mature to old," I shot back. We were falling back into the banter that had been the staple of our rapport. I'd missed this—if it was possible to miss something you'd forgotten all about.

"That explains the passed-out roommate," he said drily,

and I couldn't help but laugh.

"Marissa just couldn't hang."

"Do I know her?"

"No, she's a friend from my real life." I smiled. "Though who's to say what's real and what's fake?"

"What's give and what's take?" he replied, shaking his head as he finished the lyric. His smile revealed lines around his eyes that only made him look more rugged. The years really had agreed with him.

"Classic Golden Tiger. I had no idea how much I was missing it until tonight. Life-changing. At least for me."

Why was I telling Vince, of all people, the concert had been a life-changing experience? I was yammering away like a schoolgirl. Strike that, like a schoolgirl managing to also have a midlife crisis.

Not a good look.

The door to the room behind him flew open and the hallway filled with noise. It was a welcome distraction from my blathering, until I saw who it was. April. No last name necessary in the ranks of Golden Tiger groupies. She was the queen bee, and all the other groupies swarmed around her. I'd chosen not to swarm for fear I wouldn't be invited into the hive. Even now, looking at the older, more hardened version of her made me tug at the hem of my miniskirt self-consciously.

"Vincey! What are you doing? We need that ice stat!"

Vincey? I glanced at his face to see how he reacted to that bit of ridiculousness and thought I caught a slower than normal blink. But with Vince, it was hard to tell. Not much fazed him.

"Ran into an old friend." He pointed in my direction. Now would have been the time for me to say something clever, but instead I just stood there smiling like that same schoolgirl on picture day.

I finally noticed the ice bucket in Vince's hand, which was odd, since he'd wrapped his arms around me for a hug. But then again, I'd been too distracted by nostalgia and his scent and his hug to really pay attention.

April still wore her emotions all over her heavily made-up face. She narrowed her eyes, scrutinizing me, and then stepped forward and laid a possessive hand on Vince's arm.

"You do look vaguely familiar. Do I know you?"

Seriously? I was being mean girled by April again? I knew I wanted to relive my old life, but this wasn't exactly what I meant. I glanced at Vince, who seemed oblivious. Men usually were.

So, I held out my hand to introduce myself, stepping forward, but was stopped in my tracks when none other than Davis Scott appeared in the hall from the same room behind her. Was that door a direct portal to my past?

"There you are! I was hoping you'd find the after-after-party, doll." His bright blue eyes and black as night hair were a stark contrast to aging gracefully Vince. I hadn't noticed when we were on stage but now it was obvious—he'd had work done, and lots of it. Still, there was a delicateness to his features. He was almost too beautiful to be real. His face wasn't frozen in time, it was just frozen. Beautifully frozen. And when those eyes twinkled in my direction, well, it unfroze a thing or two, let me tell you.

It took me a full five seconds to process that he was extending the invitation to me. Just like I'd dreamed of him doing all those years ago. Dreamed? Hell, I'd downright fantasized. And here it was, happening. With Davis Scott.

"I don't know if I found it or it found me," I replied. It came off as coy, but I was really asking the universe—what were the chances that the party I'd been dying to find would be happening directly across from my hotel room?

"Well, come join us." Davis moved aside and I could see

the party was in full swing. I stepped forward, instinctively waiting for Vince to reach out and stop me.

I mean, that's what would have happened back then. It was sort of our thing.

Vince was looking me directly in the eye, another something I remembered him always doing. "Yeah, come join us."

It was that invitation, more than Davis grabbing hold of my upper arm to usher me in, that intrigued me. Up until now, I'd been floating along in a bubble of melancholy. But we were all grown up now. So, things were different, as much as they felt the same.

I was going behind the velvet rope at Vince's invitation. I couldn't help but pat myself on the back for winning this round, though it far from made up for all the other times I'd been left on the outside looking in.

Chapter Eight

Inside, the party was overwhelming, even for someone who'd been dying to get in. Only once in the thousands (okay, that's probably an exaggeration) of times I had tried had I found my way to the after-party, and this was the *after*-after-party, so it was even more exclusive.

And much more intoxicated.

There was liquor everywhere. In the hands of the roadies and groupies who were gathered in pairs or small groups. On every table or counter in the suite. Music was playing, just loud enough to make talking hard—not that anyone was talking. They were all dancing, slow and fast. No one on the actual beat, and no one seemed to notice or care.

Davis guided me to the bar and spread his hands at the array of bottles, I assumed to ask what I preferred since I couldn't hear what he said. I pointed to the whiskey and he winked and began searching for a glass.

I mean, he sort of winked at me, anyway. The botox on his forehead only let his eye close partway. I found myself staring and wondering how he slept. *On his back, perfectly preserved?* I thought. And then pushed the image from my mind. After all, I wasn't as young as I used to be either.

Movement in the mirror behind the bar caught my eye. Vince had returned with the ice. Even if I hadn't caught sight of him, it would have been hard to miss his entrance. I turned to watch the entire party hold up their arms and erupt with "VIIIIINNNNNCCCEE!" and then random hoots and whistles. Vince was still the most appreciated man on tour. And this tour was only one day old.

"Vince, my man! Saving us all again!" Davis yelled over the music. Beside me, Vince set the ice bucket on the bar.

April, who was walking so closely behind him that she was practically hidden, appeared when he reached the bar. She stepped to the side, laying a hand on his arm in a way that suggested what? Intimacy? Familiarity? Vince and April? So strange.

Davis added a few cubes to my whiskey and handed it to me before making another one, which he handed to Vince. April said something, but it was too quiet for me to hear. Vince as well, so he bent his head down closer and her hand went to the side of his face. Which was oddly possessive for her. She was a band groupie to the bone; this attachment to Vince was new. And, if I knew anything of April's opinions, beneath her.

Fascinating. Had I missed this all those years ago or had it happened after I left the tour?

Davis grabbed the bottle for himself. Not bothering with a glass or ice, he just took a swig right from it.

"Cheers, man!" he yelled, and Vince turned to clink his glass to the bottle. But his focus was on me. He leaned over to say something directly in my ear.

"Watch yourself. Davis is on a mission tonight. And Davis on a mission is a dangerous thing."

I bristled. Now this was the Vince I remembered, trying

to shoo me off.

"I can handle myself." I wasn't a wide-eyed innocent girl anymore. I'd learned a thing or two about what I wanted, or rather, what I didn't want. And tonight, Davis was not in that category. No matter that April was still glaring at me like an outsider.

He pulled back and raised his eyebrows at me. "Well, I guess if you still just want to be another notch on his mic stand, by all means."

My mouth fell open, and my annoyance built to fury as I tried to form words to reply.

"I don't need you running me off and ruining my life again." The words were out before I'd even thought about what I was saying. *Ruining my life again?*

The statement seemed to slap Vince in the face. His brow furrowed. "Okay," he said. "Okay." And without another word, he threw an arm around April and walked away.

He had some nerve warning me about Davis when he was involved with the human version of a praying mantis. I wouldn't doubt for a second that she'd pull his head off when she was done with him. I mean maybe twenty years ago, when we were kids, but now?

Davis made his way around the bar toward me. I'd played this scenario out a thousand times in my head. I'd imagined it as I slept in my car outside the venue during that tour. And as I'd driven mile after lonely mile to the next city. And, if I was being completely honest, in the dark of night in my unhappy marital bed. Whiskey on the rocks with a rock star.

I held out my glass for a toast, shoving whatever had just transpired with Vince far away.

"To a kick-ass start to what is going to be the tour of the year!" I said.

He clinked his bottle to my glass and took another drink from it. He smiled, just one side, as he always did. That sexy smirk was his trademark. Rock star sex appeal really was a thing, and this guy had it in spades.

"That's the plan. Being up there with the guys again, it was easy to forget all the bullshit we went through." He yelled over the crowd, not bending closer to be heard. So, I did. Laying my hand on his chest to steady myself.

"It was as good as it's ever been. The music, I mean. Those lyrics still hit me right where they need to, just like they did twenty years ago. God, can you write a song." I pulled back just a bit, so I could look at his face.

I expected a sultry nod, but instead his lips pulled back in a tight smile, just for a second. And then he took another drink of his whiskey and seemed to collect himself.

"That's the point, right? A song isn't anything if it doesn't mean something to someone."

I exhaled. "They mean something to me. I had forgotten that. When you sing, I feel like it's right to me." That was true, no need to be coy about it.

His eyes darted to the side, and then he was on his feet. "You want to go out on the balcony? I can't even hear myself think in here."

Without waiting for my reply, he stood and walked across the room to the balcony doors. Vince's words echoed in my head, but I stood and followed. After all, I could either go with him or sit by myself at the bar.

The whole wall was windows, so what could possibly happen in view of the entire party? Davis paused and let me pass in front before closing the door behind him. I was stunned by both the view and the sudden silence. I walked to the railing and looked out over Chicago, wishing I had my camera and cursing myself for leaving it hanging with my purse on that barstool.

He came up behind me, putting his arms on either side of me, clutching the railing. It should have been hot as hell, but in the moment it gave me a wave of what felt like panic. I took a deep breath and let it out as subtly as I could. I didn't want him to think I was panting or something. It's just that it was happening so fast, and as a recent divorcee, I was so out of practice. Flirting was one thing, but actual physical contact? Would I even remember how? I took a sip of my whiskey, trying not to overthink it. To live in the moment.

Like the old me would have. Old me? Or young me? It felt almost like it was another me. What would she have done? And how? I shook my head, trying to clear the doubts suddenly crowding it. Either way, the *former* me would have died to have this exact moment.

"I remember you. You know? From our glory days." Davis's voice was in my ear.

I doubted that somehow, but it didn't mean I didn't want it to be true. And it was, after all, why I was out here.

To finish what I started.

I took a gulp of the whiskey. If I turned around, we would be face-to-face. By the logistics alone, I would be practically kissing Davis Scott.

But instead of turning, I replied, "I'm suspicious of how true that is."

He stepped back, letting go of the railing. I turned to see that he was holding his hands over his heart as though I'd wounded him with my words.

"How can you doubt me?"

"Well, first of all, you haven't seen me in over twenty years, and secondly, in the game to vie for your attention, I was always three rows deep in the crowd."

He pointed at me with the hand that held the whiskey bottle. "I can't deny that I was a fox in a house full of hens, but that doesn't mean I was oblivious to them on a human level." He took a long drink, finishing it off. "Besides, that red hair? Unforgettable. That's why when I saw you in the front row, I had to pull you up on stage. So glad you're back on the tour. Photographer, right?"

I stared at him blankly, because my brain couldn't seem to remember how to send words to my mouth.

Back on the tour? Photographer?

He crossed the balcony, and my heart started to beat faster. It was going to happen. He was going to kiss me.

Just as Davis's lips almost reached mine, the balcony was filled with the sounds of the party again.

"You okay out here?"

Vince. Because of course. Just like old times.

Davis turned to face him. "Yeah, except we're out of whiskey. Keep an eye on her, will you?" He tried his version of a wink again. "Be right back, doll."

Doll? I could do without that.

"How about you?" Vince asked when Davis had closed the door behind him.

I scrambled to cover. "I'm fine. I can take care of myself. I don't need you to check up on me."

Vince raised his eyebrows, déjà vu in one gesture.

"I'm checking to see that Davis isn't making an ass of himself. Not that you can't handle it."

"He isn't making an ass of himself. He's just being Davis Scott. But I do think he's got me confused with someone else."

"What makes you say that?"

"He told me he was glad I was back on the tour. Which oddly had crossed my mind during the concert—try and find the girl I used to be, or some fantasy like that..." My voice trailed off.

He was nodding. "That's what you meant when you said the concert was life-changing."

Why it surprised me he remembered me saying that in our brief encounter in the hall, I don't know. But it did. I nodded.

"I just got caught up in wondering what my life could have been like." I paused here, because I couldn't believe I was going to say this out loud, to Vince of all people. "If I hadn't left in the first place."

But to my surprise, he didn't have a smart reply. "You've wondered that?"

I shook my head. "Not until tonight. I came here, to the concert, fully expecting to be swept up in the nostalgia of it, but once I was in front of that stage? I don't know, it was the only thing I could think about. Who I was, who I've become."

Vince only nodded, his silence making me feel self-conscious all of a sudden.

"But I didn't tell anyone. So, what in the hell is Davis talking about?"

Before Vince could answer, Davis burst through the door. "Vince! Thanks for keeping your eye on this little lady for me. Nice to have her back with us."

My eyes went wide. Back with us? Was I? Could I? He was saying all this like we'd talked about it. Like we'd had some history. And to be straight, we hadn't.

I opened my mouth to try and clear things up but closed it as Davis crossed the balcony toward me holding out the bottle to refill my glass. I mean, if he was under the impression we'd had something once upon a time, was now the time for me to object?

"Don't you worry, she's one of the good ones. Aren't you, doll?"

I looked around him at Vince. Without missing a beat, he replied, "Oh, I'm not worried at all."

Well, *that* made one of us.

Chapter Nine

I woke up in a massive bed with the sun shining directly in my eyes and no idea where I was. I tried sitting up, but the room tilted and swayed enough that I had to lie back down. The sheets were cool and the pillows so soft I almost drifted off again, but then I remembered.

The after-after-party.

I sat straight up again, ignoring the splitting headache and queasy stomach. I pulled the blankets down to see that I was still dressed from the night before. Whose bed was this? How had I gotten here? I was suddenly overwhelmed by a sense of déjà vu. This was the second time in two days I'd woken up with a raging hangover. I really needed to get my shit together. Newly divorced or not, this was as much wild child midlife crisis as I was allowing myself. The whole point of this second chapter was to live life to the fullest—while still being able to remember it.

Not to mention that the whole waking up in a strange hotel bed thing had happened on the last tour. Then I'd been disappointed to wake up fully clothed, this time I felt nothing but relief. If I was going to sleep with a rock star, I wanted to remember every detail of it. Though what I could remember clearly was that up close, Davis's skin was still as smooth as a porcelain doll. His features so fine-tuned and delicate that he didn't even seem real. He was like airbrushing come to life.

I sighed. And my mind settled on Vince. I'd forgotten until I saw him last night in his element that we'd actually had some pretty good times. Sure, he'd barred me from backstage, but on more than one occasion he'd stolen a bottle of whiskey to share with me, seemingly removing himself from the party as well. And we'd had that banter, that verbal back and forth that from his side always included warnings about the scene and why I was better off staying clear of it. From my side, always the reasons why he was wrong about both,

And now here we were twenty years later, and he was still warning me to stay away. And it still pissed me off.

I glanced at the mirror opposite me and gasped in horror. My perfect smoky eye from the night before was now more rabid raccoon than sexpot, and my hair was more Heat Miser than bombshell. On the bedside table was a bottle of water, but no aspirin, no cute note from whoever had put me to sleep. I opened the water and downed half of it before swinging my feet off the bed, thankful to find there was a bathroom attached to this bedroom.

I washed my face and did my best to get my hair to sit down by pulling my fingers through it. It wasn't ideal, but it would have to do. I was getting flashes of the night before.

Vince.

Whiskey.

Davis.

The Chicago skyline.

Dancing.

Toasting.

But I had no real idea what order any of that should

be in, which was not ideal. And there was something else, something that seemed important, just on the outside of the fog. I had to stop doing this to myself. Last time I'd quit my job and put my house on the market. I could only hope that the missing detail this time was less life-altering.

I needed to find my purse and a hair tie and some aspirin and, hopefully, my phone. Surely by now Marissa was awake and I could get back in our room. I put my ear to the door and heard nothing. Slowly, I turned the knob, hoping to avoid making a sound so I could find my purse and sneak out of wherever this was and back to my room. Marissa was going to kill me for not waking her up to join the party.

"Well, good morning!"

I stopped dead in my tracks.

Marissa was sitting at a dining table in what I vaguely recognized as the suite I'd been in last night. Evidence of the party was strewn on every surface, empty glasses and bottles, a stray bra or two. And my purse, hung from the back of one of the barstools with my camera.

Vince sat across the table from Marissa looking over some sort of document, no trace of the hangover I felt on his face. The table in front of him was covered with silver domed room service plates and a pot of coffee.

"Um, good morning? How are you here? I mean, how did you find me?"

Vince smiled, those damn lines around his eyes crinkling again. I hadn't forgotten that part from the night before. "Your phone was ringing off the hook. I'm surprised you didn't hear it, though, you were snoring pretty loudly."

"I woke up and you weren't in our room, and I realized I must have locked you out. I was worried so I started manic dialing, like I do. Vince answered and invited me to join you two for breakfast."

She tilted her head, her emphasis on the words "you two."

I scowled at both of them and went to pour myself a cup of coffee. "I don't snore."

"Whatever you have to tell yourself." Vince turned his attention back to the papers in his hand.

I shook my head, which reminded me of my splitting headache.

"Either of you have anything for a headache?"

"Back in our room," Marissa offered with no enthusiasm for going to get it.

"Someone is out of practice with her whiskey drinking. The Campbell I knew would be right as rain this morning," Vince snarked.

I glared at him, but that hurt my head too. "Why aren't you hungover?"

"I guess I never fell out of practice." He smiled wickedly.

"Where's April, still in bed?" I asked, matching his tone.

This brought a chuckle. "Nope, she got an offer higher up the food chain. Lucky for you, I gave you her bed."

"I doubt that?" I replied. Though I wasn't sure what I doubted.

From the confused look on Vince's face, neither did he. "I have some aspirin."

He stood and walked into what I assumed was the other bedroom, and as soon as he was out of sight, Marissa started kicking me.

"Who is the hot guy and how do you know him and what does he mean the Campbell he knew?" she whisper-shouted.

"SHHHH!" I said. "Vince is the stage manager for Golden Tiger—or he was, I'm not really sure at this point. We knew each other twenty years ago." I ignored the *hot* part.

"You *knew* each other?" She raised an eyebrow. "Did you get reacquainted last night?"

I knew from the heat in my face that I was blushing. And when a redhead blushes, there's no hiding it.

"No! Vince and I aren't like that. We're adversaries—friendly, but not on the same side."

She seemed perplexed by this information, so I continued.

"Ugh. When I was twenty, I spent the summer following Golden Tiger. Their second tour. This tour, the one they're trying to recreate."

Her jaw dropped, which in my opinion was a bit dramatic. "Wait, like you were a groupie? Like, you followed them around the country, and tried to sleep with them or something? Why am I just finding this out now?"

"No." I shook my head. "I mean yes. Sort of. I was really into the music. I had this fantasy of being some kind of rock and roll photojournalist—covering the band and their music, that sort of thing. And I never told anyone because Jack was embarrassed about it, and I was trying to live up to his—"

Photographer. Davis thought I was the tour photographer. Davis thought I was joining the tour. That was the memory in the fog. I swallowed.

Marissa didn't seem to notice. "Of course he was. Jack is *such* an ass." She handed me a piece of bacon from her plate and I sat down in the chair next to her, happy for the change of subject. Though it didn't last.

"So, what's the yes part?"

"Well, I mean they were the biggest rock band in the world." I was impressed at my witty reply since my mind was reeling. The last thing I remembered clearly from last night was being on the balcony with Vince, and then Davis. We'd done a shot to celebrate my new position. And then another one, and then the doors had flown open and the party had joined us on the balcony. The exact scenario of my dreams and I'd thrown myself into it, apparently. After that, nothing.

Vince was right—I was out of practice.

Marissa cackled and then held her hand out to fist bump me.

I met her fist and then asked her the question I had been turning over in my head since I'd stood backstage last night. "Do you ever wonder how your life could be if you'd just made one choice in a different way?"

"Deep thoughts and a morning hangover." She laughed but then saw I was serious and shrugged. "I've never thought about it. What's the choice you want to do differently? Hook up with the hottie stage manager? Is he the one that got away?" Her eyes sparkled, needling me. The thought of those damn gold flecks in Vince's eyes slammed into me, how he smelled so familiar, and how even though I'd acted annoyed, it had been nice that he came to check on me on the balcony.

But I wasn't looking for familiarity. I'd had that for the past twenty-two years.

I was looking to shake things up.

"Hell no." I shook my head, picturing Davis's piercing blue eyes and that sexy half smile. A shiver went down my spine. That overwhelming longing I'd felt for him as a girl. But this was different. I wasn't a girl anymore. "Bigger."

Her eyes widened, and I waved her quiet before she could shriek.

"Once upon a time I was a girl who had the balls to pursue a rock star. And now, I'm this." I waved my hands in front of my face. "I don't want to be just this anymore."

"You grew up, Campbell. We all have to do it."

I nodded. "But I could have had a whole different life. I want to know what happens if I make the other choice."

Saying it out loud sounded even more outlandish than thinking it.

"Are you saying you're going to become a Golden Tiger groupie again?" Her mouth hung open. "Um, don't you think that's just a little bit insane? We have to go home. You have a life, even if it is boring and safe."

I shrugged. "I know, but I chose safe last time. Maybe

insanity is what I'm looking for now."

"A little insanity is really what we're all looking for," a deep voice said from behind us.

I whirled in my chair to see Vince had returned, a bottle of aspirin in hand. My face flooded with heat. Just how much had he heard?

Chapter Ten

"It keeps us young," he sang.

How had I not known that Vince could sing? I gave him the next lyric, though not nearly as melodically. "I don't want to grow old, without having lived young."

"So, baby, let's you and me have some fun." We finished the last bit together. His voice still rough, but smooth. The hair on my arms stood up.

Marissa cleared her throat, snapping me out of what felt a bit like a trance. "This takes on a whole new meaning now that I know your sordid history."

"Better a sordid history than a boring life, which is what I have now," I quipped, opening the aspirin and taking a few with the bottle of water that was sitting in front of me. I was still reeling a bit from Vince's voice singing those lyrics I knew so well. The ones that seemed to reach inside me and pull my long-lost free spirit from where I'd buried her. I had always been certain it was Davis's voice that touched me. But the way Vince sang them? Well, let's just say it wasn't just my soul that felt a bit on fire.

Apparently, part of my midlife rebirth was feeling like a horny teenager.

"Campbell." Marissa's tone sounded more like my mother than my friend. "You can't just run off and follow a band because you think your life is shitty. You're an adult, not some wide-eyed twenty-year-old."

"I don't *think* my life is shitty, I *know* my life is shitty, thank you very much. And as an adult, don't I get to decide exactly what I want to do with it?"

I stared at her across the table, neither of us blinking. Until she stood up.

"Just because you relived your wild years for one night is no reason to recreate them. I get that your life is in flux, but this is all a little...*extreme*, don't you think? I have to go call and check on my kid and my coffee shop. I'll leave the door unlatched." She looked at Vince, sizing him up. "Thanks for breakfast, Vince." And she was gone.

I poured more coffee and started lifting the domes from the room service plates until I found one with bacon and moved it closer. Bacon made everything better.

"So, care to elaborate on your shitty life?" Vince asked, sitting back down across the table from me.

"Well, I'm recently divorced. I take children's portraits for a living at a place called Portrait Hut. Which is basically just glorified babysitting while being yelled at by moms who are overly invested in their Instagram appearance. Or, I used to. I sort of quit in a stand for artistic freedoms. And I live in a house that is completely beige and I drive a gray sedan. Not exactly an awe-inspiring life."

"There are other ways to be awe-inspiring."

I looked up from my plate of bacon to find him staring right at me, like he was trying to tell me something without saying it.

"I don't think I'm probably that, either."

"Don't be so sure." That gravelly voice made me lean forward in my seat. None of this was the Vince I remembered. He'd been fun, cool, even flirty. But he'd never been so direct when he'd spoken to me. Instead, always distant in that cool, gruff way. I didn't know what to make of it, so I looked away, fidgeting with the edge of the table.

"What about this hot mess could possibly be awe-inspiring?" My hand went to my hair, smoothing it, though I knew it wasn't going to improve my bedhead.

"Inspiration has nothing to do with perfection."

I looked up and met his glance.

"Imperfection has its merits, I suppose." I was thinking of his laugh lines, the gray hair at his temples. How men are allowed to age into sexiness but women are not. I'd slept in Spanx for crying out loud.

"I think imperfection is actually more inspiring." He let out a breath, like he'd been holding his. I took a deep breath myself. This was an oddly intimate conversation to be having with Vince of all people. He already thought I wasn't good enough to rub elbows with the band. Now, here I was telling him why he was right all along. And he was arguing my point.

"That is the exact opposite of what my ex would tell you. You probably don't remember, but meeting Jack is why I stopped following the tour that summer. I thought he was the answer to everything. Boy, was I wrong. His core belief is that there's perfection and then there're those who don't try hard enough."

Vince raised an eyebrow. "He sounds like a peach. Divorcing him was probably the opposite of a shitty move."

He wasn't wrong. The truth was, divorcing Jack was not shitty. Being recently divorced in your forties was shitty. It was a big distinction.

I sighed. "Still, maybe Marissa is right. Adults don't just abandon their lives to follow rock bands. Maybe I *am* having a midlife crisis."

"That's sort of insulting to a guy who's doing just that. Hand over some of that bacon." He laughed and just like that, whatever had been bubbling up between us snapped and floated away.

I pushed the plate across the table, relieved by the change in topic. The conversation had been too serious for breakfast. "Not the same. You have a job to do on the tour. What would I be? An aging groupie? I think I'd rather be shitty than pathetic."

Before he could answer me, his phone rang. He glanced down at the caller ID and scowled.

"I have to take this." He held up a finger, which I took as a sign I shouldn't leave.

"Harrison, to what do I owe the pleasure?"

Whoever Harrison was, he was pissed off. Vince winced and held the phone out from his ear, then punched at the screen until it was on speaker and set it on the table in front of him. He held his finger up to his lips at me before he continued.

"Harrison. Dude. You have got to chill on this. It isn't a big deal."

"It is a big deal. I specifically hired a photographer because we want to control the image of this tour. And the one bimbo Davis pulls out of the crowd has a camera. How the hell did she even get it in? Where was security? You need to find out who she is and get those pictures."

I perked up. He was talking about me. Bimbo? Was it bad that sounded like a compliment to me? That seemed bad. But the more important word in that sentence was "camera."

And it gave me an idea. A crazy, wonderful idea.

I leaned closer to the phone and Vince scowled again, but he didn't motion for me to back off.

"Hi, Harrison, is it? This is the picture-taking bimbo."

He was silent for a full ten seconds.

Then, "Vince, my man, I should never doubt you. Why didn't you say you were on top of this?" He chuckled. Was that innuendo? Gross.

Vince raised an eyebrow, the look on his face shifting to one of amusement.

"Because he isn't," I said with a confidence I didn't feel.

Dramatic exhale from Harrison. "Well, that is unfortunate."

As soon as I heard the words and recognized the tone, I smiled. I'd dealt with a man like Harrison for twenty years, and I knew a thing or two about how to handle him.

"It doesn't have to be." I stood and leaned forward, my hands on the table so I was closer to the phone. "Actually, I may just be the answer to your prayers."

"I very much doubt that," Harrison huffed, and Vince leaned forward and opened his mouth to say something, but I waved him off.

"I have a proposition for you." With Jack, I always paused after this first part, so his brain could start looking for the way that whatever I was about to say would benefit him. "How about instead of whatever random photographer you hired, you hire me instead. I have the experience you're looking for and a personal connection to the band."

The noise he made was so dismissive, I actually felt a bit of the subdued rage I generally geared toward my ex-husband. I bit my lip to keep from saying anything in my own defense. Another trick my marriage had taught me.

"I'm sure you have plenty of experience with the band, but that's not the angle I'm going for, sweetheart. The label is looking for a photographer who can produce a commemorative book of photos and anecdotes. A collector's item. Not some groupie's love letter to a rock band." His tone was condescending and expected.

I wasn't fazed. His use of the word "sweetheart" was just pouring gas on my fire. "Harrison. That is exactly what I'm not only talking about, but capable of. And, frankly, given that I have onstage photos of the opening night and your guy was a no-show, I don't see where you have much of a choice."

Vince's eyes went wide, and then he nodded slowly.

"Either you hire me or I produce my own book. And believe me when I say the band will be thrilled to cooperate." What was I saying? None of this was true.

"I think she has you over a barrel, Harrison. And I've seen the pictures. They're stellar," Vince chimed in.

I stared at him in disbelief. He hadn't seen them. Hell, I hadn't even seen them. Why would Vince lie on my behalf? To help me get a job that would put me in close proximity to the band? It made zero sense, but I welcomed the assist. Harrison was silent. And then another dramatic sigh.

"Fine. But I need to see your work. I'll need a book proposal and sample photos ASAP. It had better be professional. We have a very firm idea of how we are branding this whole tour." His voice was clipped, not defeated. "Vince, have her sign a standard contract and fill her in on the vision. And if this goes south, it's all on you." And then he hung up.

I stared at Vince. My eyes wide, my mouth open. I'd done it. I'd gotten a job with the tour.

"What just happened?" I asked, falling backward into my chair.

"I believe you just got yourself a job as the tour photographer." He chuckled. "That was some stellar negotiating, by the way. I always enjoy witnessing that parasite getting put in his place."

I laughed at the absurdity. "Trust me when I say that I can handle any man who actually uses ASAP in a sentence." My eyes widened, though, as what I'd just done sunk in. "I can't believe I did that. And you! Lying and saying you've seen the pictures. *I* haven't even seen the pictures! They could be total crap."

He shrugged. "I doubt that very much. I remember back in the day, you with your fiery red hair and attitude to match. Always a camera in your hand or framing up a shot. I'm sure they will be good. You're good. It's a good hire." He picked up a pair of glasses, put them on, and then started shuffling through the papers in front of him.

Why in the world would Vince remember that about me? I was barely noticeable on that tour. To anyone.

"Until Harrison finds out I actually have zero experience for this sort of work." I was starting to feel the ramifications of what I'd just done. I hadn't taken anything but staged portraits in decades. There was no way I could pull this off.

But Vince just shrugged. "You let me worry about that nitwit."

I shook my head. "I'm too old for this."

"Campbell, we're *all* too old for this." He paused in his paper shuffling and looked me dead in the eye over the top of his glasses. "But that's beside the point. Last night, when you talked about joining the tour, it was because you were trying to find yourself. And I guarantee the self you're looking for isn't at the Portrait Hut."

I looked down at my hands, then up at his face, sure I'd see condescension at the life I'd chosen. But instead what I saw was something that looked like hope.

He broke away and resumed his search through the papers and then finally found what he was looking for. Picking up a pen, he scribbled something out and then began writing as I sat silently with my thoughts.

He was right about that. I didn't want to be that person anymore. I wanted this. I'd wanted it for a long time, even if I'd made myself forget. But Vince going out on a limb for me didn't make sense. It wasn't who he was, at least not where I was concerned.

"Why would you do this for me?" I asked, glancing up at him again.

He stopped writing and stared right at me in that Vince way of his that was no longer jarring. Instead, it made me lean in, listen. "First off, I'm doing it for myself. I'd rather know the person documenting this tour, the band, than some young guy who probably doesn't even know who they are."

"Well, as long as it's about you."

Vince continued, his voice softer, the business edge to it gone. "Pfft. It's about the band, and you know it." I did. With Vince, it was always about the band.

"And apparently I ruined your life once, or so you said last night. Consider this me making it up to you." Our eyes met, and there was nothing but honesty there. Vince was a straight shooter, and I wasn't at all used to that. I was used to dealing with emotional manipulation.

I hadn't meant to say such a thing to Vince. Nor was I even sure I'd ever thought it before last night. But it made some sense, to me at least. His constant running me off had driven me straight to Jack in some way. Even if it was for completely the wrong reasons, Jack had made me feel wanted. I'd abandoned everything I wanted back then for a life I thought would make me feel safe but instead just made me feel trapped. If I took this job, I could go on the tour legitimately.

I could find the old me, that girl I'd been. She wouldn't worry she had no real experience. She'd be thrilled to finally have the opportunity. And she wouldn't care she was probably in over her head—the girl I'd been could always fake it until she made it.

And I'd be taking real pictures, the way I'd always intended. The only thing that seemed unanswered was why in the hell Vince was finally inviting me into the inner circle.

And that somehow made the offer even more intriguing.

"Where do I sign?" I worked to keep my voice as light as I could, but something in the way Vince's eyes lit up made it clear. He wasn't falling for it.

Chapter Eleven

My stomach churned and my mouth was doing that nonstop watering thing. I was not in good shape. Though it was hard to tell if it was the hangover or nerves. Either way, I popped a mint into my mouth and hoped it went away. Same with the constant dialogue in my head.

What the hell was I doing? What the hell was I thinking? There's no way I had the eye or the relationships or the experience to do any of this. I had to tell Vince this was a horrible idea.

Vince. That was another thing. Vince 2.0 had me stymied. What was he up to with this nice guy routine? Sure, we'd had some fun back in the day, but nothing that warranted him sticking his neck out for me like this and giving me a job that was not only going to keep me around but put me smack dab at the center of everything to do with Golden Tiger. It made no sense.

I think it was safe to rule out hangover.

"You are awful quiet for a person about to launch into the adventure of a lifetime," Marissa quipped. We were on our way to the airport so she could fly home. She had an actual life to get back to, as she'd said in her dramatic exit from Vince's room.

After I'd signed the contract, I'd gone back to our room, waving a white napkin in front of me and hoping Marissa would at least hear me out. Which she did, because she was my friend.

"I'm not judging you, but this is a little bit of a midlife crisis, don't you think?" She was lying on her unmade bed, so I flopped down on my fully made one. A reminder I'd spent the night elsewhere.

"First of all, don't say 'midlife'—that gives me a different kind of crisis. And yes, maybe it is, but it's also an incredible opportunity."

"The fact that you have some sort of job makes it fairly legit. Though, no less crazy."

I sighed. "I mean yes and no. What if the real crisis came first, when I ditched everything I ever thought I wanted out of life to marry Jack?"

"So, you're opposed to the word 'midlife' but not the word 'crisis'? Just so we're on the same page…"

I turned my head to see that she was smiling, which was at least a step in the right direction.

"Yes. And I'd also put in a plea to stop calling me crazy. It has a bad connotation. I'd rather go with outlandish or outrageous. Those words are much more fun, and fun is sort of what I'm looking for. That and freedom. Freedom to finally figure out who I want to be, now that I'm an adult and fully in control of my own destiny."

"Fine, I will be a supportive friend of this somewhat harebrained idea," Marissa said, leaping out of bed.

I breathed a sigh of relief. Obviously, I could do it without her support, but having it helped.

She reached for my suitcase and started pawing through

the clothes I'd brought for what I thought was a girls' weekend, not life on the road with a rock band.

"I'm not sure any of this is worthy of your new lifestyle choices."

"Well, it's what I have," I replied, looking at the collection of yoga pants, T-shirts, cardigans, and jeans with dissatisfaction.

She glanced at her watch. "I have four hours until my flight."

I smiled. This was her white napkin. "Are you suggesting...?"

She nodded. "Let's go shopping!"

• • •

Two hours and several disagreements later, my wardrobe had been refreshed to better reflect my new situation.

"Leopard print and a black lace cami? Am I trying out for oldies night at the strip club or attempting to be a rock and roll photographer?" I'd called as Marissa flung things over the top of my changing room door. The entire outfit made me shudder, especially when I saw the pants were made of Spandex.

"Very funny. You need to be edgier. I saw what you took from the racks back there."

"It's edgy!" I said, pulling on the jacket I'd grabbed.

"The fact that it is red does not make it edgy!" she yelled through the door. "It's still a suit. If you're going to pull this off, you need to channel that groupie you were. How'd she dress?"

I thought for just a second about the ripped jeans and the tank tops I'd been fond of back in the day, sans bra. I couldn't possibly still pull it off. Even though I'd never had kids, the girls were not quite as perky as they once were.

Jack had wanted children, desperately. And I thought I did, too, when we first got married. But as the years went by, I kept finding an excuse as to why it wasn't the perfect time. Subconsciously, I think it was the weight of the illusion of a perfect family I couldn't handle. Being the weaker link in the perfect couple was hard enough. And then it was just too late, our life too settled.

I think when your upbringing is rough, you either long to create the family you never had, or you realize that children do not create stability. I was the latter, and completely content with it. And Jack's desire to adhere to his strict schedule and routine outweighed his want for a child. Especially after he heard the stories of the messy, unruly children I photographed every day.

So, in the end it was mutual.

"I get it, but you have to let me do it my way, or I won't be able to pull it off." I shrugged the blazer off, my fingers lingering on its soft fabric. I did love a good power suit, but she had a point.

I pulled on some distressed jeans, added the lace cami (with my push-up bra on, thank you very much) and threw the jacket back on. I looked in the mirror, liking how the outfit came together. Pleased to see the shadow of my former self lingering there, just beneath the fine lines and slight bulges of the woman in her forties I was.

I opened the door. "How about this?"

Marissa's eyes lit up. *"Perfect!"*

It was, and so were the black cigarette pants and moto jacket, both in a very flattering and forgiving Ponte. I'd also gotten V-neck T-shirts in white and black and one in snakeskin that I rolled my eyes at when Marissa had insisted on it. I'd even grabbed a pair of kick-ass boots, for when I was feeling kick-ass or needed to be. And an entire new skincare routine "guaranteed" to fix my wrinkles and bags in no time flat. I doubted that, but it was worth a shot.

I'd left Nordstrom poorer but feeling much better. However, as we got closer to O'Hare, the reality was setting in. I was doing this. Leaving my whole life to go on the road with Golden Tiger.

"Marissa, is this too crazy?"

I knew she would be honest with me. She always was, even when I didn't want to hear it.

"I mean, it is crazy. But *too* crazy? I don't think so. And I thought we weren't using that word anymore?"

I took the exit to the airport and chewed on my lip as I waited for her to continue.

"The truth is, as much as I am forever grateful you married Jack and he brought you to our little town, you've never really fit there."

"You're sort of bad at pep talks if that's what you're going for." I squeezed the steering wheel slightly.

She slapped my arm. "Not like that! I mean it in a good way. I've known you for twenty years, and you always seemed to be playing a role, square peg round hole sort of thing. This morning, in that hotel room, I think I saw who you were supposed to be. Maybe that's why I was so against the whole thing at the start. It meant all these years I haven't really known you."

My eyes flooded. "You've known the me I was trying to be."

"Well, that really isn't good enough anymore." She sucked in a deep breath. "You have to go. You have to go find the real Campbell."

"That is both the nicest and the most terrifying thing anyone has ever said to me," I said. Traffic on the 190 was bumper to bumper, which was good since my tears were making it hard for me to see.

She reached out and squeezed my arm. "Well, it's true.

And you have to kick ass, if for no other reason than for all of us chugging away at the daily grind of our boring lives to get some excitement by living vicariously through you while you join the ranks of the fast and furious."

I laughed.

"Yes, life on the road is extra glamorous, as I recall." The car in front of me started to move so I let my foot off the brake, and we inched forward slowly, then faster, until we were humming along, bumper to bumper at forty-five miles per hour.

She let out her breath in a whistle. "As I recall! I still can't get over the fact that you were a groupie for Golden Tiger, and YOU NEVER TOLD ME!"

I eyed the sign for the entrance to O'Hare and merged onto the exit ramp.

"In my defense, I was pretty busy trying to live up to Jack's idea of the perfect wife. As you might recall."

She nodded. "I do recall. And let me tell you, I am all in on you not doing that anymore. There's just one condition."

We had pulled into the terminal and I maneuvered my car as close to the departures door as I could. "Anything, obviously," I answered as I put the car in park and turned to look at her.

"When you do sleep with Davis, I want details. Not stupid details like, it was the best, or he was amazing. I mean I want actual details." She made her eyes wide.

"Marissa!" I yelled. But she only smiled before reaching for the door handle, hopping out, and slamming the door. I wanted to get out and hug her, but already the car behind me was honking. So instead I rolled down her window and she came back and stuck her hand out to me. I squeezed it.

"Thanks for everything," I said, and meant it.

"Of course! What are friends for? You're going to kill it."

My stomach relaxed a bit and I didn't feel quite like I was

about to vomit.

"Safe travels," I replied, and she shot me a wicked smile.

"Oh, and my one condition goes for Vince, too." She cackled and then turned and walked into the airport.

Vince?

I sat there for a few minutes, until the car behind me started honking again.

Marissa was apparently the crazy one, not me. Vince? Um, not a chance. I'd be thrilled if the nice guy routine of the past twelve hours stuck. I'd be lying if I said I hadn't noticed how nicely he'd aged, but sleep with him? Um, no thank you. Wasn't he sort of my boss now?

Besides, Davis was my missed opportunity and that was my focus. I let my mind wander back to the details of the original tour. The music, how it affected people. The crowds, the fans. Even the band itself. It had started and stopped for me with that, and so that's where it should begin again this time. And I planned to capture it all, on film.

The band was playing another sold out show tonight before they hit the road for the next city on the tour. I wasn't sure where exactly that was, though it had to be in the Midwest since this tour was all buses and no private jets.

Just like the old days.

I had no ticket for the show, and I'd just put my sidekick on a plane home. I felt a slight flurry of panic but tamped it down. I was on my own, this was my job. I'd order in and do some brainstorming. Ideas for the book, for the way the photos should look. Would they have a throwback quality or be new and flashy?

I stopped at the concierge for a pizza delivery recommendation and was headed to the elevator when the front desk clerk cut me off.

"Are you Ms. Cavett?"

I stopped. "Yes?"

He handed me an envelope. "Sorry to chase you down. This is for you. Have a nice night."

I waited until I was in my room to rip open the envelope. Inside was a backstage pass, wrapped inside a handwritten note.

Campbell,

I don't have your number. I probably should. Here's your pass for tonight. I'd get there before eight if you want to catch the guys before they hit the stage. I'll take you to the after-party, so you don't have to find it yourself this time.

Vince

Backstage pass.
After-party.
Vince.

I reached for the shopping bags I'd thrown on my bed. I was going to need those boots.

Chapter Twelve

I stood in front of the mirror in the ladies' room trying to give myself a pep talk. Trying to convince myself I could go from groupie-wannabe to professional photographer. But it wasn't as easy as all that. Earlier, at the concert, I'd let myself fall back into the role of groupie. How could I not? Seeing the entire show from backstage? I was still a little starstruck with my whole situation.

I could hear the throwaway comments the guys made to each other, see how the people in the front row reacted to them. Strike that—how the women in the front row reacted to them. From where I stood, I could see it all.

I snapped their photos, wanting to capture their energy, their adulation. Maybe I could blur the faces. And the band? Well, they ate it all up, and then gave it back in their energy. It was like they had never stopped playing together.

Also skewed was my reaction to Vince, who was standing just a bit over from me through the whole show. I found myself watching him when the songs changed—he was even more pulled in by the music than I was. Closing his eyes, his fingers strumming an imaginary guitar as his lips muttered along with the lyrics. Clearly, he had deep-seated roots with the guys and the music. It made me realize I didn't know his origin story, which seemed impossible.

"So, tell me about your history with Golden Tiger. I don't think I ever knew how it is you came to work for them," I'd asked. We were riding in the back of a black SUV courtesy of the label. Tonight's post party was going to be a tamer event, according to Vince. Early call to hit the road in the morning meant far less whiskey for everyone.

He'd smiled slyly. "My history with the band goes back to before the band even existed."

"Well that's cryptic."

"Not really. I grew up with the guys, all of them except Tony. We brought him in at the end."

I knew this, that the guys had grown up outside Chicago, and that once they'd gotten serious, they'd auditioned drummers. I hadn't known that Vince was part of that. His use of the word "we" was interesting.

He considered himself part of the band. I tried to remember if I'd ever seen a photo of him in all those old shots, the garage band years.

"Now that's a story for you. Make sure to ask the guys about the auditions for a drummer. At that point we were rehearsing in Rex's grandma's garage, if you can believe it. She was deaf so she didn't mind, but the neighbors sure did. Up until then, we'd been acoustic, no drums. Very low profile, and then we won a local battle of the bands and suddenly people wanted to book us, but we needed a drummer."

"We? So, you were part of the original band?"

He'd been staring out the blackened window as we drove through the streets of Chicago, like he was fondly recalling the memories, but with my question he turned and faced me. Again, looking me square in the eye.

"Yes, and no. When we started, when it was about the music, yes. When they decided they wanted to be rock stars, then I couldn't get out of it fast enough."

"Why?"

His eyes narrowed like he was contemplating his answer. We were pulling up to the bar where the party was being held, and I wished for a red light, not wanting this story, or this intimate moment, to end just yet.

He pointed at the crowd outside the bar and the barricades that had been set up. "Wait and watch." We'd pulled up well beyond the front door. Behind us, the stretch SUV carrying the guys stopped right in front, and even inside our car the screams were so loud my eardrums vibrated. It only got worse as they exited the car.

"That right there, it's just not my scene. It isn't what it's about for me."

I watched as grown women pulled at Davis's coat sleeve, until it was almost off of him. He was unfazed, until another one started to climb the barricade and security had to step in. Then he retreated back to the middle of the walkway, closer to the guys. They were still all smiles and stopped outside the door to turn and soak up the adulation.

My face was hot. I'd been one of these women twenty years ago. Or at least one in the crowd. Davis and the other guys seemed to feed off it, but Vince, he looked almost scared.

"Is that why you were always such a hard-ass about who was allowed behind that velvet rope? Less people, less of a scene?"

His gaze fixed on me. "Something like that." He reached for the door handle. "Let's sneak in the back while no one's looking." The change in subject made me think there was something else he wanted to say but then stopped himself.

I followed him up an alley I hadn't noticed when we stopped. Out here, the screams were definitely worse.

"DAVIS! YOU STILL LOOK SO HOT!"

"REX! JUST ONE KISS BEFORE I DIE!" And more that I'd rather not repeat. Or acknowledge. Could you still be guilty by association twenty years later? At least I'd been subtle about trying to get noticed and never screamed at them, which was way classier. Or at least that's what I told myself.

We arrived at the back door of the bar. Vince knocked three times, and it promptly opened into the back hall by the bathrooms.

"I'm just going to duck in here and freshen up," I said and didn't wait for a response. I needed a minute to collect myself. It was overwhelming, but I was determined not to let it get the best of me.

I stood over the sink and stared at myself. I wasn't the infatuated twenty-year-old girl I had been, but I also wasn't the lost, sad woman I'd been just a few days ago. I was somewhere in between. And though I looked a little scared, I wasn't going to let it stop me.

Progress.

Chapter Thirteen

One look at me, and Vince must have seen the nerves that I was feeling. A one-off drunken party was one thing. But this was a totally different animal. Tonight I was seeing them as a professional. The photographer hired to document the biggest thing they'd done in years. Even with my bathroom mirror pep talk, I was still a bit rattled.

"Let's just go say hello."

He was waiting for me outside of the bathroom, the band having found their way through the adoring crowds and to a table where they were holding court. I gave him a grateful smile and then followed him across the room.

Tony, always the wildest of the group, as drummers so often are. He had a straw between his fingers and was spinning it like a stick. Alex, the bass player, wearing his signature dark glasses even in the barely lit bar. Rex, lead guitar, he'd always been the coolest of the guys, the truest musician. And, of course, Davis.

He looked me up and down, then up again. Which should have been a bit repulsive, but instead sent a little thrill down my spine. He was totally checking me out.

"You guys remember Campbell from last night?" Vince said by way of introduction.

I raised my hand, sort of like a wave, but also as though Vince was taking attendance. I pulled it down immediately, but not before I caught Tony and Rex smirking at me.

"Campbell, you remember the guys: Tony, Rex, Alex." One by one they raised their own hands. I was being trolled by the biggest rock band of my generation.

"And, of course, Davis." He didn't raise his hand, but instead unfolded his six-foot-plus frame out of the booth and stood beside me.

"How could I forget? This lovely creature and I had a very memorable time last night." He took my hand and pressed it to his lips, never breaking eye contact. My breath hitched at the feel of them on my skin.

My heart was pounding in my ears, and I was hypnotized by it, and Davis.

"So, Campbell. You enjoy the show tonight?" Tony asked, his voice coming from what seemed to be far away. I needed to answer him, I knew, but somehow I just couldn't pull my hand away from Davis.

Until I took a sharp elbow to the ribs.

I withdrew my hand from Davis and glared at a smirking Vince.

"It was fantastic," I replied, wishing I could sit. I felt like I was looming over the table like a lunchroom monitor.

"Settle an argument for us, then," Rex chimed in. "In 'This Stupid Lie We Tell,' did you like the new bridge, or do you like the old one?"

"That's tough. The old one, well it drove the point home, right?" The music, now *that* I knew something about. "But this new one, it sort of strings you along but it gets you there. Seems more mature. Like the song grew up."

I could tell from the looks on their faces they were shocked. They were expecting a typical groupie response of, "I don't know, what do you boys think?" purred at them across the table as I bent over and showed them my cleavage. I couldn't blame them. I *had* waved.

"Damn. That's profound," Davis said, leaning against the wall next to the booth.

I smiled. "Well, I know *your* music. That's why I'm so excited to be the one capturing the tour."

The guys shot looks at one another, and then at Vince, who nodded slightly. Always the gatekeeper, Davis looked slightly smug and in the know.

"Well, welcome aboard," Alex said, his voice as low as his instrument. I leaned back on my heels, then planted my feet again.

"Yeah, welcome to our rock down memory lane!" Tony said, drumming on the table with his fingers, loudly.

Davis took my hand again. And, as though maybe he'd forgotten he just pulled this move, raised it to his lips again. "I look forward to our one-on-one shoots." And then he turned and walked, actually strutted, toward the bar.

The thing is, my reaction to Davis was purely physical. Chemical. Illogical.

I mean, it was Davis Scott, looking me directly in the eye and kissing my hand. I wouldn't say I was transported back to the girl I had been, but rather it seemed to awaken the part of me that she'd left behind. No matter how cheesy his moves were, I was affected by them. I could barely connect my thoughts, let alone speak.

I took a deep breath, trying to collect myself. I was blowing any chance of being considered a professional by these guys. I had to get my shit together. And spending another night drinking with them was not the play, no matter how much former groupie me would argue. I'd impressed them with my musical aptitude, that seemed a better ploy than showing them I could hold my whiskey. Which, based on the past two nights, I actually couldn't do.

"I am looking forward to it..." My face flamed. "Er, I mean, I'm looking forward to the rock down memory lane, not the one-on-one with just Davis, actually one-on-ones with all of you, those I am looking forward to, if you guys are on board with that..." I was rambling. This was decidedly not getting my shit together.

The guys laughed, and Vince was looking at me like I had sprouted an extra arm or something. This was more than blowing it. This was humiliating. Fight or flight, and I was certainly not looking for a fight.

"It was really nice meeting all of you again. I think I'm going to grab an Uber back to the hotel. Early start tomorrow and all of that." And before any of them could say a word, I turned on my heel and left, hoping to make it to the door without tripping or running into a waiter carrying a tray of drinks or something.

I escaped unscathed and was licking my self-inflicted wounds on the curb, waiting for my ride, when my phone rang.

Marissa.

"Thank God it's you," I said by way of an answer.

"Sounds like things are going as well there as they are here," Marissa replied.

"I think I just made a giant ass of myself, in front of the band." I leaned against the wall of the club.

"You think, or you did?"

I swallowed. "I did. Maybe you were right. This whole thing is well beyond my skill level in so many ways."

"Nope, we already went through this. You are more than qualified, in so many ways. But that doesn't mean it's going to be easy."

I had expected her to agree with me, celebrate and tell me to come right home, and I would have. Her honesty and encouragement instead was the calming effect I needed.

"Thanks," I said softly.

"For what?"

"For not telling me I told you so and to come home."

She clucked her tongue. "The road is your home now, or at least that's what I told Jack."

"Wait, Jack? Where in the hell did you see him?" There was no scenario that had their paths crossing. Jack thought coffee out was a waste of money. Had probably even told Marissa that more than once so there was no way he'd been in her shop. Nor could I picture him grocery shopping, though, he must have to now that I wasn't doing it for him.

"He dropped off a box of what looks like your old journals at my house. I don't want to snoop, because nothing is lower than reading someone else's journal, but the covers are all decorated with Golden Tiger logos and I thought maybe they could be important."

I sat down on the bench meant as a bus stop. "Wait, he brought them to your house? That's weird."

"He said he found them in a box under a bunch of his old college books. That they must have gotten mixed up with his somehow and you should be glad he didn't burn them. He's furious, by the way, that you're selling the house. Since he 'lost it to you' in the divorce."

"Ah, so that was his angle." Jack always had an angle and I bet he *was* furious. He loved that house, he'd picked out everything in it, so he should. "If he's so furious, he can buy it."

"I said the same thing!" Marissa replied. "He didn't like that one bit. Said he'd never pay twice for the same thing. Made some reference to you being cheap that I didn't quite understand, but maybe that was because I was pushing him out the door."

"Charming as always." I scoffed. "Wow, the old journals. I always thought he threw them away. My *sordid past*, he always called it." It was an odd coincidence them turning up now, but I'd take it. More of the universe lining up or whatever. I'm sure they were awful, but still—I'd like to read them for no other reason than to get reacquainted with the person I was.

"I thought you'd be itching for them. That's why I called. I can send them first thing tomorrow if you tell me where."

"I'll get an address for the next hotel from Vince and text it to you." My mind was already spinning. Those journals were more than just a glimpse into my past. They were a road map of how I didn't want to act around the band.

"Thanks, Marissa, for everything."

"Of course. You got this, Campbell. Really, you do."

I wished I believed it as strongly as she did. But I wasn't quite there yet.

"I'm going to need you to keep telling me that, like it's your job," I replied. She agreed and we said our goodbyes.

"You okay out here?"

I turned to find Vince standing just outside the door of the bar.

"Yep, just Marissa checking in. I'm waiting on my Uber."

He nodded, then handed me a cocktail napkin. "Glad I caught you before it came. Davis wanted me to give this to you."

I took it and unfolded it to see a phone number. My hands suddenly felt clammy around it, so I refolded it, terrified my sweaty hands would run the ink.

"He said to call him to set up your deep dive." He tilted his head in the direction of the window. "As you can see, he's filled his time slot for tonight."

I followed his nod to see that the band had been

infiltrated with what truly looked like groupies. And though they'd aged, they were the exact same women who'd been around twenty years ago. Big blonde hair, big blue eyes, and big boobs. Davis had his arm slung across the one closest to him who looked quite pleased with herself.

"The three double Bs," I noted.

"How the hell could I forget that?" He laughed.

"I don't know, you coined the phrase, I just co-opted it."

He sat down on the bench next to me, still laughing.

"All those Bs, and not a brain between them."

"Yep, you used to say that, too." I stuck my chest out. "I never qualified."

Vince looked down, lingered one second, then met my eye. "That wasn't the reason. You with your camera, and your ability to hold a conversation." He tapped his temple.

It was as close to a compliment as Vince had ever given me and it pleased me more than I cared to admit. I punched his shoulder. "Aw, thanks."

He chuckled, then pointed. "Looks like your car has arrived." A car fitting the description of the one I'd ordered on my app was pulling up to the curb.

I nodded. "See you in the morning." I glanced at the window one more time before I headed for the car.

This night had started out with such promise but was ending like it always had. Davis with his arm slung over the shoulder of one of the Triple Bs and me watching from a distance.

Except I was now in possession of his phone number. That was new.

Chapter Fourteen

It was all well and good to pretend I was eighteen and could just wander aimlessly around the country following a band. But if last night showed me anything, I was going to need more of a plan than that if I was going to pull off this whole gig, since I seemed to lose my focus when I was alone with them. And by them, I meant Davis.

I couldn't ignore how quickly he had moved on to the Triple Bs, and the ensuing sense of déjà vu it had conjured up. As much as I was enjoying the whole rock and roll scene, that part was a total been there, done that moment I didn't care to relive again. So, it seemed a good place for the adult me to step in and strategize. Not that I was giving up, not even close. Davis was my "what if" and I intended to find out the answer.

He was probably just turning on the charms because I was the one tasked with getting the best optics of him. But it was something I could use. An angle to spend time with him and set myself apart from the usual groupies. Maybe he'd enjoy the chase if I took on a more professional persona?

The book. It was my angle, but it was also my job and I

had to get some concrete ideas on just what I wanted to do with it. Some sort of vision or storyboard. So here I was in my hotel room in St. Louis, holed up with my twenty-year-old journals which had been delivered to me the morning after we arrived. Marissa always came through, even at the cost of overnighting them. I was hoping for some sort of inspiration.

It hadn't started out well. The first entry had read like a letter to *Tiger Beat*.

My God! Davis in those leather pants! I think he was singing right to me, and I felt it, really felt it. We have a definite connection. He felt it too, I know he did, because he winked at me. I almost died. They're staying out at the Travelways motel. And guess who has a room there too! That's right, me! And there's a bar, so I plan to hang out there until they show up, and I just know once he sees me, that will be that. Who knows? Maybe he'll write the whole next album about our instant connection! And I'll get to be right there while it's happening. I can't wait to see just how the guys work when they are writing their songs. And I can document the whole thing! I can already picture the dim lighting and cigarette smoke. Them bent over scraps of paper. So artsy. So cool!

I didn't need to read the next entry to know that none of that had happened.

When Davis had arrived at the hotel, he already had two girls, one tucked under each arm, and he had neither stopped in the bar nor acknowledged any sort of connection between the two of us. I almost felt a bit sorry for my younger self. Except that she sounded like a naive teen. Which was basically what she was.

But there were some useful nuggets hidden in the angst. Snippets of conversations I'd had. Things I'd seen. And pictures, though they weren't the best quality thanks to my cheap camera, but they'd been framed beautifully. There was no doubt I'd had a good eye back then. When I'd been close enough to get good shots, I'd written the song they were performing on the back.

Could I recreate them? Lay the book out with the old and new photos, song by song? I was keen to make sure that the music was a big part of this. I was no writer, that part I knew for sure. But the stories of the songs had to be a part of it.

All the theatrics of Golden Tiger aside, they were kick-ass musicians. Using their own songs to tell their story was a twist I thought fans old and new would be fascinated by. Diving into the meanings or inspirations behind them, told by the band members themselves. Weren't we all trying to capture a little bit of our youth, and wasn't music the way most of us did it? Surely I wasn't the only person who could hear a song and be transported back to a specific moment. That was a universal feeling. And I could do that in photos, for sure. But a little storytelling alongside that would really make it special.

It was a start.

I checked the time and was shocked how late it had gotten. I needed to get to the venue to see what the guys did pre-show. At this point, I was well versed in what happened after the show. *Too* well versed.

I pulled on my black high-waisted skinny jeans (thank the Lord for the suck-it-in-ness of the high waist so I could leave the Spanx at home), black push-up bra, and white blouse which I left open just one button more than I was truly comfortable with. This made it edgy but age appropriate and not desperate—or at least that's what I told myself. I pulled my hair up in a messy bun, put on eyeliner, mascara, and a red lipstick I also considered edgy, and headed out.

"I'm here for the show," I told the lobby bartender at a

venue similar to the one we'd just played in Chicago. He was the only person at the club I could find.

He looked at the clock above the bar. "A little early, aren't you?"

I flushed. "What I meant to say was I'm here for the band. I'm the photographer doing a photo book of the tour. Well, more of a photographic essay book of the tour, I guess." I patted my camera bag to make my point, since I couldn't make it with my words.

Would he ask for ID? Credentials? Surely that was something most actual photographers would have.

He pulled out a clipboard.

"Name?"

"Of the book? I haven't decided on one yet."

He blinked, holding it for a long time. Much longer than a regular blink. "Your name. So I can see if they put you on the early entry list."

Was it possible to die of embarrassment? Like bleed to death because all of the blood in your body was flooding your cheeks?

"Campbell Cavett," I said sheepishly.

He ran his finger down the list and then pointed the clipboard in the direction of a door.

"Right through there. Best of luck with that title."

I chose not to acknowledge that last remark and instead walked as quickly as I could to the door he'd pointed to, pausing just inside to try and collect myself. The theater was bigger than the one in Chicago. It was dark, except for the stage. There was something sort of magical about being here without all the people and noise. It felt like the calm before the storm.

I made my way to the stage and hoisted myself up. Everything was set up for the show. The mic stands lined the front, the drum set on a platform at the back so that Tony could be seen, lording over the rest as they danced and strutted down front. Guitars stood in stands at the ready near giant amplifiers. A huge screen hung behind the whole thing.

I turned and tried to imagine what it would be like to see yourself projected larger than life on the screen while hundreds of people screamed for you. It had to be terrifying and a rush all at the same time.

I turned and walked to the front of the stage, my fingers dancing across the mics. I had never been one for attention, but still. I could imagine the thrill of it. The lights, the screaming fans. Davis lapped it up. They all seemed to.

Suddenly the spotlight turned on, shining directly where I stood. I froze, lost in my thoughts, but seemingly captured.

"Um, sorry?"

Why I was apologizing, I did not know. No one had told me I couldn't go on the stage. I had free range according to Vince. But I felt caught.

From the darkness came a hearty, recognizable laugh.

"Scared you, did I?"

I held my hand up to shield my eyes. "Vince? What the hell?"

"Just time for the light check is all." His booming voice was now closer, and then he appeared in the edge of my spotlight.

"You look pretty good in stage lights," he said, though he turned his head as he spoke, making it hard to hear for sure. But I was nearly certain, and I bit my lip to keep from smiling. A compliment from Vince was both pleasant and unexpected. I moved to where he stood out of the blaring spotlight and sat down, dangling my feet over the edge of the stage.

"It has to be such a rush to be up here and really deserve that spotlight."

Vince nodded. "Those four guys, ordinary as they come

back when I met them. Even now, when they aren't caught up in being Golden Tiger, they're pretty damn normal dudes. But you get them up on a stage and give them mics and instruments? Call it chemistry or talent or whatever you want. I call it magic."

There was something about the look on his face when he spoke—mesmerizing, dreamy. Replying felt like it would break the spell, so I nodded. I called it magic, too.

"Vince?" A loud voice boomed over the speakers.

We both jumped.

"Time for the sound check," the voice boomed again.

Vince waved a hand over his head. And then he grabbed the side of the stage and pushed himself up next to me, swung his feet around, and stood. He held his hand out to me, and I took it, surprised by how soft it felt. Then surprised that I noticed such a thing.

He dropped my hand as soon as I was upright and went about the business of checking the mics. Unsure what to do, I stepped back and watched as he worked. I'd never seen him do any of this before. Though, what did I think he did for the band all these years?

He had his head down, like he'd done it a thousand times, which he probably had. We were joined on stage by the sound crew, and he gave them instructions. He smiled as he slapped them on the back. He pointed and directed. Then, to my astonishment, he picked up one of the guitars, plugged it into an amp, and gave it a strum. Then another.

He played the opening medley of "Fall's Forgiveness," which was my absolute favorite Golden Tiger song. But he played it slower, almost hauntingly. It was certainly beautiful, and completely unexpected. Vince was a much more complex and talented man than I gave him credit for. My skin prickled.

He played, eyes closed, holding each note just a beat longer than the last, slowing it down. Humming the lyrics, with an occasional bit of singing into the mic. It was artful. Around him, the sound crew stopped what they were doing and listened. I stepped back and reached for my camera, snapping before he noticed.

It fit exactly with my vision for the book, the story that had gone untold. Little details from behind the scenes. It hadn't really dawned on me that Vince was a big part of that.

I snapped a photo, then another. I moved back, trying to get the whole thing in frame—Vince in silhouette playing in the spotlight but to an empty house.

He finished up with a grand flourish, and the crew rewarded him with raucous applause and hoots. I joined in, wishing I could whistle like Marissa. He played it up, waving his hands to encourage the applause, and then he saw me, and his face froze. Like he'd forgotten all about the fact that I was there, too. He eyed the camera that I held at the ready and that look came again, sheepish, but with a hint of something else.

It was something wistful I couldn't quite place, and my heart thudded as though it was a look we'd shared at some point. Though I knew that wasn't true. I opened my mouth to ask why it felt so familiar, but a hand on my elbow stopped me.

"Glad I caught you, doll. Let's get a start on our one-on-one time."

Davis.

Saying words I'd only ever conjured up in my fantasies. I shivered as I turned to reply, catching Vince's eye across the stage. He scowled ever so slightly, and I wondered why. It was why I was here after all. It must have just been pure habit. He was always scowling at me when we were younger.

"I'm ready when you are," I said to Davis, my plans to play this completely professionally all but forgotten as I followed him away from the stage.

Chapter Fifteen

Davis's dressing room was exactly what I thought it would be. Or should be, rather. Dark, with scarves thrown over the top of lamps to make it as moody as possible.

"Aren't you worried that's a fire hazard?" I was suddenly a ball of nerves to be sober and alone with him in his private space. Being worried about fire safety is super sexy, right?

Davis furrowed his brow in confusion. Apparently, he was so not concerned about fire that he had no idea what I was even talking about.

"The scarves. All that fabric on top of hot lightbulbs. Just seems dangerous." I pointed at the lamp, cursing myself under my breath. *Let the fire thing go.*

"Danger is what I'm all about." Sly smile. I wondered if that was a natural smile or if he taught himself to do it. I pictured a young Davis staring into a mirror, practicing different facial expressions to find the one that he thought made him look the sexiest and arriving at the side smile.

Gah! I needed to focus. Nerves be damned, this was my chance. Why was my brain trying to sabotage me?

Davis closed the door to his dressing room and turned to face me. I swallowed, but it did nothing to calm my nerves.

"It's going to make it awfully hard for me to take pictures, having the lighting this dim," I said, earning me his signature smirk, which in turn caused my nerves to activate my next lovely line of defense as I broke out in a cold sweat.

Was that more or less sexy than my earlier safety patrol routine? I needed to retreat and pull myself together before I blew this whole thing.

"I prefer a little dark, a little mystery," he replied as he walked past me, his voice still light and flirty. Which I took as a good sign that I hadn't turned him off completely. I took a deep breath and tried to remember that I was supposed to be playing at least a little bit hard to get.

"What if we start with a story? You could tell me how you guys came up with the name Golden Tiger."

There were several different versions of how they came to name the band, each more ridiculous than the last. The mascot of the high school the guys had attended had been a tiger. And though they tried as hard as they could, none of them were athletic enough to achieve varsity status, which was nicknamed Silver Tiger. So, they one-upped the jocks and named the band Golden Tiger.

Another version had the guys spray painting the mascot statue as a prank and the only spray paint they had was gold.

And yet another had to do with Rex's long golden hair and the fact that he'd somehow managed to sleep with the French teacher, who called him *le tigre*.

Like I said, each was more ridiculous than the last.

"Is that really how you want to spend our one-on-one time?" he asked. Another good sign. His flirting back.

He struck a match and started lighting the candles that until now I hadn't noticed were everywhere in the room. Talk about a fire hazard.

"I just think a good opening story is the way to really get the book started. Like a show, you know. You wouldn't open with a ballad. You want something that rocks. That everyone knows. It sets the bar for how the rest of the show will go. I want to have stories to complement the pictures, and since I'm not a writer, the stories need to come from you."

He seemed to be considering what I said as the match burned dangerously close to his fingertips. But before it could burn him, he shook it out and then pointed at me.

"I see where you're going there. It's good, setting it up like a show, building the anticipation. Stories and photos." He tapped his finger to his temple. "I like the way you think. Very rock and roll."

I sighed with relief. Setting aside the flirtatious nature of this meeting, an endorsement from Davis on the format would go a long way with the other guys.

"So, tell me. Why the name Golden Tiger?"

He made his way across the space toward a couch at the far side of the room, lighting candles as he went. I wasn't sure if he was ignoring my question or pondering it.

"It's hard for me to believe you would let the band be named after Rex's sexual prowess, so that rules out the French teacher." I crossed and settled on the arm of the couch, one foot on the ground to keep my balance. And hopefully appear interested but sexy.

Perching was sexy, right? Oh God, I had no game, none at all.

"Never count out Rex, or sexual prowess," he said with a sexy little laugh that had the same effect on me as him saying "ladies" at the concert that first night.

I moved my foot and slid down the arm of the couch so I was sitting next to him, hoping the move came off as casual and flirty and not like a lazy eight-year-old taking a seat, and wishing I could think of the perfect flirty comment with just the right amount of innuendo.

"Or sexual prowess in general," I tried, not liking how it sounded as it came out of my mouth. Sure, I wanted to be flirty, but I didn't want to come across as throwing myself at him like the groupies he was used to. And all that comment was missing was a mindless giggle afterward. I'd forgotten how hard flirting was. This whole thing was more than a little uncomfortable. I didn't know who to be.

He paused like he was considering this statement, then he turned and looked at me intently. "And here you went on and on about us not knowing each other."

I smiled. "We didn't, despite my best efforts."

He threw his head back and laughed, and suddenly I remembered why I was here and reached for my camera. The dim light, the colorful scarf blurred in the background, it was all Davis. I snapped quickly and then he straightened up and gave me his signature smirk, the moment of reality gone as his persona slid back into place.

"I should feel bad about that. Scratch that, I do feel bad about that."

I pulled my camera away from my face. "It was a long time ago," I replied, not wanting to draw attention to the fact that I was a bit of an outlier, a loser, back in the heyday.

"I guess. Though being up on stage makes me feel like it was only yesterday."

I nodded. I felt that way sometimes, too. Though his yesterday and mine were vastly different memories. "Yeah, it's hard to believe that you haven't played together in all these years. That same chemistry you've always had in spades, it's still there."

"Like fingers on the same hand," he said, and he held his up to me, wiggling them. He was back to being just a guy, and oddly I found him much more interesting and was far less affected by him. Apparently, it was the rock star personality that made me practically trip over my own lust.

"You guys lucked out. Not a prima donna among you," I quipped. This was sort of getting away from me and while this was nice and all and good for the book, I had something completely different in mind when it came to a one-on-one with Davis.

"Nothing lucky about it. The stars aligned and put us all right where we were supposed to be. Sort of like you, being in that front row the other night." His voice shifted and something around his eyes softened, drawing me in. I moved closer to him. This was more like it.

"You really believe in all that? Destiny and the universe?" I asked, my own voice unrecognizable. When Davis turned on the charms, well, who could deny it? I could feel myself drawn into the possibility that my inner wild child was about to reappear.

He nodded. "The universe has spoken, and here we are," he purred, leaning in, closing his eyes. So it had. I did the same, drifting toward him. And then my mouth went dry. I hadn't kissed anyone in decades except Jack. Was I letting nostalgia get the better of me? Should I be doing this? The ink was barely dry on my divorce papers.

But this was Davis-frickin-Scott.

I closed my eyes tighter and willed away my nerves. We were so close now, I could feel the heat radiating off of him and I hoped he couldn't hear my heart pounding because it was all I could hear. I felt his breath, hot with a hint of whiskey. I leaned just a titch forward, filled to the brim with unresolved teenaged angst, and the aforementioned something wild.

It was happening, Davis Scott was about to kiss me silly.

But then the door opened, flooding the room with light. I bolted upright and away from Davis, the sudden brightness blocking me from seeing who had joined us. Davis scowled and pulled himself to sitting.

"This better be important."

"Why the hell is it so dark in here?"

Vince. Not the universe.

"I like some ambiance, sets the mood."

"Sets the mood for what? A séance?"

Even in my slightly-delirious-from-almost-being-kissed-by-Davis-Scott state, it was so Vince. So spot-on drily hilarious that I bit my lip to keep from laughing.

"The fact that you don't know says a lot, man. And the fact that you don't know you should knock when a dude has a lady in his dressing room."

Vince nodded. "Ah, yes. You mean our tour photographer. Probably a little light would help her with *taking your photo*."

"We were doing all right, weren't we, doll?" he asked.

I really didn't like that nickname.

Vince continued, "Well, sorry to break up whatever that might be, but they need you on stage. They aren't sure my voice is the same pitch as yours and they want you to do a sound check."

Davis scowled slightly and then stood and started toward the door. Stopping in front of me, he reached for my hand and brought it to his lips.

"To be continued," he said, lip curl, half wink. His persona back in place. Then he pivoted and prowled back across the room. He paused again and punched Vince in the gut.

"Next time, knock. Or you just might walk in on something."

The punch wasn't hard, but Vince still pretended to flinch, making a show of it before he chuckled, slapped Davis on the back, then pushed him toward the door. "I'll keep that in mind."

My face was hot, for no reason. It wasn't like we'd been really doing anything when Vince walked in.

"Nothing was going on," I said as soon as Davis was out of earshot.

Vince raised an eyebrow and then shrugged. "None of

my business."

I went from embarrassed to annoyed. "I was trying to get a story for the book since the lighting was nonexistent for photos. Though I did get a couple of very Davis-looking shots. He had no interest in telling me much." I flipped my notebook closed and crossed my arms. I was rambling and I knew it.

Vince moved to the dressing table and blew out the candles. Pulling the scarf off the lamp, he shook his head and held it up to his nose.

"Burned. I have told him about a thousand times that those bulbs get too hot to throw scarves on top of them. He's going to burn himself down someday."

"I said the exact same thing! Surely there has to be a safer way for him to create his ambiance?"

"Those are the sort of hard-hitting questions he refused to answer?" Why did he look so damn amused?

"Shut up. That wasn't part of my interview. It was more my icebreaker."

Vince set the scarf on the chair. "And what did you follow up with?"

"I asked him how Golden Tiger came up with the name. He didn't answer, so I threw out some theories."

"You didn't ask him about Rex and the French teacher, did you?"

I furrowed my eyebrows. "Maybe?"

He leaned back against the dressing table and crossed his arms in front of his chest. "Davis hates that story about as much as Rex loves it. So, I'm not surprised he wasn't chatty and retreated to the whole rock star routine. How about you and I get together after the show tonight and go over some ideas. Questions that will work. How to ask and who to ask what."

I felt my whole body relax. "Thank you. I think that'll be a big help."

"I'm happy to do it."

Down the hall came the muffled sound of singing and he straightened to go. "I better make sure the sound is all right."

He checked his watch. "Doors open in twenty minutes. Why don't you watch this one from back by the bar? You'll get to take in the whole scene."

"Okay." It was nice to have Vince looking out for me like this, though I'd never in a million years admit that to him. I didn't need him thinking I couldn't do it on my own. I wanted to, and I wanted to believe I could, but a little help to get started couldn't hurt. Once I knew what I was doing, and the guys got used to me, it'd get easier. Or that's what I told myself as I followed Vince up the hallway, Davis's voice getting clearer as we neared the stage. Someone had set up a bar just in the wings, and Vince reached into a tub of ice and handed me a beer.

"It'd help if you loosened up a bit, I think. Try to be more like you are with me. One of the guys." He paused and smiled here, a real smile, not that tight one he used when he knew he should be smiling. "Not that your whole sexy high school newspaper girl thing isn't great, but you're going to have to take a softer hand when it comes to Davis. Let him think it is all his idea." He pointed at my notebook and pen and walked backward toward where Davis stood before spinning on his heel. He slapped him on the back and said something I couldn't hear and they both started laughing.

Sexy high school newspaper girl? I flushed. Was that a compliment? From Vince? What was he playing at, and what were they laughing at? If there was one thing I'd learned because of my divorce, you couldn't let someone always have the upper hand. I needed to even the playing field. Or find some sort of home field advantage if I was sticking with the sports analogies.

We were in St. Louis and thanks to my journals, I knew just the place.

Chapter Sixteen

"I thought we were meeting in the hotel bar?" Vince eyed me suspiciously. I was waiting for him backstage with my keys in my hand. The show had been fantastic again. These small venues really let the audience be a part of the show, and the energy between the band and the crowd was palpable. I had gotten great shots with the band soft and out of focus in the background, with a crowd in front that was really feeling it. I was rediscovering the eye I used to have for this sort of photography, but with a quality camera this time around. It was exhilarating. I felt like I was possessed up there. Someone else.

There were times when all I could hear was the click of the shutter, which seemed impossible as loud as the music was, but it was true. It was so good to be back taking the kind of pictures that gave me life, instead of the kind that drained my will to live.

The guys had left, riding the high. Off to wherever the after-party was probably already raging. Davis with his arm slung around the shoulder of a Triple B, me already forgotten.

Which I guess was for the best. I needed Vince's help, and tonight was the night he was offering it.

It was just shy of midnight and because there was only one show here, the whole stage had to be broken down. I'd had to wait for Vince until that was done, spending the time jotting down notes about the show, which song went with which photo. I had the idea to focus on a different member of the band with each song, and then change it from show to show. I was hoping by that alone I could start to figure out which meant more to who.

I had so much on the line with this project: showing my ex that I could stand on my own two feet, showing myself that I was capable of supporting myself with my art. Showing that ass Harrison I was right for the job. Having to tap Vince in to help me wasn't ideal, but it was a concession I was willing to make. He knew the guys better than anyone.

I shook my head at Vince as I turned to walk toward the door. "Nah, better idea." I didn't bother to see if he was following me.

He was, I knew, because I heard him sigh as I pushed open the door to the lobby. Well, he could sigh all he wanted. Joining this tour was supposed to be about me rediscovering who I'd been, and how I'd allowed her to get swallowed up by someone else's idea of what her life should be. Not to repeat the pattern.

"The Tipsy Rooster?" Vince said as we pulled up in front of the twenty-four-hour diner.

I nodded. "Don't pretend like you aren't thrilled that I remembered it."

"Thrilled isn't the word I'd go with." His voice was tight. I'd forgotten how much Vince hated not being in charge.

Well, it was good for him to stretch his comfort zone.

I flashed him a big sarcastic smile. "Oh, you're going to love it. Trust me."

I put the car in park and turned it off. The streets were empty, the only sound coming from the distant freeway. We were as alone as we could be in the middle of a big city, and it was a feeling I had always loved. Small town or metropolis, everyone slept in the middle of the night. Or at least that's how it always felt to me. I wanted to run and stand in the circle cast from the streetlight, but Vince already seemed leery, so instead I just pulled the door open.

It was exactly the same. A place before its time, a diner that served booze. Booths lined the walls and there was an island of them in the middle. Above each a light hung from a chain, the only lights in the whole place aside from the ancient neon jukebox that sat against the back wall.

"It's just like I remember," I said as the hostess approached us, yawning.

"Two?"

I nodded. "Just two."

She grabbed two plastic menus from the side of her hostess stand. "Follow me."

There was just one other table of people and she sat us a booth down from them. "You're lucky they beat you in here." She nodded at the couple. "I had to wake up Eunice and she was none too pleased. But now she's had her coffee and should be all rainbows and unicorns again." She laughed at her own joke as she set the menus down and left us to take our seats.

Vince was still looking around like he was an amnesia victim.

"Why are you acting like you've never been here before?" I asked as I slid into the booth.

"It may surprise you to know that I don't remember every place I've ever dined in my life." He took off the jacket he was wearing, an old leather thing that looked like it had been around as long as he had, in fact I was pretty sure he had been wearing it on the last tour, now that I thought about it. He threw it on the bench before sitting down across from me.

I was struck with a strong sense of déjà vu.

Though, when we'd been here last, we hadn't come together. Just like tonight, the show had been amazing and just like this tour, they'd only been playing here for the one night. I'd camped outside the tour buses where the after-party would rage until they all passed out and the bus drivers could make their way to the next stop in the peaceful dark of night.

It had been so early on the tour, and I'd been hopeful. My hair teased, my T-shirt ripped just so, I'd stood on the outskirts of the group trying to figure out who was getting in and how. Once I'd collected enough information to know that I had to appear drunk enough to be fun, but sober enough to last the night, I'd made my move.

"Hold up there. Where do you think you're going?" Vince had said. The first time he'd ever actually spoken directly to me.

"On the bus. For the party," I'd said, trying to make my voice breathy and flirty like I'd heard the other girls do.

He just shook his head and pointed his finger away from the bus, and I'd skulked away. Mortified with embarrassment at being dismissed like a child, I'd gotten in my car and driven away, pulling into the first place that was open in the middle of the night. Thrilled to find booze and pancakes to soothe my wounded pride.

It had been about thirty minutes later when Vince had shown up, thrown his jacket down, and slid in across from me. Like he just had tonight.

"I always wondered how you found me here that night," I said, lost in the memory. But before he could answer, our waitress appeared.

"Who's drinking?" she asked in a voice that sounded more sex phone operator than diner waitress. And, I might add, blonder and twenty-two, not the full gray and pushing sixty that she was.

"Eunice!" Vince exclaimed. And I mean exclaimed, like Eunice was his long-lost aunt or something.

She eyed him skeptically. "Is that a yes on the drink or have you had enough already tonight, hon?"

He laughed. "All these years, and you're still on the job. We'll take two whiskeys."

She shrugged and wrote the order down on the green pad in her hand. "Where else would I be?"

"So, you remember the waitress, but not this place?" I asked when she'd walked away, I assumed to get our drinks.

He handed me a menu and then opened the one in front of him. "I may not remember the place, but I never forget a face. Eunice looks exactly the same. If memory serves, you better be ready with your order when she gets back with those drinks."

He was right. I remembered that too. I perused the menu quickly. There were all sorts of fancy new items—crustless quiche and avocado toast—but I'd come here for the pancakes.

Eunice returned with our drinks and took our orders, waffles for Vince, pancakes for me. Bacon for both of us, and she was gone again.

"I wonder what she puts in her coffee?" he asked as she walked an unsteady route back toward the kitchen.

"People in glass houses," I said, raising my glass for a clink, which he obliged.

"And to answer your question, I hadn't been looking for you, I'd been looking for a drink and some food. Finding you here was just a pleasant surprise."

That was news. A pleasant surprise? "You mean you didn't set out in the dark of night to apologize for hurting my feelings and then hurt them worse by telling me to get over myself, get a life, and stop following a rock band?"

"That last bit does sound like me, and if I'm being honest, I do remember how hurt you looked when I told you to move along that night. And I believe it only made you more determined." He pointed at me and then took another drink.

That it had. I took a sip from my whiskey. I hadn't been lying when I told Marissa that Vince and I had an adverse relationship. We had, but we'd also had moments like this that I'd completely forgotten about. Something about his gruff outside, the way he tried to always act like he was annoyed with everything and everyone, it was endearing to me. Maybe because it was so familiar. I was pretty hard on the outside, too.

"You told me I had to have more going for me than I could find in the back of a tour bus. Or maybe you said on my back in a tour bus. It's hard to remember now."

"Now that sounds even more like me!" He laughed. "I'd seen you around, with your camera. You could hold a conversation, that was the buzz around the roadies. You talked to them like they were people, not just an in with the band."

I nodded. "I wanted to know about the equipment, why Rex switched guitars when they all looked the same to me. How many sets of drumsticks Alex went through in a show."

"Even then, you got it." He looked me dead in the eye, and something in my belly tilted just slightly. I took a sip of my whiskey.

This spark, this connection, I had no memory of whatsoever. But it held me enough that I didn't break eye contact, no matter how much my buzzing brain was telling me to.

"Here we are. Pancakes for the lady, waffles for the gentleman. Are you a gentleman?" Eunice elbowed him a little after she set the plate down.

"Or maybe I should ask the lady." She winked and then

slid down into the booth next to Vince. "Mind if I sit for just a second? My feet are killing me."

Since she'd already sat down next to Vince, it was a rhetorical question, so neither of us answered. I wasn't sure if I was upset or relieved.

"I've been doing this for quite a few years at this point as you so kindly pointed out earlier." She winked at Vince. "I have to say the couples who seem the happiest are the ones who aren't cookie-cutters." Vince looked as confused as I felt.

She pointed at our plates. "Pancakes and waffles. Not the same. You two are a perfect match."

I had busied myself buttering my pancakes and pouring the perfect amount of syrup on each, but at this I paused. "Oh, we aren't a couple."

Someone at the table behind us yelled out for service and Eunice stood up slowly, laughing. "Not as far as you know anyway." She shuffled off in their direction. "I'm coming, keep your pants on."

We sat in silence for a few minutes, both of us doctoring up our food. Until finally I couldn't take it. "So, waffles, huh?"

"And pancakes." He pointed, and a smile spread across his face.

"I don't know why. It isn't like I come from some family where my mom made them homemade on Sunday mornings or anything. You?"

He shrugged. "I just always wanted a golden retriever named Waffles."

"So, you eat them?" I deadpanned.

"Well, when you say it that way, I can see that it's a bit odd. I think they're both just things that I find comfort in. Things I think of when I think of a real home."

A real home. I wasn't even sure what that meant for me. The one I'd grown up in couldn't qualify: my family never quite had enough of anything, and no one seemed to particularly like each other. The home I'd made with Jack had been sterile and run by strict rules of appearance, and the like thing seemed to apply there too.

Had I known a real home? I didn't think so.

"Did you have a dog growing up?"

He shook his head. "My dad was allergic. Davis had a dog, a mutt. Cute as could be, but not very smart. Sort of like Tony before we got him."

"Tony is cute." I chuckled. "I don't think I've ever talked to him so I can't speak to his intellect."

"Trust me on this one. Back when we were kids, when he first joined, the rest of the guys had convinced him that a bag of pink insulation was cotton candy. I stepped in just as he was about to take his first bite."

"Stop it! Didn't he notice how sharp it was?" My mouth hung open.

"They told him it was well done."

"Okay, I hate to judge, but that is not very bright."

"He means well. He has a good heart, maybe the best of them all. I think you should talk to him first."

I set my fork down. "Why?"

Vince finished his bite of waffles and then cut another. "For a few reasons. One, he'll bend your ear with the stories he can tell." He stabbed at the bite he'd cut with his fork. "And two, once Davis sees you spending time with the other guys, he'll settle down with the whole rock-star-sex-god act." He put the waffle in his mouth.

Is that what I wanted? Davis to stop his seduction? If you could even call it that. Sure, in the moments it was happening I rarely knew how to handle it. When he turned on those rock and roll charms, it shot straight to my veins and I turned into a quiet, wanton creature of some sort. Did I truly want him to stop? Not until something had come of it. But admitting that to Vince seemed a little raucous and unprofessional.

I was starting to feel like my two pursuits—Davis and pulling off a book that would pass muster—were two entirely different goals. Two roads that were never going to intersect. How was I going to pull them both off? Would one be a sacrifice to the other, and how in the hell would I ever choose?

"Unless you don't want him to settle down?" Vince asked, pulling me out of my own head, his question the very one I was asking myself—further evidence of the connection that seemed to be buzzing around our booth.

That direct stare of his felt like he could see into my soul. Which, if he could, would be somewhat embarrassing given my current train of thought.

And since I didn't want to answer, I took a bite of my pancakes.

Chapter Seventeen

The rest of our late-night dinner was small talk and polite laughter. Whatever connection we'd had disappeared like whiskey and pancakes. And when we'd said our good nights on the elevator, he'd gotten off a floor before me, I'd felt like there was something I should say to acknowledge it had been there, but I wasn't sure just what it was. Or if it was all in my head. Maybe this was just what having a male friend felt like? I wouldn't know. It hadn't been allowed when I was married.

I spent the rest of the night ruminating on it and the realization that my goals were at cross-purposes. I tossed and turned in my bed, unable to make my mind turn off, finally drifting off to sleep around four a.m.

In the light of day, a full travel mug of coffee in my cup holder and my eyes focused on the taillights of the tour buses, I had decided that Vince was probably right. Getting Davis to cool his jets was probably best for the book, but was that what was best for me?

Could it be enough to know that Davis had found me worthy of pursuit? Yes, but also no. For a woman who'd been trained over the years to feel what she wanted was unworthy, I just didn't think it was enough. Would sleeping with Davis solve that? Would doing that make me feel better or worse about myself? Would I lose all of his respect if we did "the deed"? What about my self-respect?

It was also clear that Davis wasn't being all that authentic with me. Maybe he just wanted the focus of the book to be about his sex appeal? That seemed ridiculous. Golden Tiger, for all its hype and theatrics, was at its core a rock band with songs that meant something to millions of people. How could he want the book to be so shallow? Especially when the flashes of his real self I got were so genuine and interesting. Maybe he just didn't want the book to ruin his rep as a rock star and all that was assumed to go with it?

So many questions.

I jotted them down in the notebook I kept open on the passenger seat. Not exactly the safest way to drive, but neither was keeping them buzzing around in my brain. It was distracting.

Since there was no show tonight, I was looking forward to getting to the next city and staying in with nothing but my thoughts and the internet full of old photos. When it came down to it, I was having a crisis of conscience. Was I on this tour to change a choice from my past, or was I really serious about creating something that would capture a band I thought was iconic and doing them justice? And by doing so, hopefully cementing my future.

It seemed I was leaning more toward the latter, but if that was really true, how did I square that with my vow to stop seeking the comfortable way out? Being in that dressing room with Davis had been uncomfortable, but wasn't that what I was after?

I had no answers and nothing but miles of highway ahead of me. I thumbed through my music until I found what I was looking for. Music always served to quiet my mind. And this time was no different. It had been years since I'd listened to *Tour Bus Taillights* from beginning to end.

I'd forgotten that it told a story when you listened to it that way. It was, hands down, my favorite. Even though it came out after I'd left the tour and I'd only ever listened to it when Jack wasn't around. Maybe that was part of the allure. The secretness of it all. Like I still was connected to the tour, the band. My wild side.

My brain started to churn with more questions, but then Rex hit the perfect chord, and Davis hit that one note that made my heart squeeze and I let them go. I rolled down my windows, the hot summer air pushing the air-conditioned chill from the car.

I felt human, alive. Like I was finally doing something that fed every part of me: my heart and soul. My creativity. It piqued my curiosity and pushed me to learn more, do more. The constant stream of questions in my mind were proof of that. Even if I had no idea how to answer the questions, I let that be okay and just enjoyed the music and the scenery as the miles flew by.

When we reached Kansas City, the sun hung low and orange in the summer sky. We were staying right downtown, and though the crowd outside the hotel was nothing like it would have been twenty years before, there were still a good chunk of fans waiting for the band to arrive.

Davis, never one to disappoint, had the bus pull right up to the front door to let them out. I opted to park in the lot and walk through the side door to avoid the inevitable scene. I was exhausted and wanted nothing more than food and my bed. The trouble was I had to find Vince to find out what room I was in, which meant the lobby and the circus. I pulled my bag behind me through the maze that was the first floor of the hotel and hoped that by the time I reached the front desk, things would have settled down.

My duffel bag slid from my shoulder and I stopped to readjust it when a woman came bursting out of her room and ran right into me.

"I am so sorry, but oh my GOD! Did you know that Golden Tiger is staying in this hotel?" She looked at me wild-eyed. And I smiled. She was about my age, normal looking—no ripped jeans or T-shirt or thick black eyeliner. And she was downright giddy.

I nodded. "I did know that."

She smiled. "I feel ridiculous about how excited I am. They were my absolute favorite band when I was a teenager. Those songs? Right? Every girl wanted to be the one Davis Scott was singing about. Every time I hear them, it takes me right back."

I wasn't the only one. Other perfectly normal-looking women still loved Golden Tiger.

"It's the same for me. I think it's generational. At least for those of us with double X chromosomes."

She laughed and then touched my arm conspiratorially. "Glad to know I'm not alone."

"Definitely not alone." I smiled.

We started walking.

"I think I played *Tour Bus Taillights* until it wore out." She was smiling.

"Absolute favorite album. Hands down," I replied.

The noise level had increased so the guys must have made it inside. "Are you in town for the show tomorrow night?"

She shook her head. "No. I was here for work. I had no idea they were even touring. I'm sure it's sold out."

We reached the lobby and I breathed a sigh of relief as I

saw Vince standing with a stack of keys in his hand. I turned to my new friend who stood silently and not screaming as the guys strutted by and into the elevators.

"I'm with the band. I'm doing a photo biography on them and this tour. I'd love to sit and talk to you about what the music has meant to you, and what you think of them now compared to then. Take some pictures of you at the show."

She turned her wide-eyed stare in my direction.

"I can get you a ticket is what I'm saying. Then we could go for a drink after and chat."

She threw her arms around my neck and then stepped back, embarrassed. "I am so sorry. I should not have done that. I just, you have no idea. My job sucks and I spend so much time in hotels doing nothing but work. A Golden Tiger concert is like the antithesis of my life right now."

"Actually, I do." I handed her my notebook. "Just give me your name and room number and I'll leave your ticket at the front desk."

She scribbled quickly and handed it back. "I have to go call someone—no wait, everyone. They'll never believe this in a million years!"

As she skipped back down the hall, Vince walked up and handed me a room key and a piece of paper. "Your room and a list of questions I think would be a good start with Tony." I took them both and smiled.

"Thanks. Do you think it'd be possible to get an extra ticket for the show tomorrow?"

"Marissa coming to check up on you?"

"Nah, just trying to help someone else bust out of their shitty life."

He raised an eyebrow.

"A fan I met, someone a little less hysterical than the groupies. Thought it'd be a good angle for the book."

He nodded. "Anything for the book, right?"

He stared at me with his burning intensity and it only made my desire to hole up in my room alone even greater.

It was such a loaded question, and I had no energy to follow up, so instead I merely replied, "Thanks, Vince," then turned toward the elevator.

The first thing I did when I got to my room was strip off my sweaty clothes and take a shower, then I slipped into a camisole and sweatpants and ordered up some room service. I hoped I was ahead of our crowd, that it wouldn't take hours to arrive. My stomach grumbled with hunger. On the nightstand my phone buzzed with a text and I flipped it over to see it was from Marissa.

Checking in. How's life on the road? Anything exciting to report?

I had no energy for that either. No matter what I said, she'd want more, and I didn't have more. I only had a constant stream of questions I couldn't answer. I flipped the cell back over and left it where it was. I piled up the pillows at the top of my bed, grabbed my notebook, and snuggled in.

I needed to get a handle on the myriad of questions that were flooding my brain, both personal and professional. Was what Vince had asked me true, would I do anything for the book? Because it seemed like if that was the case, I'd need to stop my fantasy of sleeping with Davis.

Which left me both disappointed but also excited. Not sleeping with him meant I could keep things professional, whereas sleeping with him probably lost any hope of that. But that also assumed eventually he would want to sleep with me. I couldn't even begin to consider how it would feel if this whole thing was just a repeat of the last tour.

I just needed to keep my focus on the music, I rationalized. It was a partial solution to the problem at hand that put off me having to choose between my two goals. And that shouldn't be all that hard. I could give Davis his larger-than-life rock-star section, if he could give me a glimpse into the boy who'd written the songs that still managed to go off in me like fireworks. And I could still hold on to the fantasy of him setting me off like fireworks at some point.

I glanced at the questions I'd scribbled while driving. Most of them had to do with certain songs and lyrics. A lot of it was a jumbled mess. Writing and driving was really not a match made in heaven.

I hoped I'd be able to decipher them when I listened to the album again. And it really was about that one album. Golden Tiger had put out five in total. They'd had a debut that had gotten them noticed, led to them going on tour as an opening act. Then there'd been the follow-up, that was the one that got them their own tour, this tour. Most people thought that had been their debut. But most people were wrong.

The follow-up to that, the third, was *Tour Bus Taillights*. The one I could and did listen to on repeat. And then the next one, which sold well but almost had a different sound entirely. And then the last, which had been so awful even a devoted fan could barely listen.

What had happened? Why had the music changed so drastically? Different from any other band, they hadn't broken up, hadn't turned on each other. They'd simply packed up their guitars and mic stands and gone away. It was a mystery I was itching to solve.

There was a knock on my door. "Room service." And as I crossed to answer it, I spied Vince's notes under the key. I grabbed them and let the delivery man in.

"Thanks so much! I was worried it would take forever with so many people checking in from the tour at once."

He nodded as he wheeled the cart over to the far side of the room. "It's a little hectic in the kitchen that's for sure. Who is this band?"

"Golden Tiger," I replied, expecting the same reaction I'd gotten from the gal in the hall. Instead it was the exact opposite.

"Never heard of them. Are they old?"

The look on my face must have made him concerned for his tip because he scrambled to cover. "I mean, old school? I don't listen to a lot of old school rock. Except when we have cover bands in the bar. I love those. I bet I'd know their music if I heard it." He looked to be all of nineteen, so I cut him a break.

"I am sure you would. I bet your parents played it all the time when you were a baby." I held my hand out and he gave me the bill to sign, which I did quickly and sent him on his way. I grabbed the domed plates off the cart and sat back down on my bed. Jack would have murdered me—burger and fries with ketchup and mayo on the bed!

I smiled as I bit into it. I may not have all my answers, but my life was starting to feel a little more my own again.

I unfolded the list of questions from Vince. They were pretty generic, standard stuff:

What's the best thing about being back with the band?

Who has changed the most and who is exactly the same?

Tell me about your first time in front of a live audience.

What's your favorite song?

What would you play if you didn't play drums?

What's the wildest thing you remember from the first tour?

The whole thing read like the outline for the most generic

"where are they now" article. There were no guts to any of it.

Maybe they were suggestions to ease my way into the band? A jumping off point until they got used to me? Or maybe he doubted I could even do this after seeing me with Davis last night? That whole respect thing maybe spilled over to what Vince thought, too.

More questions.

I ate my burger and stewed over them. By the time I finished eating, all I wanted to do was curl up and quit thinking about any of it. I set the plate on the ground, turned off the light, and fell immediately into a deep, dreamless sleep.

It felt like it had been minutes when I woke up to a pounding on my door. But what door? I had no idea where I was. Was it day? Night? Had I slept through something important? I jumped out of bed, kicking what remained of my room service and the fancy domed platter across the room. The clatter reminded me where I was, but who the hell was at my door?

"Hold on, I'm coming!" I said as the banging persisted. I undid the chain and pulled open the door to find Vince on the other side, his face red.

"What the hell, Vince? Is the hotel on fire?"

"Worse. Davis is missing, and you might remember, Davis missing in Kansas City is not the part of this tour we want to recreate."

Chapter Eighteen

Davis going AWOL in KC was the stuff of legends, but not the good kind. Last time it had been at the whim of a lady. A very attractive and very crafty woman who had plied him with good tequila and convinced him it was true love. He'd been gone for more than twenty-four hours before anyone had realized it. Everyone had just assumed he was holed up on the bus, only to find the lump in his bed was Rex's guitar case. And that had been discovered a mere three hours before the concert was supposed to begin.

"At least this time we have almost a day to find him," I said, glancing at the clock. It was one in the morning so maybe not a whole day. I waved Vince inside, wishing I had a sweatshirt or something on over the top of my cotton camisole. I felt exposed, though from the frantic look on his face I don't think he noticed my, ummm, floppiness.

"I'm not going to lie, I was worried about this happening. Kansas City is not a place that holds good memories for him. You know, they only played here on that tour. They never came back."

I had thought Vince was annoyed at Davis, but he was actually concerned about him. I softened a little in my own irritation of being so dramatically woken up.

"I'm sure he's just gone somewhere to get a drink. To have a little privacy."

Vince rolled his eyes. "Davis hasn't wanted privacy since he had to change out of his gym clothes when we were in seventh grade. Puberty came late to America's rock and roll heartthrob."

"TMI, Vince. TMI!" I grabbed a sundress from the top of my unopened suitcase and walked past him into the bathroom. "Give me one minute to change and then we'll go find him."

In the bathroom I pulled off my sloppy lounge clothes and threw on the dress and a bra. My hair was piled on top of my head in a messy bun and there it would have to stay. Once it was up, there was nothing outside of a shower that could save it. I had no interest in going glam, but if we were going out in public, I didn't want to look like I'd crawled out of the tour bus. A few swipes of mascara and a little powder would have to do. I reemerged from the bathroom to a pacing Vince.

"Took you long enough."

"It took me less than five minutes. Calm down. This isn't like last time. There weren't even any groupies on the bus."

He pointed to his temple. "Nope, learned my lesson on that one. When the buses move, only people getting paychecks are allowed on them."

I grabbed my purse and my keys. "Okay. So, where do we start?"

He followed me out the door and down the hall. "Should we start at the end?" he asked nervously.

I stopped dead in my tracks and turned around. "Vince. There's no way that Davis is at the airport waiting to board a plane to Vegas to marry some conniving groupie."

Twenty years ago, we'd arrived just in time to pull him off the plane. That was back when security allowed anyone up to the gate. And thank the Lord they had. That groupie had made April look like a saint. I'd only gotten to go along because I had a car.

Actually, that part was the same, I guess.

We crossed the parking lot, and without a word I handed Vince the keys. There was no point in fighting over who was going to drive. I happily slid into the passenger seat as Vince threw himself into the driver's seat and fidgeted with the controls until he got the seat to go backward. He looked ridiculous behind the wheel of my car, and I started to say so, but then he turned and looked at me.

"No one can know about this. Just you and me, swear."

He was so serious.

"I swear. Vince. He's fine. If he hasn't gone somewhere to be alone, then he's probably just blowing off some steam. How do you even know he's gone?"

"He isn't in his room, or the bar, or with any of the guys. I could see the look in his eye when we got here. He hates Kansas City."

He started the car and the music blared through the speakers.

If you're going to leave and break my heart in two, at least take a piece of it with you.

The guitar revved up into the bridge and Vince shook his head. "*Tour Bus Taillights*, really?"

"It's my favorite album," I said. "I was listening to it on the way here. Chronologically it almost tells a story. How did I not notice that before?"

"Not the time, Campbell." His voice was tense.

Of course. The story was about a girl who broke a rocker's heart while they were on tour. It was about this very thing.

Davis's heartbreak in Kansas City.

I leaned forward and snapped the radio to off. "Sorry. I'll focus. Okay, there has to be a bar or something around here. He couldn't have gone far. He was on foot, and he's Davis freakin' Scott."

He pulled out onto the street and it was only two blocks before we saw a lit-up sign that said "Bar". I smacked Vince on the arm.

"I see it," he snapped and pulled the car to the side of the road before turning to me again.

"I just can't stand to see that dude hurt. That's the thing. He can be his own worst enemy, since we were kids. Something sets him off, and he's all in. Like he has zero common sense. We just have to find him before he does something really stupid."

I wanted to ask him if he ever got tired of it—taking care of this bunch of overgrown teenagers. Of course, this was not the time, but the time would come, and it was a question I was going to get answered. What did Vince get out of all this? No fame, no glory. Just running around in the middle of the night putting out fires.

We walked into the bar and it was pretty much deserted. Just a few sad souls on barstools and country music blaring. Way too low key for the Davis I knew. Vince glanced around and then headed to the bar.

"Any of you seen Davis Scott tonight?"

"Who the hell is Davis Scott?" the bartender replied in an accent so southern he had to be a transplant. I almost expected him to spit on the floor in disgust.

"He's that rock star. Playing at the Truman tomorrow night," one of the men on the barstool chimed in and the others looked at him a bit bewildered.

"What? A guy can't listen to country and rock and roll?" he replied then turned to Vince. "He was in here earlier. Sat alone in that booth over there. But he didn't stay long."

I glanced at the booth he was pointing to, the only one that had a light hanging over the top. Of course.

"He probably left because no one here knew who he was," I said to Vince, who took in a deep breath.

"Is there any place more his scene that'd still be open?" Vince asked the guy who stared back blankly so he continued, "A rock and roll bar, maybe a biker bar?"

I raised an eyebrow. Maybe back in the day Davis could handle himself at a biker bar, but one look at his smooth forehead and they'd eat him for lunch.

"Or maybe a karaoke bar?" I threw out.

This was met with a scowl from Vince.

"You never know!"

"If it's come to that, then we have bigger problems. If someone gets a video? Imagine the label's reaction to Davis singing karaoke in the middle of the night in Kansas City."

Vince pulled out his wallet and threw a twenty on the bar. "Let me buy you a round, for your troubles."

The guy reached for the twenty. "There's a couple of places. I'd steer clear of the biker bars. He wouldn't get in anyways—you have to know someone to get in there." He listed two other places, one around the corner and the other one a few blocks down. With barely a nod, Vince turned to leave.

"Thanks for your help!" I called, running out behind him.

"You could have said thank you," I said breathlessly as I tried to catch up with him.

"I thanked him. I bought him a drink, probably more than one by the looks of that place."

"Your people skills have not improved in twenty years."

"People haven't really improved in twenty years, so it works out."

I didn't mean to laugh, but I did, and just the hint of a grin crossed Vince's face before he scowled again.

"It took twenty years for the label to agree to another tour. All they want are adoring fans and sold-out concerts."

I slid into the passenger seat. Though Vince could come across as surly and gruff, I could tell that he was trying to hide his true concern behind this talk about the label. Vince was worried about Davis. Not lead singer Davis, but his friend Davis.

I laid my hand on his arm. "He'll be okay. We'll find him. This tour is important to Davis, too. He won't do anything to jeopardize it."

Vince looked at me with grateful eyes, but then he shook his head. "I wish that were true, but Davis has never been able to say no to attention. Good or bad, he doesn't seem to distinguish between the two."

"Well, then, let's hope that this time around, Kansas City is only serving up good." I hadn't taken my hand away, and Vince didn't do anything to shake it off as he put the car in drive.

Vince drove the two blocks to the next bar, which unlike the last one was packed to the rafters. The music blaring was club music not even close to the rock we were looking for, and the dance floor was overflowing.

"How would we ever find him, even if he is in here?" I asked.

Vince scanned the place. "He isn't in here. There's too much going on for him to be spotted and that's what he wants, or he would have stayed at that last place."

We were both so busy eyeing the room that we missed the woman wearing a banner that read "Newly Divorced" who sidled up and threw her arm around Vince. "Buy me a drink, handsome?"

Vince stared at her, almost startled by the attention.

"Ummm. No, thank you? I-I'm not staying..." he stammered.

"Actually, it's we, we aren't staying." I stepped forward and took her hand and removed it from his neck, replacing it with my own. I jutted out my hip, so I could press myself as close to Vince as I could.

"Oh, sorry about that. You don't have to mark your territory. I get it." She turned on her heel and left us standing there. Vince started to laugh.

"Were you going to pee on me?"

"If it came to that, I guess."

"Well, I appreciate it, *I guess*." He smiled and reached for the back of my arm, aiming me for the door. It was the lightest touch, but the hair on my arm stood up. I rubbed it back down and tried to convince myself that it was just the blast of the air conditioner.

The next place was full-on karaoke, and though it wasn't a madhouse there were a good number of people there. Vince made his way to the bar while I scanned the booths.

Nothing. Not one sign of Davis. When we'd started this, I was sure Vince was worked up over nothing, but now I wasn't so sure.

"He was here," Vince said, handing me a drink. "He sang."

"Oh, no." I took a drink. Whiskey.

"Yep. But no one really recognized him, so he ordered a drink and left."

This was not good news. "This is the only other place on our list. Maybe he went back to his room?"

Vince took his drink down like a shot.

"I said no one *really* recognized him, but *someone* did. The bartender said after he ordered his drink a woman sat down next to him and asked if he was the real Davis Scott. He left with her."

I shot the rest of my whiskey. This was starting to feel a

lot like twenty years ago.

"So, do we go to the airport?" I asked.

"And what? Buy a ticket on the next flight to Vegas? This isn't like last time. We can't just barge onto a plane and drag him off. Nope, I can do a lot of things, but I can't put the toothpaste back in the tube."

I reached out and squeezed his arm and his face softened a bit. "I need another drink. Many other drinks. Let's go to the hotel bar so we only have to stumble upstairs."

I followed him out to the car, and we drove silently back to the hotel. Inside we found the bar locked up for the night.

"I have a bottle in my room?" Vince said. I looked at my watch. Three thirty. If there was any hope for sleep, I'd need a nightcap.

How quickly this had all come back to me. Up all night, dirty bars, and nightcaps. But somehow I felt so much more myself than I had in twenty years of a regular bedtime and a cup of tea.

We got to Vince's room and he handed me the ice bucket. "Do you mind? I'm just going to call the guys. I didn't want to sound the alarm before, but now it seems like they should know that Davis has gone AWOL."

In Kansas City again. I finished the sentence for him in my head, noting the worry lines that had gathered on his forehead. It was endearing, the way he cared and worried about Davis. But it was also a bit jarring to see this crack in his tough guy facade.

"Not one bit." I took it from him and headed out in search of the ice machine. It was around the corner and I was shocked to see someone else using it.

I was even more shocked when she turned around and it was the woman from the lobby.

Wearing the shirt Davis had on earlier in the day, and nothing else.

She blushed when she recognized me, or else she was just glowing.

"Davis?" I asked.

"Can you believe it?" she said in an excited whisper.

I didn't want to spoil it for her. "Actually, sure I can! You're awesome."

She walked back down the hall and I made quick work of getting the ice and did the same. I pushed open the door to Vince's room.

"Found him," I said, and watched Vince's face go from disbelief to relief.

"Where?"

"With a woman. In his suite." I handed him the ice bucket.

He fell onto the couch. "You might have been right. We are too old for this shit."

"Speak for yourself!" I replied, blowing him a kiss, and was rewarded with a hearty laugh. Oddly, I wasn't in the least bit jealous or sad that the lady from the lobby had slept with Davis while I ran around town with Vince.

Let her have the rock star experience. The look of relief on Vince's face made me feel better than Davis's sultry half smile. At least in this moment.

Chapter Nineteen

Different venue, different view. And I wasn't referring to my half-closed eyes. Sure, I was exhausted from last night's adventures. I'd stayed in Vince's room for one nightcap. We were pretty much delirious—both of us unable to stop laughing over our wild goose chase.

"Next time, maybe we just camp out in front of his door?" I'd said as Vince was showing me out.

"Not a bad idea," he'd said, and then he'd stopped me on my way out the door, patting me awkwardly on the shoulder. "Thanks. For tonight. For coming along without even questioning it. I get a little paranoid where Davis is concerned." His mouth formed a tight smile. "I guess I need to be less protective of him."

That last part had stuck with me. I knew they were friends from childhood, but it somehow seemed more than that. I wondered why he felt such a need to look out for Davis, more than the other guys. I'd scribbled the question down in my notebook before I'd crawled into bed and finally slept.

Thank God for high quality blackout curtains in good

hotels. I'd slept until noon, like some sort of rock star. But I wasn't quite used to flipping my days and nights, so I was still feeling tired.

My exhaustion was not tamping the excitement of my companion, Mandy.

As I sat and listened to her gush about her one-night stand, I had a touch of FOMO, even though I knew she fell into his usual type, his usual pattern. The one and done variety. Mandy had slept with Davis Scott, and now I was going to hear all about it. Whether I wanted to or not.

"After I met you in the lobby, I just couldn't settle down, so I decided to go out for a drink. I asked the concierge where I could find live music close by and he gave me the address and off I went. You can imagine my disappointment to find that his idea of live music was karaoke." Here she paused and rolled her eyes. I hoped she was taking a breath, too. She was talking so much and so fast, there was a real chance she was going to pass out.

I was trying to remember if I'd asked her for this story. I think my opening was a simple, "How are you?" This was apparently how she was.

"I was at the bar getting another drink. I had my back to the stage, and then I heard him. I knew it was Davis Scott before I turned around. He had on sunglasses and a baseball cap, but any real fan would know it was him. Though, I think I was the only real fan in that place."

She smiled slyly at me, like I was also a real fan like her, which I was, I guess, though I considered myself more of an insider now. Like I'd had a peek behind the curtain and knew a bit more than an average fan.

"He was singing 'Silverdollar Sunset.' It was all I could do to not start screaming when he got to the chorus. I mean, it was like the most insane experience, but no one else was even noticing! There was Davis Scott, giving it his all and people were just sitting around drinking their beers!"

"Well, it was a Sunday night. Most of those people were probably just regulars having a drink."

She looked at me like I had three heads, and then she continued.

"When he was done, he made his way to the bar and I went right up and told him I knew who he was, and that I wouldn't blow his cover. And he was so appreciative! And he bought me a drink, and we started talking. He was just so charming!"

I'm sure he was very charming. I'd seen that charm and knew what it did firsthand. After she'd gushed about knowing who he was, which is what he'd been on the hunt for, a little voice in the back of my head wondered why he hadn't called *me*, but I dismissed it. Davis had been looking to blow off some steam, and that wasn't possible if the woman was currently touring with you.

"Anyway, I am not the kind of woman who sleeps with someone she just met, but he invited me back to his room, and one thing led to another. And, well, here we are!" She threw her hands up in the air and flashed me a big commiserative smile. Except we weren't commiserating.

This was not at all the angle I was going for when I invited Mandy to this concert. I was hoping to talk to a woman who had a somewhat normal love of the band and the music. Not this. This was the same fangirling, or fanwomaning I should say, all over again. What was it with women and Golden Tiger? Did the band make them forget themselves, or were the women who loved Golden Tiger already inclined to let it all loose? I pulled up my camera and snapped a quick photo of her to ponder this question later. Maybe I could dedicate a few pages to this sort of devoutness?

The lights went down and the crowd noise went up, saving me from having to continue the conversation. I glanced at the side of the stage, trying to get a glimpse of Vince, though he'd never allow himself to be seen. He was there. I knew that with certainty, just outside the reach of the blazing stage lights.

Last night had been manic, but also endearing. I guess I always knew that Vince's primary role was to look out for the band, protect them from wild women and poor decisions. But until last night, I hadn't realized how much he really cared about them. Especially Davis, although maybe that was because Davis was notorious for making bad decisions. Vince had been visibly relieved when he'd been located, but only after I'd assured him that Mandy was not some sort of stalker.

I glanced to my right where she was screaming "I LOVE YOU, DAVIS!" at the top of her lungs and wondered if I was wrong about that.

No, I think it was just back to my earlier question—did Golden Tiger attract insanity or cause it? I jotted that down in my notebook and then slid it into my purse so I could enjoy the show. Mandy's enthusiasm was contagious.

Pot meet Kettle.

When the last song had been sung, and the band had taken their final curtain call, we were sweaty and hoarse from dancing and singing. Mandy's smile was so big it reached her eyes.

"Do you want to go backstage and see Davis?"

Her eyes widened a bit. "Not looking like this, I don't!"

I laughed. "You look fantastic. Like you had an absolute blast at their concert."

Still, she shook her head. "Can we go freshen up and then find them at the after-party? I'm assuming there will be some sort of after-party?"

I actually had no idea. Our next show wasn't for three days, in Denver. Which meant the buses weren't going anywhere tonight. More than likely, there would be a party somewhere. And, unlike the last time I was in search of it, now I had someone I could ask. I pulled out my phone and thumbed a quick text to Vince.

After-party locale?

Davis's suite. After last night, there's no way I'm letting him leave the hotel. God I cannot wait to be out of Kansas City.

I had to smile.

See you there! I shot back and was rewarded with a winky face. A winky face. From Vince. It made me feel oddly warm all over.

"Let's go back to my room and you can get freshened up. The party is in Davis's suite which is just down the hall. We should be able to hear them when it gets started."

Mandy nodded and followed me out of the venue to my waiting car. It was a quick drive to the hotel, and I used the valet to save time. I wanted to get her instant feedback on the show, organically, not after she had time to think too much about it.

And I wanted some background information on her, too. That had been the point of my invitation before Davis had gotten himself involved and the whole thing had tilted to idol worship.

I stopped as we reached the door to my room. Is that what he'd intended to happen?

"Mandy, did you tell Davis last night that you were coming to the show with me and that I was going to put you in my book?"

She smiled slyly. "Of course I did! I didn't want him to think I was sleeping with him just to get tickets!"

That sly dog. He was way smarter than I'd considered. Using Mandy to highlight his rock god image, I had to wonder if going AWOL last night had been all about finding a pawn and not having a rocky trip down memory lane.

Inside my room, she went straight to the bathroom to, as she said, "fix her face." I went straight to the minibar and pulled out a tiny bottle of whiskey. If Davis had used her like I thought, he was not going to be happy to see her a second night in a row.

One of the perks of being a second—actually, if I'm being honest, third—tier groupie was that I got to observe a lot of things from afar. Including what happened to the girls who made it on the tour bus or up to the hotel suite. Without question, they were one and done. Especially with Davis. For some, that was heartbreaking. Those were the naive, wide-eyed innocents who were certain he was as in love with them after one night as they were with him. The heartbreak was real when he forgot their names the next time he saw them or instructed Vince not to let them into the party the following night. I'd consoled many a tearful girl and had even driven a few of them to the bus station in the middle of the night.

There were a few who took it in stride and moved on to Rex or Tony. But the way Mandy was going on and on about the connection she'd felt with Davis, it was obvious that was not a possibility.

"Do you want a drink?" I asked, interrupting her story about how she knew deep down he was singing "Green-eyed Lady" directly to her.

Her eyes were brown.

"Sure! Do you have any chardonnay?"

I walked back to the minibar and produced a tiny bottle and brought it back to her.

"Glass?" she asked.

I took the one that was still upside down on the paper coaster next to the sink and poured the wine.

"Classy," she replied but took it from me and held the

glass out for a toast. "To the first day of the rest of my life. Speaking of which, I need to email my boss and let him know I'm going to be taking a leave of absence for at least the rest of the tour."

It took everything in me to keep from rolling my eyes. "What do you do, Mandy?"

"I'm in sales. Medical equipment. That's why I was in town, at this hotel, it's right near the hospital I call on. I usually stay somewhere else, but it was sold out. And now I know why...FATE!" She took another sip of her wine and stared at herself in the mirror. "Maybe I should just tell my boss I quit."

I started to tell her I'd hold off on that, but there was a knock at my door.

"Party is starting," Vince said as soon as I opened it. From his tone I could tell he was less than enthusiastic. Behind him, Davis walked by, his arm slung across the shoulders of a blonde I didn't recognize.

I stepped aside so Vince could see Mandy staring at herself in the mirror.

"Going to be just like old times for you, Gatekeeper," I replied drily.

He exhaled slowly, and I truly felt sorry for him.

"Got anything to drink?" he asked.

Chapter Twenty

It went about as bad as expected. Vince tried his best to convince Mandy to not come to the party. Gone were the days of him just outright telling a woman she couldn't go, the old softie.

Which was great, but also, in this case, terrible.

"I'm out of practice being that level of asshole, I guess," he said as we led her down the hall to what felt like an execution. It would be, though just of her pride. At least Davis didn't wait around and drag it out. The minute we walked in, he started making out with the blonde. Poor Mandy stood shell-shocked just inside the door while the party raged around us. Vince disappeared momentarily and returned with three shots of something that was most definitely not chardonnay.

"Drink this. It'll help," he said as he handed it to her. I wasn't sure if he was talking to Mandy, or me, or himself. It didn't actually matter since we all took them, Mandy slamming hers down on the credenza.

"I'll take another if you've got it," she said. Vince looked from her to me and then back again. I shrugged.

"Might as well just get the bottle," I called to his back as he went in search of more booze.

"And to think I have a resignation letter in my draft folder. For my job! What was I thinking?" She was staring right at Davis as she said it, seething.

"You were thinking that you'd slept with Davis Scott, and more often than not, that act alone leads to all sorts of not thinking," I replied.

"Are you speaking from experience?" she asked.

"Actually, no." I watched Vince making his way back toward us, bottle in hand, and I felt a sort of thankfulness toward him. He'd saved me from this level of humiliation, and I'd always resented him for it. "But I've seen it happen too many times to count."

"My God. And I was going on and on to you about our connection and fate! How mortifying. You must have thought I was a complete idiot."

I shrugged. "Nah, I mean at some point I have to believe one of the women he's with will stick. Who was I to say it wasn't you?"

Vince had finally reached us and held out the bottle for our glasses.

"Well, it wasn't," Mandy said, throwing back another shot.

Vince opened his mouth to say something, but I laid my hand on his arm.

"Davis is a romantic, that's obvious when you listen to his songs. No one can sing about finding love the way he does and not believe in it. His way of looking for it is just different than most people," I said. She eyed me, slightly hopeful. "And now you have a memory that thousands of women would kill to have. Davis Scott chose you. Flirted with *you*, and then seduced *you*. Something he sings about every night."

She nodded. "You're right. It is one hell of a tale to tell

my friends." She set her glass down. "Actually, I think I might go call a few of them now. While it's still fresh."

She pulled me into a hug.

"It was great meeting you, Campbell. And if you use my story in your book, please leave out all that bullshit I said about fate." She paused. "And maybe my name?"

She nodded at Vince and then she was gone. I sort of wished I could hear how she crafted her story. The spin she'd put on it that would leave out the humiliation and heartbreak. Maybe I'd follow up and ask her.

Across the room, his arm still slung over the shoulders of the blonde, Davis winked at me and then lifted his hand to wave us over. The pull I felt was different than it would have been only a few nights ago. Then it had been wrapped up in lust and nostalgia, now I just wanted to see how he'd act toward me with his arm around another woman, after the one he bedded last night hugged me on her way out.

I mean, I knew he was all about notches on his mic stand, but this was a whole new level.

"We are being summoned," I said to Vince, pointing toward where the band had gathered in the kitchen area.

He glanced over his shoulder. "Did you get a chance to look at those questions I gave you? I think you could use them for any of the guys really." He put his hand on the small of my back and guided me toward the group, not waiting for my reply. I had to hand it to him, he never seemed to lose focus on all the moving pieces. And there were a lot of moving pieces.

Including me, apparently.

"VIINNNCCEE!" As always, he was greeted with cheers and raised glasses. He held his up for the toast and then did his shot of whiskey.

I, on the other hand, took a sip of mine. Tonight was not a night I wanted to lose track of.

"You are looking mighty fine tonight," Davis leaned over and whispered in my ear, while still keeping his arm around the blonde.

"Why thank you," I replied, ignoring the fact that he was flirting with me when he was obviously already spoken for, at least for the night.

"Did you enjoy the show?"

"Yep. So did my friend, Mandy? You met her last night." I tilted my head to the side, made my eyes big and innocent, though my comment dripped with sarcasm.

He smiled, not an ounce of sheepishness to him. "She looked mighty fine—last night."

Here's the thing, in any other circumstance, with any other person, my skin would have been crawling at a comment like that. Maybe it was because it suited this persona he put on, but when Davis said it, it just came off as the right amount of cocky. It was almost endearing.

"You are incorrigible. You know that, right?"

Now he cocked his head to the side, his eyes glancing up, feigning his innocence, and for the first time I felt we were making an actual connection. I was starting to get Davis Scott, not just lust after him.

"Thank God she looked mighty fine locally and not so mighty fine you wanted to fly off to Vegas with her," I replied and he smiled—a full smile, not the usual half.

"Man, I wish I had remembered that. I would have done it again just to mess with our man Vince."

"Mess with me about what?" Vince leaned over me and grabbed a bottle of beer from the ice bucket.

"Going to the airport, or at least having my driver take me there. You would have absolutely freaked."

I wanted to chime in that Vince had in fact freaked, without bringing the actual airport into it, but that felt like throwing him under the bus.

Vince pulled up a stool and sat down at the bar. "You're lucky I care enough to freak, or at least I used to care." This brought forth a burst of hearty laughter. They all knew Vince still cared that much.

"What, are you going to start practicing tough love on us all of a sudden?" This from Tony, who of course was tapping his fingers on the edge of the counter as he spoke.

"I worry that tough love with you would only be a turn-on!" Vince shot back and Tony nodded in agreement.

It was easy to see how much they all cared about each other, especially when they were out of the public eye. One by one, the women who had been at their sides wandered off until it was just the five of them, and not one of them seemed to notice. They threw insults and compliments around the table like kids because they had known each other since they were. It was a perspective I'd never had before. Not one of them was acting like a rock star. They were just themselves, a bunch of old friends, easy in each other's company.

I stepped back, and as nonchalantly as I could, raised my phone, wishing I had my camera but knowing I'd miss the moment if I went to get it. I took a few quick shots of this scene. One that I thought captured exactly who they were and what they meant to one another.

It felt like I was finally an insider, and I knew with certainty that I could just have easily been one of those girls who was drifting away from the table but making sure not to fall out of sight. To not be forgotten.

Glancing at Vince, in the thick of it, I wondered if he hadn't orchestrated it somehow. After last night, I'm sure he was relieved to have them all gathered around one table with a bottle of whiskey, even if it meant he had to take the brunt of their teasing. Of course, he'd never admit to any of his behind-the-scenes string pulling. Only shrug and move on to the next thing. But those lines around his eyes would deepen with the hint of a smile if you were paying attention.

Watching them now, I was glad I was. Vince's connection to the members of this band was fascinating. And I wanted to know more.

There had only been one time he'd been almost forthcoming with me, and as fate would have it, that had been outside of Denver. The next stop on our tour.

I leaned over his shoulder. "This seems to be turning into a boys' night."

He chuckled then leaned in so he could whisper in my ear. I shivered slightly. "Makes my job a hell of a lot easier."

I glanced around the perimeter and wondered how long those women would hang out and hope to be taken home. All night, probably.

"I think I'm going to head back to my room. Long drive tomorrow for those of us who are actually driving it and not riding on a bus."

"I can always get you on that bus, if you'd rather."

"That would have been music to my twenty-year-old self, you know."

He raised an eyebrow. He knew.

I shook my head. "I like driving. Gives me some time to clear my head."

"I can't imagine why you'd need your head cleared with such a calm and stable working environment."

"Oh yes, my working conditions are ideal for crafting a book. Artists in general crave chaos and loud parties while they are creating their vision."

"So, you're calling yourself an artist now, are you?"

My cheeks felt hot—that had been a slip. Sure, I was trying, but I still had no idea what I was doing. For the most part I was just snapping pictures that spoke to me and taking notes about what they said. It seemed like there should be way more to it than that and I could feel the pressure of the project. That thought made me cold with panic. But I didn't really want to get into that with Vince. Something about the way he was tonight. With me, with the guys, I wanted to go back to my room and sit with it.

"I'm going to call it a night, let you guys have your fun."

He nodded and started to stand. "I can walk you to your room." It was such a nice gesture. But it was also Vince making sure all the loose ends were tied. Nothing personal. Him sitting here with the guys? That was personal. I shook my head.

"Nah, it's just down the hall. I can make it. You stay here and enjoy yourself."

Did he look disappointed or did I just want him to?

I glanced at Davis, who was looking at us intently, as if he was seeing me differently somehow. Gone was the half smile, the wink, and in its place seemed to be a look of actual attraction. Like if I'd nodded my head in his direction, he would have followed me out the door. Which on any other night I might have done. But having seen him break one heart tonight, I found I wasn't all that interested at the moment. My mind was elsewhere on the space-time continuum that I so often was finding myself on.

It was good to leave him wanting for a change.

"Okay," Vince replied. "Buses are leaving at nine."

I nodded. I actually planned on hitting the road a little early. The other good thing about having my own car was I could take my own drive down memory lane. There was somewhere I wanted to find. If I could, maybe I could make some headway on seeing if this new friendliness I was feeling where Vince was concerned was real, or all in my head.

Chapter Twenty-One

I was glad there were some off days between shows on this leg of the tour. It had taken some doing, but I had found what I was looking for and was thrilled to find it still standing.

An old roadside motel on a two-lane highway just outside of Denver. The sign still lit up in neon, "Mountain View Motel." Not a broken down, murdery-looking place but a family-run, honest-to-goodness motel. With doors that opened to the parking lot and an ice machine on each end. Freshly painted and flowers in the window boxes.

It was much quainter than I remembered. Though, twenty-year-old me may not have noticed all those details. Someone still loved this place.

"Where are we going again?" Vince asked as he buckled himself into the passenger seat of my car.

"Remember how I followed you, no questions asked, on your wild goose chase for Davis the other night?"

He gave me one of his patented long blinks.

"This is you returning the favor."

He sighed, but I caught a glimpse of a slight smile. I

pulled out and made my way away from the city. We were staying on the outskirts, so it wasn't all that long before we hit the country road. Vince rode silently beside me, taking in the landscape. My brain, on the other hand, was far from silent.

What if he doesn't remember this place, or this night? Am I setting myself up for failure? Embarrassment? Both?

I told myself this was nothing more than a research mission, using the element of surprise to try and get Vince to open up a bit. And the photos I would get would more than make up for it. But if that was true, why was I so nervous?

As we reached the curve in the road before the motel, I slowed and put my signal on. Vince sat up a bit in his seat, as though leaning forward would show him where we were going that much quicker. And when the motel came into view, he fell back into his seat.

"Holy shit. The Mountain View. How in the hell did you remember this place?"

I released my nerves with a laugh. "My old journals are proving to be a wealth of information." I pulled into a parking spot in front of one of the rooms and put the car in park.

"Did you get us a room?" Vince asked in the same playful tone he'd been using with the guys last night. Was that a good sign? Vince treating me like one of the guys?

"I sort of had to or they would have wondered about the random car parked in the lot." I opened my door and he did the same. "But that isn't where we're going."

I popped the trunk and walked to the back of the car to pull out the supplies I'd stashed inside while Vince took his time getting out. The sun was just starting to reach the tops of the mountains in the distance. The timing was perfect. I handed him the cooler and slammed the trunk.

"This way, in case you forgot."

"You're kidding, right?"

I stutter-stepped, waiting for him to continue.

"Not a chance I could forget."

We rounded the corner to the back of the motel to find what looked like, but could not possibly be, the same rickety ladder leaning against the wall. Vince put a hand on it, and a foot on the bottom rung, before turning to look at me.

"This time, I'll go first." He smiled and my nerves settled a bit.

That night, I'd found this ladder and cooked up a plan to finally have some alone time with Davis. I was feeling a bit sassy and confident because he'd winked at me after the show, looking at me, not past me, and I had taken it as a sign as I followed the buses to this motel. I wasn't checking in, because money was scarce, and I needed to save what I could for gas if I was going to keep following the tour. I was more than used to sleeping in my car and I'd pulled around back, away from the noise of the highway, to do just that. That's when I saw the ladder. I'd climbed up and was rewarded with the most beautiful view of the valley and the mountains. I'd taken pictures and thought they were good enough to get published somewhere. (Spoiler alert: they were not.)

I'd hatched a plan to get Davis to meet me up here. We were in the middle of nowhere, I'd reasoned. He didn't have anything better to do. I stuck a note under his door, climbed the ladder, and waited. But he never came. I was used to the rejection, but this one stung a bit more for some reason, and when I'd tried to climb down the ladder, I'd knocked it over, trapping myself on the roof. It was Vince who'd heard my cries for help and come to my rescue. But not before joining me on the roof.

"Age before beauty," I said, waiting as he started the climb, slowly with one hand. He paused.

"That's my line."

"Is it? Seems like I've heard it somewhere before you?"

He got to the top and leaned over to set the cooler down

on the roof before slinging a leg over the wall.

"You're not going to believe it, but the chairs are still up here," he called down, and I scrambled up the ladder after him.

"Be careful there, we don't need a repeat of last time," he said, reaching out to grab my hand and helping me over the edge.

"It wouldn't be like last time. Last time I got stuck up here by myself," I said as I swung my legs over and stood up. Vince was still holding my hand, and the area all around us was lit up by the setting sun.

"Wow." Vince, understated as always.

"Sort of takes your breath away," I said, finally pulling my hand away.

"Yeah, until later when the sky is so dark it looks navy, dotted with a million stars."

I smiled. That's how I remembered it too.

I walked to the edge, pulling my camera around from where it hung over my shoulder, and started snapping. Moving slightly to change the angle, flipping from horizontal to vertical. Lost in the colors, the mountains. All of it. When I turned around, Vince had set the cooler down next to the chairs and was watching me.

My face red, I walked over and flipped open the cooler.

Beer. Sandwiches, and a bottle of whiskey.

He raised an eyebrow. "We may need that room if we drink all that tonight."

The thought of Vince and me in a tiny motel room made the skyline tilt a bit. I sat down.

"Not if we pace ourselves."

"Valid. What can I start you off with?"

I glanced toward east. "Whiskey with the setting sun."

"It's called alpenglow," Vince said. His voice was low, and it seemed more gravelly than usual.

I turned to see he was staring at the same thing I was, still standing, his hands shoved in the pockets of his jeans, his face transfixed by the beauty we were witnessing.

"Alpenglow?" I looked back at the mountains, now lit up even more pink than just seconds earlier.

"When the sun dips just below the horizon, it throws its rays on the mountains opposite." He nudged me and handed me a glass of whiskey on the rocks. Then he sat down next to me and in silence we watched as the sun finished setting, the pink fading to black.

"I had no idea it had a name. I remembered it as something almost mystic from years ago. I wanted to see if I had made it up, if my memory was making something more amazing than it actually was." I was still staring at the void and not at Vince. Even without the glow it was hard to tear my eyes away. "But that proves it wasn't all rosy retrospection."

"Rosy retrospection? That's quite a turn of phrase." Vince chuckled, and I turned to look at him.

"I had the opposite with you, you know."

He tilted his head. "Do tell."

"Well, I had you painted as the bad guy in my memory of that summer. The one who kept me from doing what I most wanted to do. Who thought I wasn't good enough to be a part of the in-crowd."

"The in-crowd? Is that what you thought of that pack of wild animals?"

I wasn't sure if he was talking about the band, or the groupies, or the entire scene. Either way, it was an accurate description.

"Back then, yes. And at the party that first night, yes. But I'd forgotten all the good times we'd had."

"Like this." The way he said it, he remembered, too.

I nodded and took a sip of my whiskey. "The night I got stuck up here was pretty rock bottom for me. That's how I remembered it: stood up and left out. I could hear the party raging below me, and I felt so sorry for myself. I remembered that feeling, but not this one."

Vince was looking at me with a strange intensity. I motioned back and forth between us. "Not just that night, but the others. You might have kept me out, but it's becoming clear to me that you weren't doing it because you thought I wasn't good enough."

He shook his head. "But because I thought you were too good for the whole scene."

"I get that now. Though, you have to admit, looking back at it, you were sort of a dick to think you got to decide *for* me, right?"

He took a deep breath and rattled the ice in his whiskey.

"I can see that. I was young then, too. I'm sorry. I guess I shouldn't have butted in where you were concerned. But you have to know I thought I was doing the right thing."

"Not back then, but I do now. Back then Campbell? To her you were enemy number one."

He looked away from me, silently. Just sipped his whiskey, so I did the same.

A car went by on the road below and then he spoke. "We had some good times back then. I can't believe you forgot them."

"Didn't fit my narrative. I'm starting to realize that revisionist history is my specialty."

"What was your narrative?"

I swallowed. This was more honesty than I'd planned on. But the setting, the mood seemed ripe for it. Something about sitting side by side in the growing dark. "Well, I came on the tour back then to take and try to sell photos of the band. And because their music said something to me. I wanted to understand that, to belong to something. Because I'd never had that in my life. But then I got so swept up in the whole scene, I forgot why I started following them in the first place."

"You always were a sucker for the music."

"A sucker? Is that what you thought of me?" I sipped the whiskey, smooth but bitter.

"I mean that in the best way possible. Even now, we got in your car the other night and you're playing the album that was the beginning of the end for them."

"I love that album. Davis at his finest."

"Do you really believe what you said last night to that Mandy?" Vince asked, taking a sip of his whiskey. "About Davis being a romantic?"

"Sure, for the most part. I mean when he sings? Absolutely, without a doubt. Who could write songs like that and not be a hopeless romantic? But it doesn't seem to translate to who he is off stage. His idea of seduction is a sort of full-court press. And maybe I'm just out of practice, but it's not exactly sexy, more an idea of what *he* thinks sexy should be."

Vince was silent for a minute. I wasn't sure if he was trying to figure out what he wanted to say, or what he didn't want to say.

And then, "That's why I'm always looking out for him. The Davis he is off stage is a whole lot closer to the guy I knew growing up." He sighed.

"So, you're with me that the whole rock star, womanizer thing is an act?"

"I think at some point along the way, he listened to people who just looked at him as a way to make money and was convinced that was how he had to be to carry this whole thing."

This was news. "Care to elaborate on who that might be?"

From the look on his face, it was clear he thought he had said too much. "Nope, I'd rather keep elaborating on my transition from villain to savior in your book."

I laughed. "Do you mean my memory book or literally in this book that you convinced me I'm capable of putting together?"

"Is it wrong if I say both?" He chuckled in that way you do when you know the answer to the question you are posing.

"Not wrong, but maybe optimistic. I'm still searching for the perfect angle for the book." It was so nice, so easy, this way between Vince and me as we slipped right back into rhythm.

"Speaking of the book, did you get a chance to look over the questions and photo suggestions I gave you?"

Back to business, then.

"I looked at them, and honestly, Vince, they're pretty mundane. I think the fans want something deeper."

"I think Golden Tiger displays nightly that they don't really have a deeper." Something in his voice had changed; we weren't waxing nostalgic anymore.

"I disagree. Seeing you all around that table last night, five guys who grew up to be the biggest rock stars in the world and then disappeared for no reason, but still love each other? That's what I want to show."

He shook his head. "I think you'd be better off sticking to the simple stuff. This tour is about their glory days, not their glorious implosion."

There was something in his tone, a warning maybe? It was an immediate trigger that sent me spiraling back to Jack telling me what was and wasn't acceptable. And though I'd just spent the better part of the evening gushing that Vince was one of the good guys, it sure didn't feel that way when it came to my book.

Not to mention, *glorious implosion*? This was new ground, and it made me dislike his question suggestions even more.

Vince knew something, something big. So why was he trying to hide it?

Chapter Twenty-Two

The turn the conversation had taken was killing the vibe. A fight with Vince was not anything I was interested in. So after a few minutes of uncomfortable silence, I remembered the food. Maybe our blood sugar was too low.

"There's dinner, remember?" I said, pointing to the cooler. And whether he was actually hungry or wanting the distraction, I'm not sure. But he opened the cooler and pulled them out.

We ate the sandwiches, each having a beer to wash them down, and then Vince poured another whiskey, taking note of my still relatively full glass.

"I see that the sipping-rule of whiskey is another thing you've remembered," he said, the smile on his face reaching the crinkles around his eyes.

Phew, argument averted.

I laughed. "Of all the things I've remembered, that might be the most important." I held up my glass, the amber liquid below the level of the now melting ice cubes. "It only took waking up a few times with no knowledge of the night before for me to remember—sip, don't shoot."

"Mantras are best when they're simple like that. Look at all the things you're learning about yourself. And you thought joining this tour was running away from being an adult. There are things to learn everywhere." He winked like the wise old sage he was pretending to be, and whatever friction had been starting melted away.

It seemed neither of us wanted to let our impasse ruin the whole night. As nostalgic and magical as this rooftop was, it served to soften the edges of our opposing sides. We'd lapsed back into stories of our days on the road. Mostly I think he wanted to remind me of the good times, since I'd confessed I was just now remembering that we'd had them.

I let him top off my whiskey, cranking my head back to look at the stars.

"In my humble opinion, stargazing is best and easier when you lie on your back. Unobstructed view." He motioned to the blanket I'd brought. I nodded, and he stood and spread it in the space in front of the chairs, then lay down.

As strange as it felt to lie so close to Vince, I joined him. Thinking all the while that if Davis had said this same thing it would have felt like a come-on, but with Vince it really was about the better view. Plus, I think both of us wanted a change of subject, or no subject at all.

"This sky makes me want to say something profound, but all I can come up with is how tiny it makes me feel. That seems so trite."

We were lying side by side, not touching, but I could feel his warmth beside me.

"I know what you mean. Some things are just hard to put into words."

I sat up and reached for my phone.

"That's why there's music." I thumbed through my playlists until I found what I was looking for. A bootleg acoustic version of the album I so loved. I hit play and then lay back down. And even though the song had nothing to do with endless nighttime skies, or millions of diamond lit stars, it was still just right.

Davis sang about loneliness, about the love he wanted and the girl who never saw him.

"Perfect," Vince said softly beside me. And then, "So, marriage, huh?"

"Talk about killing the mood."

"It couldn't have been all that bad. You were together almost two decades."

I shifted to my side, propping my head on my elbow so I was looking at Vince's profile.

"It won't make sense to you—hell, it barely makes sense to me. Sometimes, I don't even believe it *was* me. Or that those years even happened. It's like I was on the tour, there was a pause, and now I'm back. My married years? They feel like that was someone else entirely."

He turned his head while I was talking and was looking me dead in the eye while I spoke. Listening. And since this felt like something I was figuring out as I went along, I continued.

"It was easy at first. There were rules. I followed them. Life was steady, no drama. Which was a comfort in the beginning. Coming from the family I did, the situation of my childhood where things were far from steady. But it was also hard, if I actually thought about it, that life made me feel like I was suffocating and financially I was trapped. Jack was shocked when I told him I was unhappy. He thought there was no way I'd go through with it. We had money. We were content. To him that made life good."

"What made you realize you wanted out?"

I rolled onto my back and looked up at the stars. "I caught a glimpse of myself in the mirror one day when we were out to eat. At first, I didn't recognize it as me. You know how, in your head, you think you look a certain way?"

"Yeah, it's the gray in the hair that always shocks me." Vince laughed.

I shook my head. "It wasn't just the added years. The reflection I saw was a woman who looked absolutely miserable. And I just, I don't know." I turned my head to meet Vince's eye. "I had to do something to save her." I sighed. "Maybe because letting someone else do it all those years ago had cost her everything."

"I'm glad you did," he said. Our eyes locked, and we stayed that way, his words hanging in the air along with what felt a hell of a lot like anticipation.

He shifted and for a brief second I thought he was going to wrap his arms around me or maybe I just hoped he was. But then his breath evened out.

He'd fallen asleep. Or more likely passed out. Was I disappointed? Relieved? This was all so confusing to someone who had been living purposely on emotional autopilot. Instead, I tried to let myself enjoy the moment for what it was. Which was something I'd never been very good at—always letting my mind wander to how I should be doing it better. Old, ingrained habit.

The entire sky looked like someone had thrown a bottle of glitter on a midnight blue felt board. My eyes focused and unfocused on the stars that actually twinkled from up here. It was as comforting as Vince's solid warmth beside me. I sighed, and then I was drifting off, too.

• • •

We woke with the sunrise, wrapped in each other's arms.

"Shit!" Vince almost shouted as he scrambled up, yanking his arm from beneath my head, which bounced off the ground because I was only half awake and had no real idea what was going on.

I sat up and rubbed the back of my head. The look on his face was confusion, and slight panic. It would have been sort of funny if it wasn't mortifying. Was it really so awful to have woken up with me in his arms to the rising sun?

Yes, apparently.

I hurried to stand and started packing up the things from the night before without saying a word. Mostly because I wasn't sure what to say. I mean, his reaction was a little humiliating. That was hard to ignore. My back was stiff from sleeping on the roof and I had a knot in my neck. My ability to relive my glory days was an emotional trick only. My body was clearly not on board.

Vince, having stopped swearing and pacing around, went to work picking up the beer cans and other garbage and when there was no evidence left, he turned to me and smiled slightly, enough for the lines around his eyes to crinkle.

"Gets pretty cold up here at night, I guess."

"Is that your way of justifying wrapping yourself around me like an afghan last night?" The words were out before I could think to stop them.

Vince chuckled, and I felt some of the horror drain away.

"Good to know you'd be willing to sacrifice your personal space to keep me warm if we ever get stranded in the actual mountains," I said. I grabbed the blankets and headed toward the ladder. I was glad we were joking about it since I wasn't prepared to deal with the mortification that these feelings, if they were really a thing, were one-sided. I didn't need Vince acting weird about it.

Plus, I really, really needed to pee.

Once that was taken care of, I'd focus on how I'd gone from remembering that Vince and I had once been buddies to wanting him to take me in his arms on a motel roof. And if I was being honest, my fantasy hadn't ended there. My face flushed just thinking about it. I was glad I was making my way down the ladder so he couldn't see my cheeks.

"Do you think they'd let me use the bathroom?" I asked when he was on the ground next to me.

He shrugged. "Just go use the one in the room. You said you reserved one, right?"

I had. "All this fresh air must have made me forget." I fished the keycard out of my pocket and held it up.

"I would think this place would still have actual keys. You know the kind with the kite-shaped plastic tags? Remember those?"

I nodded. "Of course. Printed with 'If found, drop in any mailbox. We guarantee postage.'" I stopped at the door to the room and waved the card in front of the handle. "Imagine it being that easy to be returned to where you needed to go when you're lost."

Vince clucked his tongue. "The things you say, Red."

Red. Had he given me a nickname? My face flooded again.

I stepped in the room and dropped everything I was carrying on the bed and made a beeline for the bathroom.

Closing the door behind me, I leaned back against it, trying to get my wits about me.

But my bladder, having sensed proximity to relief, threatened to burst. This was yet another reminder that I wasn't a kid anymore. I barely made it to the toilet and only after I sat down did I glance around and wonder if I shouldn't have laid a foundation of clean toilet paper before sitting.

The locks might have been updated, but nothing else about the room had been. There were rust stains around the drains in the sink and the shower, and the towels were thin and scratchy and had been numbered in sharpie for some reason. There was also a very threatening note Scotch-taped to the corner of the mirror.

Don't steal our towels! We'll know who has them if you do!

I washed my hands and splashed cold water on my face. For having just slept on a roof with nothing but Vince's arm for a pillow, I didn't look nearly as bad as I should. I tucked my hair behind my ears and went back into the room.

"They obviously have a problem with petty thieves," Vince said, pointing at a note on the vanity mirror exactly like the one in the bathroom. Though *towels* had been replaced with *linens*. There was also a sign on the TV, and the phone of all things.

"Who's stealing a push-button phone? Is there a market for that?" I asked.

"I have no idea. This place is a trip." Vince stepped around me (was he being careful not to touch me or was I just being paranoid?) and went into the bathroom. "It has a real unsolved-murder vibe."

"And you think the things I say are out there. Who even thinks that?" I asked and moved to where I'd dropped the blankets and busied myself folding them until he returned, looking at his phone.

"I gotta bust it back. The stage crew needs me for setup, and Davis is about to call out the National Guard since I haven't answered one of his thirty-seven texts or fifty-three calls."

"Hmmm. Maybe a taste of his own medicine is good for him," I replied, picking up the blankets and heading toward the door.

"I'd agree, but the whole *do as I say not as I do* philosophy is lost on him."

We'd reached my car and I fished for my keys. Vince held out his hand. "Mind if I drive us back?" I handed them over without a peep. We shoved all the stuff in my trunk and climbed in, my music clicking on as soon as he started the car.

He reached to turn it off, but then his hand hovered above the dial.

"Any chance you mind just enjoying the silence? It's a little early for me," he said.

I glanced at the clock. It was only 6:02. Of course. Sunrise came early when you were sleeping outside.

I nodded and then shifted my gaze to the window.

"Have you been looking out for Davis since high school?"

"Actually, it started out the opposite. We met on the playground—elementary school. I was the new kid. Skinny, not athletic at all. An easy target for the bullies out there on my own. Davis invited me to the top of the monkey bars with him. It was a good vantage point, from up there we could see the whole social structure of recess. He told me who to avoid, who would avoid me. And he invited me over after school. He had a mom who brought us Oreos and Nestlé Quik. I didn't have that at my house. Single mom who was always either at work or with her latest boyfriend, who wasn't ever interested in her kid. It was nice at Davis's house. Normal. I kept coming and she didn't seem to mind."

I nodded. "That sounds familiar. I wasn't the new kid, and my parents were still together, but mostly it seemed so they had someone to fight with. Didn't make me want to spend much time at home. And I didn't have a Davis to take me in, I was on my own."

We pulled up to a stoplight and he turned to look at me, that direct way of his zeroing right to my core. "I always figured that about you."

"How?"

He took two fingers and pointed in the direction of my eyes, and then back at his own. "It's in the eyes. You have that lost soul look in them, same as me."

I didn't know what to say to that. It was true, I had felt lost or lonely for most of my life. It was probably what drove every decision I made. Important ones anyway. Trying to find a place I belonged.

The light turned green and the car moved forward.

"It's changed though," he continued.

"What has?"

"That look in your eye."

"How?" I cleared my throat, which was hard to do since I'd spent the night inhaling roof dust and had forgotten to pack any water.

This seemed an oddly intimate conversation. The second we'd had in the past twelve hours, and I was glad we were having it in a car so we could both stare forward.

"Well, when I first saw you in the hotel hallway back in Chicago, you still had it. Actually, it was what made me recognize you right away. Like recognizes like, you know?"

I did know. Maybe that was what drew me to Vince, without knowing it.

"And the next morning when I gave you the job, you still had it but tinged with terror. Since you joined the tour? When you're holding your camera or setting up a shot? You have a fire in your eyes now, reminds me of the guys when they get on stage."

He turned into the hotel, pulled the car into the valet line, and put it in park.

"But *you* still have it," I said. It wasn't a question, because I knew the answer.

He looked at me. "I'm still working on that." His smile was a little sad, and he opened his mouth to say something else, but before he could, the valet opened his door.

"Guest of the hotel?" he asked.

And just like that, the moment was gone.

Chapter Twenty-Three

Something shifted between Vince and me in the days after that night on the motel roof. We smiled more easily when we saw each other, like we were in on the same jokes, which maybe we were. After all, like recognizes like. A phrase I don't think I'd ever thought about much, never fully understood until Vince had said it about us, but now brought a jolt to my chest every time I thought of Vince saying it to me.

Not that I had much time to dwell on it. After a successful few nights in Denver, the tour rolled on to Phoenix and I found myself in the hotel restaurant after I'd checked in, having a drink and working on questions for my upcoming one-on-one with each of the guys. I had finally managed to nail them down. I knew the pictures were good, but I didn't have much material that lined up with the way I wanted to do the book. With their stories told, not the stories told about them.

I'd printed out some of the photos I'd taken from the previous shows and was going through them, looking for the best of the best to show Harrison.

"Homework?" Vince asked. I knew it was him without looking up, thanks to his familiar scent.

Was that weird? Or gross? Maybe a little of both.

Also, what the hell and why the hell was I smelling Vince?

"Just stuff for the book." I was actually glad he'd shown up. I'd told him I didn't think his questions fit for what I was going for, but I hadn't shown him why. Now that I had some things sketched out, I hoped that showing him would make him understand better why I'd rejected his input. I scribbled down the question I had come up with before I forgot it.

"I don't want to interrupt you." He started to slide back out of the booth. "I was just going to get a plate of truffle fries and maybe a drink or two before I checked in."

"No interruption." I set my pen down. But of course he *was* interrupting, so why was I saying that?

"If you're sure?"

"Of course. I'm up for anything." I took a sip of my whiskey. None of this was true. I was supposed to meet with Rex in the morning and I wanted to look professional, like I had my shit together, so I had planned on an early night.

But I also wanted to sit across from Vince and drink whiskey and eat french fries.

"You two need anything?" This waitress was young, no flash from the past there. I doubted she even knew the biggest rock band in the world had checked in.

"I'll have a whiskey on the rocks, and an order of your truffle fries, extra crispy. No need for that aioli, just ketchup will do."

"Actually, bring the aioli, too. Some of us are civilized." I put my hand on Vince's as I interrupted him as if it was the most natural thing in the world. Then pulled it back after realizing what I had done.

"You know it's just mayonnaise, right?" Vince said drily. If he was bothered by my hand touch, he didn't show it, and

I relaxed.

"I don't care what it is, it's amazing."

"That's the trouble with the world today, everything has to be fancier than it needs to be."

"Says the man ordering truffle fries." I waved my hands around the bar we were sitting in. "A little fancy now and then isn't going to hurt you."

He looked amused. "I only ordered truffle fries because that's what they offer. I would have been fine with plain old regular fries."

"As long as they're burned."

"Extra crispy." He pointed at me. "There's a difference. Only a maniac likes limp fries."

"If memory serves, you like all your food burned: pizza, burgers, bacon."

He nodded, then, "If you're going to have someone cook your food, it should be cooked all the way."

I laughed. "Maybe my next project can be a Vince Caparelli lifestyle coffee table book?"

He raised an eyebrow. "Your next project? Someone's feeling confident."

I could only nod. Telling him that the confidence I was feeling had come after our rooftop chat seemed a bit too confessional, and we hadn't had nearly enough whiskey for that. But the night was young.

The waitress brought our drinks and Vince held his out to me.

"What are we toasting?" I asked as I tapped his glass with mine.

He shrugged. "How about that whatever memory road we get dragged down on this stop is a pleasant one and not a nightmare." I clinked in agreement. Though, I'd had just as much fun chasing Davis around Kansas City as I'd had waking up on that roof in Denver.

Because they shared a common denominator: Vince. And since he kept coming around, I had to think he thought the same thing about me.

"I'm trying to remember what sort of trouble we got up to when the tour rolled through Phoenix," I said, sitting back and wrapping my hands around my glass.

"Well, much like this time we were here in the heat of the summer. It involved the pool, the ice machines, and a significant lack of appropriate swimming suits."

"Oh my God. Yes. I remember now!" It had been too hot for the buses to travel during the day so we'd gotten stuck here, waiting for the sun to go down so we could move on. The guys had commandeered the ice machines and dumped it all in the pool and then gone skinny dipping.

"You might notice that this hotel does not have a pool." He tapped his finger to his temple.

"Always one step ahead," I replied.

"I have to be, or they'd put me in an early grave."

I so wanted to jot that down so I wouldn't forget it. I wondered if I could locate that old hotel, that pool. The fries arrived and I quickly scratched a note to myself before I moved my things out of the way for the food.

Vince was right, extra crispy was the way to go, but so was aioli. We polished off the fries and ordered another round of drinks. In the corner of the bar a band started playing, cover songs of all things.

"They aren't too bad," I said to Vince as they finished their first number.

He nodded. "No escaping rock and roll. Maybe this is tonight's adventure?"

As if on cue the opening bars of "She's Come Undone," a Golden Tiger cult favorite, began to play. It was a slow haunting start that gave way to a driving beat and I'd had just enough whiskey. I slid out of the booth and stood at the end of the table.

"Let's dance." It wasn't a question, which was so not like me, and I held out my hand to Vince, who was quick to shake his head in protest but then stood and took it. We waded onto the dance floor and joined the group shaking and stomping what our mamas gave us all in good fun. We even tried our hand at a bit of swing dancing, if that could be done to rock music.

It could, actually, just not very well.

Neither of us cared as he spun me and dipped me in time to the driving beat. It was more fun than I'd had in years. So much fun that when that song ended and another began, we stayed right where we were. And when that one gave way to a ballad, I turned to head back to the table, but Vince grabbed my hand and pulled me close.

"You have something against slow dancing, Red?" he asked gruffly, and I could only shake my head and let him pull me in. Keeping hold of my hand, his other went to the small of my back, and I settled in against him.

I don't know if it was the whiskey or all the time we'd been spending together, but it felt so natural, so right. I leaned in so I could hear him singing softly in my ear, captivated by his rough voice, and the tenderness with which he caressed the words. Vince, tender? It made my heart ache and took my breath away.

When the song was over, we both stayed like that as the band launched into another upbeat rocker. It was only after we'd been bumped into from all sides that we finally let go of each other.

And for a second we stood there and stared at each other blankly. Confused.

What was happening? Was I falling for Vince? Was he falling for me? Was any of that a good idea? Were we both just being nostalgic, caught up in these moments we kept creating and recreating?

But even as I wondered, we were ambushed. Rex, Tony, Alex, even Davis descended upon us.

"You trying to ditch us?" Rex said, throwing an arm around Vince's shoulders, banging his head up and down to the beat.

"Now why would I do a thing like that?" Vince replied loudly, but the sarcasm was lost on them as they all started moving with the music. He glanced at me, but I couldn't tell if the look on his face was relief or annoyance. Which was, frankly, relatable.

The guys were actively dancing around us and into us, really giving us no choice but to join in. I was dancing in a bar with *Golden Tiger*. Which wasn't exactly where I thought my night was headed, but I couldn't complain. We were a circle of people moving with the music, shouting out lyrics. Dancing, laughing, and drinking. I was so sucked into the moment, I didn't worry about how bad my rhythm was or how ridiculous I looked.

This was the magic of music.

It was chaos and fun, and I was disappointed when the song ended and the band announced they were going to take a break. The guys followed us back to the booth we had abandoned for the dance floor. At first trying to squeeze in six of us in a booth for four did not work so well, though not for lack of trying. I was pressed up against the wall with Rex across from me and Davis beside me. Tony and Alex slid in, smashing Rex into the wall, which I think was the point. Vince took one look at the puppy pile of overgrown man-children and chose to remain standing at the end of the table.

"Pass me over my drink, will ya?" he said to the trio across from me, but as they were jockeying for position, it was hard to see just which one of them was closest. Finally, I reached across and pushed it his way. He nodded in appreciation, a slight shake of his head that I interpreted to mean that he was a bit disappointed our booth had been crashed. And I smiled in return. It was nice, our inside joke.

"What's this?" Rex asked, flipping my notebook around so he could see it.

"Just some lists of questions for our one-on-one time tomorrow," I replied, the words coming as easily as if I'd asked about the weather.

"OOOOO!" was the response, because at this point the juvenile male behavior was taking over.

"Trying to make me jealous by paying attention to the other guys, are you?" Davis asked, throwing his arm along the top of the booth behind me. He said it without a trace of his signature smirk. Kidding with me like he would have with any of the others, and the small smile I'd shown Vince grew wider.

"You wish," I replied, shifting away from his arm, my back against the end of the booth so I could look right at him. His other hand went to his heart as though I'd wounded him. As if I could do such a thing to Davis Scott. It was a little surreal, this bantering with him, but so natural. As if he wasn't who he was, just some guy out with his pals. It almost made me forget that he'd been the object of my desire for all of my teenage life, with a few lonely adult years' worth of fantasies thrown in for good measure.

"What, are you reading my mind now?" He laughed.

"I don't need to, it's written all over your face." I was laughing as I said it, at the absurdity of the comment, this teasing that was just shy of flirting. Which was once again received with a bellowing, "OOOOOO!" from the rest of the group. I glanced at Vince, expecting that he was in on it, but the look on his face wasn't one of amusement.

Which was odd. Wasn't this what he'd all but told me to do? Try to fit in and be one of the guys? Right now, I felt as far from my groupie days as I'd ever been, and I'd once been a children's portrait taker. In Iowa.

"I've never been much of a test taker," Rex was saying, pulling my attention away from whatever the hell was going on with Vince.

"What test?" I asked. And he pointed to my notebook.

"Why would you think it was a test?" I asked, sipping at my whiskey. Vince was fidgeting where he stood and hadn't said a word, and I glanced at Rex to see that he wasn't paying one bit of attention to it. So, I didn't either.

He shrugged. "It's questions that I have to answer. Seems like a test to me."

"I'm not trying to trick you, any of you," I replied, looking around the table.

"Oh, so it's going to be more of the 'what's your favorite song' or 'what's your favorite memory on stage' kind of BS questions we've all answered a thousand times."

"Not even close," I said. It just reinforced that Vince's angle for the book was not only overdone, but it was also boring. I opened my mouth to point this out, but the hard stare Vince was giving me shut me up. What was his problem all of a sudden?

"I want to know about the inspiration for the songs, not just the lyrics, but also for the notes, the chords, the harmonies." I looked at Tony. "The rhythms."

"I want to know about the stories you intended to tell, not just in the songs, but in the layouts of the album. How you came to write them, and why. And I want the whole thing to be laid out like liner notes. With the photos showing the evolution, not just of the band, but of each of you. And the songs."

My face was flushed when I finished, and I was too nervous to look up. I'd been staring at the table while I laid it all out. What if they thought it was ridiculous? They were, after all, all about the show.

But then they erupted again in a chorus of "OOOOOOs!" and the charge of that, of my idea not only being accepted, but that they were excited about it, was one hell of a rush.

Until I looked to the end of the table to see that Vince was gone.

Chapter Twenty-Four

The guys were continuing to hoot and holler, though at this point it seemed more about the hooting and hollering than the book. It was nice to be so enthusiastically received. It helped me to try and ignore the disappointment that Vince had just up and left. Had I made up whatever was happening between us during the slow dance? That we'd been building to something since that night on the roof and that tonight, that dance was the start of something between us?

Did Vince disappearing mean he didn't and would never see me like that? I closed my eyes at the thought.

Had I let myself believe that the ease between us meant something more than it did? Maybe because there had been no ease at all between Jack and me in those last few years. Was I just projecting? Maybe my divorce had me more emotionally vulnerable than I'd given it credit for. I should probably try and figure that out.

But the men of Golden Tiger were all in. Alex jumped up from the end and returned with five shots of whiskey.

"It's going to be a hell of a book, doll." Davis smiled in a way that started with his signature smirk, but then moved to his whole wide face, then he handed me a shot. They all held them up and then threw them back.

I, having learned my lesson on shots, simply threw it over my shoulder, hoping no one was sitting in the booth behind us. There wasn't, and none of the guys seemed to notice.

"What the hell happened to Vince?" Davis asked as he slammed his shot glass back down on the table.

Alex shrugged. "He was headed to the elevators when I got the whiskey." My disappointment confirmed. I sort of wished I'd taken the shot now.

"That dude needs to lighten up," Davis said, though I could see the look on his face was one of concern. "I'm gonna go find out what crawled up his ass." He pulled his arm away as he slid from the booth, stopping to squeeze my shoulder.

"We'll have to save our one-on-one for another time, doll."

I swallowed. The last one-on-one I'd had with Davis had been less than professional, what with my practically drooling over the idea of him kissing me. There'd need to be some parameters for this one. At the very least there would be lights and no candles.

"I'll let you know when." He winked and then turned away.

Tony and Alex followed him, stopping at the bar as he walked out the doors.

Only Rex stayed, but Vince disappearing had sort of taken the celebration out of me.

"Why would Vince just leave?" I asked.

"How could anyone know? Vince keeps it all locked and loaded." He knocked his chest with his fist.

That he did. I shook my head. All the fun we were having aside, the laughs and the fries and the dancing, the truth was even in all of that Vince never let his guard down. Sure, there were moments where he did, but they didn't build on each other and when they came, I was caught off guard. It was more frustrating than I'd let myself admit. I'd actually planned to work all night. Once again, I had let myself be distracted from what could actually change my life by some emotional fantasy of Vince only to have him storm off for God knows what.

I'd seen this act before, and I wasn't interested in a replay.

Obviously, Vince was not interested in me. Which explained his reaction when we'd woken up in each other's arms on the roof. I was a buddy, a pal. We were just friends, someone to spend the hours with happily out of the spotlight while the real stars took to the stage. He had no interest in anything deeper. He wasn't sending mixed signals, I was making up whatever this connection I thought we had in my head and I needed to put a stop to it.

I'd let myself get detoured by a man once before. But this time, this new amazing opportunity? I wasn't about to be derailed again.

• • •

I was up early after a fitful night of little to no sleep. Vince's abrupt exit from the bar bothered me even though I kept trying to tell myself to let it go. He hadn't even sent a text to explain himself. Surely he wasn't that pissed I'd dismissed his line of questions? It was my book after all. My vision, my salvation. Though, that was probably a bit dramatic. But as I got farther and farther from my old life, the more I felt it was true.

I expected, especially with how close we'd gotten in the past week, that he'd be happy for how my idea for the book was received. By the guys. But maybe I was wrong. Or maybe it was bad and he didn't want to tell me? It was infuriating that he was leaving me hanging like this. Doubting myself, again.

He was, in some way, the one who'd convinced me I could do this job. And now he was pulling some sort of disappearing act? Because I'd somehow hurt his feelings?

At some point in the night, as my mind spun out of control, I actually envisioned Vince throwing a tantrum.

That was when I knew I'd lost my mind. Rex was right. Vince was not overly emotional. Vince was the definition of even. I'd finally fallen asleep around four, but my dreams had been a dramatic mix of my ex-husband and Davis in a lip-sync battle at the dive bar in Kansas City.

Somehow Rex was also involved and when I'd woken with a start, it was in a full-on panic that I wasn't going to be prepared for my session with him. So, I ordered a pot of coffee from room service and dug in, pushed Vince's disappearing act as far out of my mind as I could, and focused on my plans for my time with Rex. Photos I wanted to get, and questions I wanted to ask.

Rex's story was interesting in that he was the only member of Golden Tiger who had continued performing after the band had broken up. Which was really no surprise seeing as how he was off the charts talented. He joined other bands, played other tours, charity gigs, but he never released his own original work. Not an album, not even one song. He didn't so much as change a riff of a song on anything he played in the past twenty years. Golden Tiger or anything else.

Why and why not? He had the name recognition, the talent, and the following. He could have had a huge solo career, but he didn't. It was fascinating to me, and what I planned to focus my one-on-one time talking to him about. I wanted to know why. I was also hoping I could get him to play me a few songs, to photograph. I was thinking acoustic, black and white. On an unmade bed, or against the windows with the mountains as a backdrop.

Feeling good about my plan, I pulled out all of my clothes to decide what sort of look would be best. No ripped jeans or leather pants, too rock-star chic. The red power suit was off the table, too uptight. I finally settled on some black cigarette pants and a white shell. It was long enough to cover my ass. I know the fashionable thing to do was not worry about such a thing, but I did. Comfort over fashion was the way I was going.

I finished the look with the black boots. It was the perfect mix of rock and responsible, which was my new philosophy.

With my ducks in a row, I hung the clothes on the back of the bathroom door for a quick steam and jumped in the shower. I wanted to be on time, but more than that I wanted to feel calm and confident, professional even. The last thing I wanted was to show up late and harried.

I was standing in the bathroom, wrapped in a towel finishing up my makeup (light and professional, no thick black eyeliner or tarantula eyelashes for me), when a pounding erupted at my door. So loud I jumped, and without thinking of what I was wearing—or not wearing—I raced to open it. Obviously, whoever was making such a fuss was having a true crisis.

"What's the emergency?" I asked as I pulled open the door, immediately wishing I'd taken a second to check the peep hole before throwing it open.

Vince stood on the other side, and if he was surprised to find me in a towel, I couldn't tell from the expression on his face. Like I said, even.

I had managed to push him so far out of my thoughts that the shock of seeing him there almost made me drop that towel.

"No emergency, just checking in." This was not the Vince from the rooftop or the dance floor. He was distant, professional. Talking to me like I was a hotel employee or something. Like we hadn't been slow dancing the night before, right before he'd disappeared into thin air. It was irritating, but I didn't have time to unpack it.

"Checking in on what?" I asked, crossing my arms.

"You. Rex. The session?" He looked around me and into my room. "Do you want to let me in so we don't have to go over the questions out here in the hall, while you're umm..." He cleared his throat. "Naked?"

I pulled my towel tighter. Having Vince in my room was actually the last thing I wanted.

"No need. I'm all good. Just have to finish getting ready, so..." I matched his professional tone. "Thanks, though."

He gave a curt nod that was my dismissal.

I shut the door before I said something I'd regret. Then leaned my back against it and closed my eyes. What had happened? Even in the million replays of the night before in my mind, I couldn't work out his abrupt departure any more than I could figure his asking me for that slow dance. Everyone and everything he had to keep track of was in one room. Leaving was against everything I knew about Vince.

Maybe I didn't know him at all, and I couldn't keep thinking about it like some sort of lovesick girl with an unrequited crush.

I had a job to do.

The lump in my throat would just have to get over itself.

Chapter Twenty-Five

By the time my hair was done and I was dressed, my focus was once again where it should be. Or it was, until I stepped out of the bathroom and saw that Vince had shoved a note under my door. I recognized his handwriting from the first note he'd left when I joined the tour. Way back in Chicago. It was so oddly artistic for a man.

I thought about just leaving it where it was—I couldn't think of one good thing that could come out of reading it. Because the Vince who'd left it hadn't been the one who'd pulled me into a slow dance, but the one who'd shown up like a stranger at my door this morning.

A stranger, somehow, after all the late nights and long easy conversations. Vince was back to being someone I didn't think I knew at all.

So, in the end, that teenage girl who had taken up residence in my head, the one who still had hope that the note from the boy would answer all the questions, forced me to bend over and pick it up.

She was sorely disappointed when I opened it:

Red~

Just in case you change your mind on the questions, here are my ideas again. Let me know how it goes.

~Vince.

She might have been disappointed, but I was downright pissed off. How dare he show up at my door looking just as aged to perfection as he always did, make a dry joke about me being naked in the hall, and then leave me a list of his inane questions?

The questions were inane, elementary, juvenile. I'd all but told him so when we talked briefly about them on the roof in Colorado. So why was he still pushing them on me? He had no such suggestions of the photos I should take, so was it just that he didn't think I could pull off the writing portion? Or was he really so set on controlling everything to do with the band that he couldn't for a second trust that I knew what I was doing?

Well, no, thank you. If I wanted to be told how to create art, I could have stayed taking family Christmas card photos. I crumpled the note into a ball and tossed it in the garbage can. Then I pulled on my kick-ass boots, grabbed my camera bag, and went to kick some ass.

Rex's room was on the top floor, another suite, though smaller than the one we'd partied in that first night in Chicago. Only a living room and a bedroom, no giant conference table or second bedroom. I had no idea if there was a balcony because his curtains were drawn tight against the desert sun—so much for my shot against the mountains.

"You want me to order some food or something?" he asked as we sat down.

I shook my head and grabbed a bottle of water from the coffee table. "I'm good if you are."

"I'm good. Had breakfast early, after my workout. Usually I have some sort of snack late afternoon. I don't like to play on a full stomach. It makes me feel tired, bloated."

Rex's signature outfit was a leather vest with nothing underneath and jeans that hung so low it had to be uncomfortable. And involve some manscaping. It wasn't a stretch for him to pull it off, his stomach was as chiseled and flat as it had always been. I made a note to ask about his workout routine in case we ran out of things to talk about. In my experience, people who work out enough to have those kinds of abs *really* liked to talk about it.

"Grab your guitar." I walked past him and into the bedroom, relieved to see the bed still unmade. "I want to get some shots here."

"If I was Davis, I'd say something like, 'I never turn down a lady in the bedroom' but I'm not." He laughed at his own joke and sat down on the edge of the bed.

"Thank God. I don't think I'm in the right headspace for that right now." My cheeks felt warm; already I was letting my personal get in the way of my professional. I cleared my throat.

"Start sitting all the way at the top against the headboard. Look at the guitar. Can you play for me?"

Rex looked like a kid who'd won the spelling bee after being asked to spell "rhinoceros." "Any requests?"

I pulled my camera up to my face and shook my head. I was not sad when he launched into "When All Is Said and Done," a party anthem that, done acoustically, was rather haunting.

He played, I shot, both of us lost in the song. When he finished, I pulled open the room-darkening curtains and had him stand against the sheers. The light was incredible, clouds outside filtering in. He started playing again, this time a ballad. "We Can't Come Back."

I was done before he was, and I let my camera down and just listened to him play. Hoping the emotion on his face had transferred to the photos.

"That's it?" he asked when the song was finished.

"Well, like I said last night, my plan is to add stories and anecdotes from you guys to make it a little bit more than just a book of photos," I said. "You good with that?"

"I'm game." He walked back into the living room and sat down on the couch. Thankfully, not patting the space next to him.

"So," he started, leaning back. "You want to talk about how it feels to be back on stage with the guys, and how we became Golden Tiger in the first place."

"Actually, I'm way more interested in why, in all the years the band was apart, you kept playing but never put out anything original."

His eyebrows shot up, and a slow smile spread across his face. "And here I thought this was going to be nothing more than a formality."

"Meaning?"

"Meaning, I thought you were going to ask me shit you could find on the internet with one Google search. You actually know your shit. No one's ever asked me that before, or as far as I can tell noticed."

I could feel my own smile grow. "Well, I mean, you're listed on the liner notes as a writer on every album. So, I know you can write. I want to know why you didn't."

He shifted uncomfortably. "First of all, we're all listed as writers on those albums, just to be clear." He took a drink of his water. "Secondly, all I ever wanted to do was play music. Good music. No matter what. And I'm not saying there was drama over the band calling it quits, but I just wanted to play. So, when other artists and bands gave me that opportunity, I took it."

I wrote while he spoke, my brain trying to sort through what he was saying—and what he wasn't.

"But that doesn't answer the question of why you never put out anything original after Golden Tiger." I kept my eyes on my notebook, hoping it would help him to be more honest.

"Plainly—and I don't know if I want this in the book, but I'll tell you and then we can decide—I didn't want to deal with a label. Seemed easier to just keep playing other people's music."

Interesting.

"Did the label tell you what you could and couldn't put on your records back then?"

He coughed. "I didn't say that. I'm just saying that dealing with those stuffed shirts was a pain in the ass. And I didn't want a pain in my ass. I just wanted to play." His hand rested on the guitar that was next to him.

He had said it, in a roundabout way. I made a note to ask the other guys about the label, and their manager. Had that been why the last record had flopped? Why they'd broken up? It was a far better story than the guys imploding because of competing egos. Or at least that's what the fan in me wanted to believe.

They were still just as close as they'd always been. There was no faking that sort of kinship. So the mystery remained.

None of this really fit into the pretty picture and backstage yarns book I was planning, but I couldn't stop myself from wanting to know. Even if it was to satisfy my own curiosity and nothing else.

Rex shifted nervously. "I don't want to come off as unappreciative to the label. I mean, they signed us and helped us blow up. They are the ones who have us back on this tour. So don't make me sound like an ungrateful dick, okay?"

Rex was far from a dick, but I decided to go another direction and put him at ease.

"Of course. So, for you it's about the music. Playing the music. So why don't you tell me about that?"

He seemed to relax and launched into stories of being on stage, from high school to London and every big city imaginable. Telling story after story of the music, from his perspective. All of this would fit in with my vision.

But he'd laid a thread about the label, and the hell if I wasn't going to pull it.

Chapter Twenty-Six

My chat with Rex and his slip about the label lit a spark in me. I had to know more. About the band, about their chemistry, about their breakup.

I remember when the news broke, splashed across the tabloids at the checkout stands. How I'd been heartbroken, but also slightly relieved. Even as I settled into the boring life I'd chosen, I still had a hard time thinking that the band, that life on the road, was going on without me. I'd read those glossy magazines and trashy papers while I waited to pay for my groceries, never buying them and bringing them home—Jack wouldn't have liked that—so I got the story in tiny bits. I'd always thought that was why I didn't have a grasp of the whole thing. But now, I wondered if the whole story had never been told.

The thought gave me a thrill.

Because then maybe I was the one who was going to get to tell it. Maybe I could do it through the pictures I took. Soul-baring performances, as they bared their souls? Something like that. I didn't fancy myself much of a storyteller, but I knew no better narrators than Golden Tiger.

They could tell it. I would shoot it.

After I'd finished with Rex, I'd raced back to my room and started googling. He was right, there was article after article about the guys growing up together. Their high school days where they practiced in his grandma's garage, the talent show win, the club scene, the label discovering them. And then their massive stadium tour and eventual plummeting sales and scathing reviews of their final album. But no actual story of the breakup.

Some stories asked the question of why, but not one of them answered it. And while Rex had continued performing, the rest of the band had faded into oblivion. There was never a mention of Vince. Not anywhere.

No rock star worthy drunken meltdowns or bankruptcies that had any of them working at a fast-food restaurant. They went from the biggest rock band in the world, to oblivion, to this tour. And while I joined the throngs of people thrilled by their return, apparently I was the only one who wondered just what had happened to make it all come to a screeching halt.

I spent the rest of the day holed up in my room scribbling lists of questions and trying to strategically figure out who I could ask what in order to get just the right amount of information. Like Rex, I had the curtains pulled tight against the hot summer sun, so I was shocked when I leaned back to stretch my aching back and glanced at the clock on the bedside table. 7:03.

The concert started in twenty-seven minutes. For a brief second, I considered just skipping it altogether. But then I remembered the location of this one. A mid-size amphitheater in the desert. Twenty years ago, it had been like magic to hear the music stretch out into the endless night. And it was hard to argue with magic.

I opened my suitcase and gave my clothing choices

the once-over. My beloved miniskirt was on the top, but it seemed suddenly more like a costume than an outfit choice. Like it was part of who I was trying to be, not who I was. I tossed it on the floor and dug for my jeans. Slightly distressed, edgy, but comfortable too. I topped them with a plain black T-shirt, pulled my hair back into a ponytail, and was out the door in five minutes.

Vince had us staying near the place, so the drive was quick, and because I was so late, most of the traffic had died down. I flashed my ticket and was pleasantly surprised to be led down not to the front row, but to an area in front of that, one marked for VIPs only.

Not going to lie, the VIP made me wish I could go back in time and tell my awkward self that one day, I'd be the epitome of cool.

"Ma'am? Can I bring you a drink?"

Ma'am? So much for cool.

But still. "I'd love one. Whiskey, on the rocks, please." The waiter nodded and disappeared to wherever the drinks were going to come from. It was the perfect angle for focusing on Rex, which is what I intended to do at this show. I felt good, confident. When the waiter returned with my drink, in a real glass no less, I laid my hand on his arm. "Thanks, but next time, how about we forget the ma'am and you can just call me Campbell."

It came out flirtier than I intended, but he'd still blushed slightly.

"Sure thing ma—err, Campbell," and then he was gone.

Cool again!

As the stage lights went black and the crowd roared, I was really feeling myself. Even more so when I noticed the women just off to the right of me. They were at every show. Maybe not these exact women, but some version of them. Groupies, some aging more gracefully than others, but still.

These women weren't trying to remember their glory days, they were trying to recreate them, so it wouldn't surprise me if they were following the band from city to city. To me, they'd always been the goal, they were confident and sexy with a bond among them that I could never quite break into.

Tonight, they were all dressed in black. They looked like a girl version of the *Sons of Anarchy* crew in various forms of leather with windblown hair that was not from actual wind. More like hundred-dollar blowouts and an Uber ride with the windows up tight. Seeing them made me feel even better about ditching that miniskirt.

And, with a nod to personal growth, thankful not to be one of them.

I sipped my whiskey and waited for the show to start. And when it did, I focused, like I intended, on Rex. With my camera at the ready, I got some good shots to go with what I'd taken earlier. I had always been drawn to Davis during a show. He was, after all, a master showman. Watching the concert without paying attention to him gave me a whole different perspective, one that I was thoroughly enjoying.

Focusing on Rex was focusing on the music. And he was one hell of a musician.

Before I knew it, the show was over. As they came to the edge of the stage to take their final bow, I couldn't help but feel a rush as Rex pointed in my direction and then did a perfect air guitar for my camera. Rex had a little showman in him, too.

The lights went up and the adorable waiter appeared at my side again. "Campbell," he said and paused like he was really, really proud of himself for remembering. I wished I'd asked his name, but having nothing to call him, I just nodded.

"Rex would like you to come backstage."

It was such a formal invitation. I nodded and gathered up my purse and the jean jacket I'd brought.

"What about us?" one of the groupies called.

Waiter boy shrugged. "Nothing for you, ma'am."

I glanced to see how that landed. Hands were on hips, and eyes were flared. So, that would be a "not good."

For once, I was the one going backstage while they had to scheme to figure it out. I smiled uncomfortably. Because even though it was a bit of a high, I felt badly for them when it clearly meant so much to be asked backstage.

"I'll see what I can do!" I yelled, with an awkward wave to get their attention. This was met with wide eyes and open-mouthed stares, but I kept waving as I walked away. Unable to just stop for some reason.

"Can you see about getting them backstage, too?" I asked the usher, showing him my credentials. "It would really mean a lot to me." I said this last part sort of breathlessly and smiled, hoping a little flirting would help my cause.

He shrugged. "I can see what my boss says, ma'am, err, Campbell." So much for what I thought was turning on my charm.

The scene was different than the usual post party. Mostly because it was set up outside. Sure, the venue had dressing rooms and enclosed areas, but it also had a fantastic outdoor patio space. There were couches and other seating scattered around, a bar in the corner. Strings of Edison bulbs were hung elegantly, giving enough light to move around, but not so much to make it bright. The vastness of the desert stretched out behind us. It was calm, lovely. And it must have had the same effect on the guys because they were mellow. Stretched out on the furniture. Not the fist-bumping "long live rock and roll" that usually went on.

"Campbell, over here!" Rex waved an arm in my direction and I headed over and sat down on a chair next to where his lanky frame was stretched out on the couch. It was the only seat available, actually—Tony and Alex were likewise sprawled on the others. My eyes scanned the darkness for Davis, but then I decided this was actually my best-case scenario. They were all calm, reflective. Maybe it was the desert air? The newness of being back on stage was rubbing off? Either way, something was decidedly calmer about them.

"So, that was a fun show," I opened with.

Fun? Was I twelve? I might as well have waved like I had that first night I'd met them.

I swallowed my horror and was relieved that none of them seemed to notice. Instead they nodded, sipping their drinks.

"When you hit that riff right before the bridge on 'Saturdays and Sunsets,' it felt like you poured gas into my veins," Rex said to Tony. Who, shockingly, didn't have anything resembling a drumstick in his hand. Which had to be the first time I'd ever seen him without.

"Yeah, that energy tonight was wild. Maybe it was being outside? The universe or some such bullshit?" Tony laughed, and then, restoring my faith in him, drummed his fingers on the low table in front of him before reaching for his drink.

"Is it normal for you to change things up when you're on stage? Or do you stick to how you wrote the songs in the first place?"

Rex shrugged. "When we started out, we stuck pretty close to the original, but as the years have gone by, and we've played some of these songs hundreds of times, mixing it up keeps it fresh. Gives it new energy."

"Except some songs. The big ones. We can't change a thing on those, or the fans would probably storm the stage," Alex said and they all laughed a bit.

"I remember one of our last shows in the before times, we tried an acoustic version of 'Climb on Top' and the crowd fell completely silent. And this was a big-ass crowd—like an arena-size crowd," Tony said, leaning back and stretching his arm along the back of his chair.

"I remember that!" Rex said, a wide smile on his face.

I was glad I had only had one drink during the show. I wanted to remember this story.

"We thought they were into it, awestruck. But then they started booing!"

Rex laughed then, hard. "We hadn't been booed like that since we were kids!"

"Remember Davis turned around and almost shit his pants."

They were howling now, and I sat back in my chair hoping they'd just continue storytelling.

"Of course, because he'd have been on the front lines if they started throwing things or storming the stage. He was so pissed that night when it was over."

"That alone was worth it. Nothing like a Davis hissy fit for entertainment."

"Where was this?" I asked, wondering if there were reviews or anything about it online.

"Was it Vegas? I think it was Vegas. I remember the suite had a view of the strip and Davis stood in front of the window as he ranted about it. Said Vince would have known it was a bad idea."

"Vince always knows what's a bad idea." The voice was familiar, though it was out of character for Vince to speak of himself in the third person.

I'd been so wrapped up in the story, I hadn't noticed that Vince had joined our little group. I'd worked hard, without really paying attention to it, to put him and whatever had happened the other night out of my mind, but seeing him appear—calm, collected, welcome like he always was—made my heart thud against my chest.

Rex held up his hand to high five him, which should have been awkward, seeing as how Vince was standing behind him. But somehow it wasn't.

"What was I so smart about this time?" He leaned on the back of his chair, taking in the scene with one cool gaze.

"Changing 'Climb on Top' to acoustic in Vegas on that last tour."

Vince glanced in my direction without looking at me, and something about it made me sit up in my seat.

"I wasn't there to make that call," he said tightly, and his glance fell to somewhere between the couch and the table. Like he was trying to appear focused on what we were talking about, but the conversation had taken his mind elsewhere.

"Yeah, dude. That was the problem. You would have told us not to do it." Rex took a long pull from his beer. "But you'd up and abandoned us—or so the legend goes."

The rest of the guys joined in laughing, giving Vince shit about it. And though he tried to join in the merriment, something in his facade had cracked.

He looked sad. And as irritated as I was with how he'd been acting the past few days, my heart went out to him. But it didn't stop me from wanting to know just why the hell, if he always knew what was best for the band, he'd left them to their own devices.

Back then. But the other night in the bar, too. It just didn't fit. Whatever made him flee was more important than looking out for the band. There was not one thing I could think of that mattered to Vince more than the band. So where had he gone, and why had he gone so cold?

Chapter Twenty-Seven

I took a step up and onto the bus, another dream come true. Another fantasy I was finally living out: I was riding the Golden Tiger tour bus.

Just after Vince had arrived, so had Davis, and the guys had started telling stories of the bus, one after the other.

"Surely you remember that, doll?" Davis had purred in my direction. We were back to that, apparently. When I'd told Vince I was well aware that this was part of Davis's act, I hadn't told him that even with that awareness, when he really turned up that Davis sex appeal, my body responded in spite of itself. My pheromones stood at attention against my better judgment and free will. Even when he called me doll.

"Can't say that I do. I never got so much as a toe on one of those tour buses," I'd said, staring directly at Vince. And while up until a few days ago, this might have resulted in a jovial back and forth, this time there was none of that.

He'd just shaken his head in reply.

We'd gone over this. I'd even thanked him for keeping me away, but now, with this wall he had put up, it was as if none of that had happened. It was maddening, but I refused to let it spoil the mood of the evening. The slight seemed related, then and now. I'm sure I was projecting but somehow I was angry about being kept off the bus all over again.

"What the actual fuck? How is that possible? A hot little number like you?" Davis had purred again, throwing his arm on the back of the couch and looking at me in that way he did. Inviting me to join him. Vince noticed too. I could tell in the way he narrowed his eyes.

"Apparently not hot enough." I'd emphasized each syllable and Vince stared in my direction, but just as he opened his mouth, chaos descended in the form of those aging groupies from out front.

Whatever he was going to say—whether it had been a return to our easy banter, or maybe outing himself that he had purposely kept me away from the band—none of us would ever know. Without thinking twice about it, the women dotted the empty spaces on the seating areas next to the band. Like locusts to a field, not that anyone but me minded. Our quiet, intimate fireside chat was over. Talk about no good deed going unpunished.

I marveled at how they all just assumed they had a place in this group. How easily they slid into the scene, and the conversation went from the guys razzing each other to posturing and rock star strutting. I felt on the outside, as usual, but this time it was my own doing. Davis had, after all, invited me to join him on the couch. But that spot was now taken by the blondest of them all. I took a deep breath. None of this should matter. We had different goals: I wanted to see behind the scenes of the world's biggest rock band, and they wanted to be between the sheets with the world's biggest rock band. It was fine, really.

Personal growth really was a bitch.

"Blew it again, Campbell," I had muttered to myself as I

turned to take my leave. Sure that no one would notice.

"Hey, Red!" I'd stopped in my tracks at the sound of Vince's voice, the use of the nickname.

"How about we change that *never* to a *now*. You can ride the bus to Vegas. Tomorrow."

I'd turned to find the band looking at me with a bit of anticipation, and the groupies looking from me to each other in horror. Only Vince's face remained neutral.

"I'd love to, but I have my car."

"I can have a roadie drive your car. If that's cool with you?" His voice was even. Gone was the familiarity we'd established hanging out. But still. Was this an olive branch? Did it matter?

"That's just fine by me." I'd pointed back at him. "I'll leave my keys with the front desk." Then I pivoted slightly so I was looking at the guys. "And I'll see you on the bus." Then I'd turned back around as quickly as I could before they saw the giant smile that had spread across my face.

I had no idea what had prompted the invitation, but all these years later, I was finally going to find out what sort of magic happened on the tour bus.

• • •

As it turns out, not a lot. Or at least not a lot first thing in the morning, if you could count eleven a.m. as first thing in the morning.

No one spoke as they stumbled up the steps and fell into various seats on the bus. Not at all how I'd imagined the raging party on eighteen wheels.

Did a bus have eighteen wheels, or was that only a semi?

The bus itself was amazing. Like a traveling hotel suite with crushed velvet sofas and a bar that filled one entire side. The windows were covered by thick, dark curtains and everything was lit from underneath with soft lights. In front of the bar was a giant table and that's where I planted myself, my back to the bar looking out over the couches and chairs. I was hoping to get some work done if the guys were just going to sleep the entire time. As luck would have it, the bus had wifi.

I wanted to pull back the curtains and scope out who Vince had driving my car. Would he do it himself? Or did Vince ride the bus, too? Why could I not stop thinking about him? Why had he changed his mind, offered me this access and opportunity especially when he didn't agree with my vision for the book?

Part of me hoped he'd climb aboard and settle across from me and we could step back to the easy way we'd had with each other in the bar that last night, but part of me hoped he'd stay away. I needed to focus, and I didn't need him and his ridiculous ideas and easy, even way distracting me.

One step forward. Two steps back. Though I wasn't sure what I was walking toward. Was it Vince or the book? And why did it feel like I was having to choose? And when had it become Vince and not Davis?

All of that was put to rest as the hydraulic doors sighed and whistled closed. Vince wasn't riding the bus. I wondered if that was because I was, though I couldn't imagine him not wanting to chaperone my first voyage. But that was the old Vince, the one who wasn't keeping me at arm's length. It wasn't even like we'd switched to a professional relationship instead. He'd just gone ice cold. I let out a breath I didn't know I'd been holding and fired up my laptop.

I typed "Golden Tiger tour bus" into the search bar and let myself fall down the rabbit hole of stories and pictures from days gone by. There were plenty of them. *Rolling Stone* had done an article on rock and roll tour buses with pictorial spreads. The first bus was not nearly as fancy as this one. From there, a few clicks led me to fan sites where there were grainy black and white candid shots of bus parties that looked much more like what I imagined this scene to be. It looked like the party from the first night in Chicago, though with many more topless women draped over everything. I squinted and leaned in close, and there was Vince in the thick of it.

I wondered how he squared that in his head, that he was enjoying the scene he had said he always scorned. What was that about? What did it say about his standards and his ego? Or was this just keeping tabs and keeping them all safe from their worst instincts?

Why did I care?

"What's that you're looking at?" Rex said from behind me before sliding into the seat across from me. He must have come from the bunkroom in the back.

"Research. On the tour buses of old."

He raised his brows, then took a sip from the cup of coffee he was holding.

I nodded at it. "Things are a bit different on this tour bus, from what I'm reading. Unless that's full of whiskey?"

He laughed. "Well, on that first tour, the wild one, we traveled at night so we wouldn't have to spend the money on hotel rooms." He took a sip of the coffee. "So yes, things were a little different than this."

"What was different?" Tony asked, sitting down next to Rex.

"Red was just commenting that this experience isn't quite what she was expecting from a tour bus. From what she's read." He pointed at my computer, which I closed, feeling a bit self-conscious about what I'd found with my Google search.

"Ah, and I'm sensing that different is not good, in this case?" As usual, he tapped his fingers on the tabletop as he spoke.

I shrugged. "It's not *not* good. I just was expecting…" I glanced around the bus, to where Davis and Alex sat sleeping sitting up. "Less snoring?"

They both laughed.

"Give them a bit. When Davis wakes up, I think it'll be more like what you imagined. Though, less topless groupies. Unless…"

I could feel my cheeks flood. "That's a hard pass. Especially since all I've had to drink away my inhibitions is sparkling water." This brought a satisfying round of laughs.

"I mean, we can get you something stronger if that's what it'll take." This line of conversation was light, funny. Tony was no more being serious about me losing my top than Vince had been about me needing to practice my whiskey drinking.

"Why doesn't Vince ride the bus?" I asked before I could stop myself.

Rex shrugged. "He always rides with the roadies. I can count on one hand the number of times he's graced us with his presence."

So, it wasn't me. Was that relief?

"It's never really been his scene. I mean, I've never seen anyone who can hold their whiskey like Vince. And he'll stay up and bullshit for hours if that's what's going down. But the wild parties, the women, and all the rest? He just never fell into that part of it."

"The rock and roll lifestyle?" I murmured more to myself, remembering my conversation with Vince in the limo on the way to that after-party in Chicago.

"Something like that."

"So, if that's true, why do I see him in some of these old pictures?" I flipped my computer around to show them.

"I thought you told me you and Vince weren't a thing?" I jumped at the sound of Davis's voice as he slid into the chair next to me.

"We aren't!" I replied, a bit too emphatically. It was hard to miss the glances that shot among the guys. I was about to be relegated back to groupie-in-waiting status if I didn't do something.

"So, now that everyone is awake, what were you saying about giving me a real tour bus experience?"

"I can help with that." Alex was awake now, too, and went behind me to the bar. I heard the sound of a champagne cork popping. And then he was setting the bottle down on the table in front of me with flutes to go with it.

"This seems awfully high-brow." I reached for a glass, and Rex grabbed the bottle and started pouring.

"Best way to wake things up in the morning," Tony said, pulling a deck of cards from his pocket and setting them on the table.

I glanced at my watch. "It's one o'clock in the afternoon."

Davis laid his arm along the back of my chair. "That's considered morning on the road, doll."

I shifted away from him. I didn't want to insult him, but doll was really the worst nickname.

I reached for the cards. "How about this, if I beat you, you never call me doll again. And if you beat me, we can change this game into one that looks a hell of a lot more like the photos I saw of the last tour."

Rex's whole face broke into a ridiculous smile. "You mean…"

"Yes. Strip poker."

There were whistles and yelps as they settled themselves around the table with full pours of champagne as I shuffled the cards.

"What's the game?" Davis asked, his arm still on my

chair, and he let his thumb trail down my neck. I shivered.

"Five card stud, hi-lo eight."

I have to say, the look on all of their faces as they realized I was not messing around was priceless. I had to squelch my smile as I dealt the cards. The benefit of having a dad who lost his entire paycheck at the casinos was that he needed his child to know the game so he could practice. And so he could feel good about himself when he beat me.

I hated losing to him. So, I practiced. Dealing out the hands and playing each of them against the dealer until I got good enough to beat him. Of course, then he stopped asking me to play. But the skill remained. It had been decades since I'd played, another thing I'd stopped doing at the behest of Jack, but now it came right back to me.

I won the first hand easily, and the second. Davis dropped his arm from the back of my chair and inched closer to the table.

"I need to focus, dol—errr..." He curled his lip, remembering he'd lost the privilege of calling me that horrible nickname.

"Red," Rex said with a wink. "Is that one fine with you?"

I nodded. "And since I already got what I wanted with my first win, I'm fine to switch this to your game of choice. Strip poker, wasn't it?"

Davis chuckled. "You got lucky with those. But now that I have something to play for, watch out."

"I'll do that," I replied slyly and then called the game and dealt the cards.

Rex took one look at his and folded. Alex and Tony both bought in immediately. Which was what they'd done the first few games, too. Neither of them showed any skill at all at bluffing, and they were almost always overly confident in their hands. Davis, on the other hand, could and did bluff pretty well. I was working out his tell.

"I'm in, Red," he said smoothly. I was watching him carefully as I flipped the first three cards.

"Damn flop," Tony said, throwing his cards down.

"I'll check." Alex was next, trying a little too hard to be confident. He was so bad at bluffing.

Davis eyed him, and then me. "I'll raise." He pushed a pile of chips into the middle.

The flop hadn't strengthened my hand at all, but still I had two kings so I matched the bet.

Alex laid his cards down, showing his garbage hand and confirming he'd been bluffing all along. "Too rich for my blood," he said, punching Tony in the shoulder like that was the funniest and most original thing anyone had ever said.

"Guess it's just you and me then, Red."

I flipped the fourth card, eyeing Davis. If he was bluffing, he was way too dramatic a dude to not have a tell, but his face was like stone. Maybe that was it? His tell was that when he was bluffing, he was serious? Not that it mattered, the card was a king, which pretty much guaranteed my win. I flipped a chip into the pile.

"You're awful confident," Davis replied, matching my bet.

Funny, I was. And not just in my cards, but in my ability to hang with these guys. These men, who had gone from revered to somehow just buddies in these past few days. Even at the expense of the closeness I'd had with Vince, I still was pretty happy about it. And sitting there, I was also pretty sure it was going to help me turn out a pretty kick-ass book.

I flipped the last card, and then laid down my hand. My three kings beat the pair of jacks Davis held. So he hadn't been bluffing, but he had been overconfident.

"Read 'em and weep, my friends. Everyone takes off something!" I laughed.

Eyebrows were raised, and the champagne was replaced

with whiskey. There were general complaints made about hating to lose.

"I think you better get used to it. I'm feeling pretty lucky today." I raised my eyebrows as one by one they all threw some sort of clothing in a pile. Socks mostly, but Rex went with his shirt.

And by the time we reached Vegas we were all more than a little tipsy and everyone but me was down to their underwear.

Which is how Vince found us when he came on the bus to hand out room keys.

And I wasn't mad about it. Not in the least.

Chapter Twenty-Eight

"I'm coming! I'm coming." My drunken tour bus ride had come to its inevitable climax of me passing out in my hotel room. I had been keeping my drinking to a minimum since I'd officially joined the tour, but this was totally worth how horrible I felt right now. I'd waited years to ride that damn bus, and I'd beat the entirety of Golden Tiger at strip poker. And they'd let me shoot some pictures of it all.

Win/win/win.

Because it was Vegas, the curtains were heavy, and my room was as dark as night. So dark in fact that I hit my shin on the bed as I stumbled toward the pounding on my door.

I tried to yank it open, only to have the safety latch catch which only added to my annoyance. The kind of annoyance that bubbles up when you are awakened from a dead drunk sleep with a hangover at seven fifteen at night. So, needless to say, it was an annoyance that I had never felt before.

Also, the noise it made when it caught hurt my head.

I finally got the door open, ready to let whoever was on the other side have it, but was rendered speechless by a squeal that made the door bang sound like a whisper.

"SURPRISE!"

And I was. Stunned, actually.

Marissa.

"Oh my God! What are you doing here? Who's watching Sasha?"

She pushed past me and into my room. "To surprise you, like I said. There's a direct flight from Des Moines to Vegas. And Sasha is spending the weekend at a lake house with her bestie, so I thought I'd come see mine!" She marched across the room and pulled back the curtains. "Why is it so dark in here?"

I squinted, blinded by the sudden burst of light into the room. "How did you find my room?"

She turned and looked at me carefully. Taking in every detail to the point that I felt naked, even though I was still very much clothed in what I'd worn on the bus.

"I texted Vince. So I could surprise you. Were you asleep?" She glanced at what was obviously an unmade bed.

I crossed the room and sat down on the edge of it. "How do you have Vince's number?"

"He gave it to me, in Chicago." She shrugged. "What's going on? Why aren't you answering my questions? Why are you in bed at seven o'clock? Are you sick?" It was nice to have someone concerned about me. And though I wanted to know how long Vince had known she was coming, I was also just so damn happy to see her.

"Not sick, hungover. I rode the bus with the band from Phoenix." Her eyes widened and her mouth fell open. I'd rendered her speechless, which was as rare as an evening hangover.

"OH MY GOD!" she shrieked again, and I grabbed at my head.

"Shhh. You must be quieter! Or get me something for this headache."

She fished in her purse and came out with a bottle that she crossed the room to hand me. "There, now spill it."

I took the aspirin and then lay down on my bed, propping myself up against the wall. Marissa sprawled out on the end, giving me her rapt attention. I launched into the tale of the backstage bonfire and how that had led to me hopping a ride on the tour bus.

"What about your car?" she asked, which was the most Marissa question there was. Always concerned about the practical details of life. She was such a perfectionist that I knew she wouldn't pay attention to one more word unless I answered that question.

"I'm not sure. Vince took care of it."

She scrambled to sit up. "Vince took care of it? Why did Vince take care of it?"

I shrugged. "Because it's his job."

Her brow furrowed. "Interesting. His job? Not just because he was looking out for you?"

"No! Because it is his job. I don't need Vince to take care of me. Why are you so focused on Vince? I haven't even gotten to the good part of the story yet!"

She crawled up the bed and lay down next to me. "Fine. Get to the good part, but don't think for a second that we aren't coming back to Vince. Or that we're spending the night in your hotel room."

I knew that was coming. All I could do was drag out my story to try and give myself a little time for the medicine to fix my headache. I took a long drink from my water and launched into a very narrative version of the bus ride, with anecdotes and side stories that had her laughing and shaking her head. And then I culminated with Vince boarding the bus to find his beloved bandmates in their skivvies and me drunk but victorious.

"He shook his head, handed me my key, and I stumbled

off the bus before he could reprimand me or insist on walking me to my room."

"Why wouldn't you let Vince walk you to your room? What's going on with you two?"

I turned my head to the side so I could look at her. "I just told you the very exciting story of me riding a tour bus and beating the entire band, our favorite band, Golden Tiger, at strip poker, and you want to know what's going on with Vince?"

She raised an eyebrow. "The only person you left out of the story was Vince, so yeah, I'm curious. When I went home, there was obviously some sort of sexual tension between you two. I want to know if it flamed or fizzled. Or if you're still in the process of figuring that out."

"Marissa. I've only been divorced a month. I'm not figuring anything out, with anyone." I said it emphatically, like I actually believed it.

"Not even Mr-Davis Woulda-Coulda-Shoulda Scott?" Her eyes were wide.

I sighed. "The thing about Davis is, while he is still so incredibly sexy, it's like he dials it in, and my body reacts, but then..." I paused, resigned. "Nothing."

"Nothing?'

"Nope. The times I've been alone with him, it's like I'm trying to talk myself into the mindless chemistry, but then it just fizzles. He seems to want me to want him way more than he actually wants to sleep with me." I shrugged. I'd known this for a while, but I hadn't said it out loud. Marissa was my confessional.

"I really do like him though, as a person."

She looked downright bewildered at this. "As a person. Davis Scott, the sexiest man alive?"

"Yep. It's a damn shame." I wasn't sure I believed this, but at least we weren't talking about Vince anymore.

She clucked her tongue, Marissa-speak for ending a

conversation when she thought she was right and didn't want to argue about it.

Which was fine by me. Because I didn't want to talk about it anymore either.

She jumped off the bed. "Okay, enough of lying around! I'm here for forty-eight hours. I want a taste of your newfound rock and roll lifestyle! I want to do something that has to stay in Vegas!" She narrowed her eyes at me. "Go get in the shower. I'm calling room service for a hangover special. It'll have you back on your feet in no time!" She held out her hands and pulled me into a standing position. Then turned me and pushed me toward the bathroom.

I didn't want to know what her hangover special was, nor did I want to know why she of all people had one. But a shower did sound pretty good.

"But don't wash your hair! We don't have time for a full-on blowout. Nothing but dry shampoo for you!" I heard her pick up the phone as I closed the bathroom door, her questions about Vince still ringing in my head.

And why was that? He was keeping me at more than arm's length and that stung. Even if I'd read the whole thing wrong, why weren't we still friends?

I turned on the shower, which was almost as big as my entire bathroom at home, stripped off my clothes, and stepped underneath the rainfall showerhead. Which might have been the most delightful thing I had ever experienced and I tried to push the question out of my head and focus on Marissa being here and what I'd said to her before. That I hadn't been divorced long enough to think about anyone in a romantic way.

But was that my head talking? What about my heart? I'd spent twenty years with my head running the show and my heart taking a back seat...eventually making it so I felt nothing at all. I didn't want that to be my reality anymore.

This connection I thought Vince and I had established had stopped me in my tracks a bit. Partially because it was so unexpected. It sort of rocked my world, this new Vince I'd gotten to know. He was easy to be with, and obviously easy to look at—I couldn't pretend I wasn't attracted to him. Very attracted to him. And it seemed like it was mutual…

Until it wasn't.

What was going on with me and Vince?

Honestly, I had no idea. Thank God Marissa was here to distract me. Sure, she might push the matter, but I could ignore that for forty-eight hours. We were good enough friends that she'd stop asking eventually. Or so I hoped.

I shut the shower off and climbed out, drying myself with one of the most decedent towels I'd ever used. So soft and fluffy, it was amazing that it even absorbed the water, but somehow it did. I slid on the robe that hung from the back of the door and used the sleeve to clear the fog from the mirror. And looked at myself in the small circle.

The reflection wasn't the girl I'd been twenty years ago, nor the shell of a woman I'd been ever since. But I wasn't *not* them either. Maybe that was the problem. I couldn't live on nostalgia alone, and it would be oh-so-easy to fall back into being the woman who stopped feeling anything at all so that she never got hurt.

The circle filled back in from the heat of my face and I could only see my outline. It was all so deep and dreary. Too deep and dreary.

The door to the bathroom flew open. Saved from deep and dreary by the Marissa bell.

"Good, you're out. Food should be here shortly. Let's figure out our game plan." She grabbed my hand and pulled me back into the hotel room where she had my suitcase open on the bed and had clearly been rifling through it.

"What's with all the manhandling?"

"Obviously, now that you are a day drinker, you need a little push to get things going." She winked, and I relaxed. Whatever melancholy had overtaken me in the shower faded away at her cheery tone.

"I am fully capable of picking out my own clothes," I started to object but then sat down on the bed in silence when she shot me a look.

"Again, I only have forty-eight hours and I have a pretty good picture in my head on how I want those to go."

I looked at her outfit and decided that it was better to just go with it. She handed me an off the shoulder blouse, and my boots.

"You seem to have forgotten the other half of this outfit."

She smiled wickedly and opened her own suitcase. Right on top was a bag that she threw in my direction. "You're welcome."

I opened it with trepidation but was thrilled to find a pair of designer leather pants that I knew had to have cost her a fortune. And they were age appropriate and mid-waisted— no butt crack or stomach pouch to worry about. The kind of pants that suck in at all the right places. They were perfect.

"Marissa. You can't be serious. There's no way I can accept these."

She rolled her eyes. "Whatever. They were on sale and have your name and this situation written all over them. Now, put them on while I fix my face. Then I'll do yours." She walked into the bathroom and I did as I was told, the soft leather molding to my body in a way that I had never experienced before. Maybe designer was the key. I pulled the blouse on, which was cut just low enough that you could see the lace of my bra. Which was red, as assigned by Marissa. It was daring, sexy. Exactly who I wanted to be, even if I wasn't quite there on the inside.

This was Vegas, after all.

Chapter Twenty-Nine

As we entered the rooftop bar of our hotel, I was sure the guys would still be nursing their own hangovers or taking it easy elsewhere. Instead, I discovered that I couldn't have been more wrong. Not only were they there, they were in a roped-off VIP area, complete with bottle service.

"Red!" they all yelled as we approached, and without hesitation the bouncer unhooked the rope and stepped aside so we could go join the party.

"Red?" Marissa whispered.

"I know, but believe me when I say it's an improvement."

She nodded, and I could tell by the look on her face she was having a bit of star-shock.

"Guys, this is my friend from home, Marissa. Treat her like she can also kick your asses at poker." This brought hoots and objections, and then they all introduced themselves. Davis, giving her the full-on Davis effect charm offensive. Kissing her hand and flashing his sexy half smile. She giggled nervously, and then asked for a drink. Which promptly appeared and the guys fell back into whatever they had been discussing before our arrival.

"Don't look now, but Mr. I-Don't-Want-To-Talk-About-Him has arrived."

I turned to see Vince pausing to assess the situation before unclipping the velvet rope and letting himself inside. Because of course he did. No one told Vince where he could and couldn't go. He caught sight of Marissa and a slow smile spread across his face.

She turned to me and whispered in my ear. "If there's nothing between you two, then I'm sure you won't mind if I make a play?"

My heart thudded in my chest and before I could formulate an answer, she pulled back to look at my wild-eyed expression.

"That, my friend, was a test. And not surprisingly, you failed." She smiled. "Nothing going on between you, my ass."

Marissa wasn't kidding when she said I failed. And I continued to fail the entire night.

The band had five nights in Vegas, so this would be the longest stay on this leg of the tour. From here, we'd go on to L.A. for two shows, then a break for a week before we picked back up on the East Coast and made our way back to Chicago for one final show where it all began.

All of that to say, this first night was a see and be seen affair. Arranged by the label. Vegas was going to be a bit different than the other stops. They were still playing the small club they had on that first tour, but the label wanted the guys more visible in their downtime to gauge how much interest there might be in a comeback album. Something more than just the greatest hits.

Or so Rex was telling me in our roped-off VIP section

of the club. I was having a hard time focusing on him, my eyes drifting over his shoulder to where Vince stood talking to Marissa. Our earlier exchange sat like a rock in my gut, because Marissa shot from the hip. And she was seldom wrong with her blunt honesty. No matter how much I wanted her to be.

So, as I stood talking to one of the best guitar players in the world about the implications of this tour on a future comeback album of arguably the best rock band in my lifetime, instead of taking mental notes for my book, I couldn't stop my eyes from darting to Marissa and Vince. He looked at ease with her, like he had with me before the dramatic bar departure.

And I'd say I wasn't jealous, except I was totally jealous.

It was like being in high school at a party in someone's basement all over again, though much, much worse. Because what I was worried about as I stole another glance their way wasn't that Marissa was hitting on Vince—it was that she was telling him to come hit on me.

Which was horrifying.

"So, that's why the dog and pony show. To see if we're still relevant." Rex took a long drink from his beer and then pointed toward the rest of the bar.

I tore my gaze away from Vince and Marissa and looked in the direction he pointed. What I saw was a combination of general club antics, but also quite a few people snapping photos of our section, and the usual number of women in tiny dresses dancing as close to the velvet rope as they possibly could.

"It feels a little like being part of a zoo exhibit," I replied.

Rex laughed that deep throaty laugh of his. "Don't let Davis hear you say that."

"Hear what?" Davis tumbled into our conversation, throwing his arm over Rex's shoulder. I shot a glance to see if Vince had noticed, and to my complete horror locked eyes with him. Had he looked over because Davis had joined us? Or had he been looking at me? What was Marissa saying to him?

I might actually murder her when this was all over.

"Campbell here was saying this setup feels like a zoo exhibit."

"Was she now?" He turned his sultry look in my direction. "Campbell, are you calling us animals?"

I raised an eyebrow at him. Something had changed between Davis and me on our bus ride. He was really piling it on thick, playing the part of the over-sexed rock god a glint of challenge in his eye. But I'd seen a bit of the regular human side of him while I was kicking his ass in poker. Maybe that was why. Maybe he was overcompensating.

"That might be an insult to the animals," I volleyed.

"Well, someone is feeling a bit feisty after their big poker win. Or is it that your gorgeous wingman has landed?" He nodded at Marissa, who did look gorgeous tonight. Her black hair was pulled back in a ponytail that if I wore, I would think looked much too young for me. On her it looked hip and glamorous. Marissa was the kind of gorgeous that was both natural and unbelievable at the same time.

"Easy, tiger," I said, but then had to roll my eyes at my own clichéd statement.

"Oh, no, she didn't!" Rex yelled and then started hooting, loudly. My face flooded.

"Shhh!" I smacked him on the arm.

"Oh, yes she did!" Davis growled back and hooted himself.

"What is happening? Why are you yelling?" But they didn't answer because Tony and Alex had joined us, and they too were hooting and hollering.

"What is going on?" I shouted, utterly confused. Now

they were jumping up and down like we were in some sort of sports huddle and had just won the big game. And then just as soon as it had started, it was over. At least the huddle part. The guys continued their hooting as they followed Rex in the direction of the bar that was for our VIP use only.

I watched them go, my confusion only growing.

"You said it, didn't you?" My breath caught. Vince. And for the first time in days he was talking to me without that edge in his voice. I turned to face him, relieved to see the edges of his mouth turned up in that slight smile.

"Said what? Please tell me why they are losing their minds because I have no idea what is going on."

"Easy Tiger."

A smile crept across my face, and I nodded. "Is that what this is all about?"

Vince chuckled to himself. "Golden Tiger rules clearly state that if anyone, at any time, utters that phrase, the person to whom it was said will face quick and somewhat severe punishment." He pointed toward the bar and I noticed that Marissa had somehow become a part of the spectacle. "Yours seems to involve booze. We'll see if that's all they come up with."

"Golden Tiger rules? How am I just now hearing about those?" It was so good to be having this normal conversation with Vince after so many days of feeling at odds, I could feel the twinkle coming from my eyes.

"Well, I guess you're truly on the inside now, doll." He winked at that last part and I burst out laughing.

"So, you heard about the poker then."

"Oh, I heard the whole story, which is why I doubt whatever punishment they come up with is going to end with that tray of shots headed your way." He nodded to over my shoulder and I turned to see the whole crew headed back my way, Davis in the lead balancing a tray of shots in one hand. I braced myself for their arrival. Being the center of attention had never been my thing, but there was no shying away from this one.

"I guess I should just embrace it," I said more to myself than to Vince.

"You reap what you sow," he replied, which seemed strange. I mean Vince was sort of an old-sage-advice kind of guy, but this seemed oddly biblical and completely out of context.

"Meaning?"

He shrugged. "Meaning, there is a consequence for everything we do in life. Good or bad and there's no avoiding it, so you're right. Better to embrace it."

They were closing in fast, but still, I couldn't keep myself from digging. "Are we still speaking rhetorically, or is there something specific you think I deserve a consequence for?"

"Not everything is about you, you know."

The edge in his voice returned, like a slap to the face, but not the kind you get during an argument, more like Cher to Nicolas Cage in *Moonstruck*. The "snap out of it!" kind. Whatever adolescent mooning I'd been doing all night dissipated with his surly remark.

I turned to receive the group, and my shot.

"Red," Davis began, holding up a shot glass and waving the others to join him in his toast. Marissa behind him mouthed the word "Red" and then waved her hand like she was all hot and bothered about it, which I ignored. "You have broken one of the most sacred rules of the band. We never, and I mean NEVER"—he paused here, and the rest of the guys joined in—"go easy!"

They clinked their glasses and took their shots and I did the same. Whiskey, the familiar burn. The smart move here would have been to pretend to do it, but with Vince's eyes on me, I didn't particularly feel like being smart.

"Do I apologize? I'm not really sure of the protocol for breaking a sacred rule of a rock band?"

Davis waved us all to hold our glasses out and produced a bottle from somewhere and filled them again. Even Vince, who scowled while he joined, but he did it.

I was for sure about to be drunk for the second time in one day. Which was not at all smart, but as I'd rationalized in the bathroom, sometimes it was okay for my head to take a back seat. For me to live a little. This was a good time for that. Vince's hot and cold act was giving me whiplash, and frankly, I was tired of trying to figure it out.

And the book, I couldn't forget about the book. Or maybe, just for tonight, I could. Maybe I was owed just one night of not putting thought to everything I said or did. Maybe, for one night, I could just do.

Not like that first night, when I'd been trying to recreate my past, but with a confidence of a woman who knew her worth. I wasn't trying to prove anything to anyone. I just wanted to cut loose.

I took the second shot with a smile.

"So, getting drunk is my punishment?" I asked.

They all laughed at this, and then Tony turned and began a drum roll with his fingers on the high-top table behind him.

"Nah, that's just standard operating procedure. It's actually been some years since anyone has broken this protocol," Rex said. "We had to do some thinking as to who it was last. Usually they get to decide the punishment, but since none of us can remember, we decided that Davis can do the honors, since it was him you invoked on."

Invoked on? I wasn't sure that was proper grammar, but my head buzzed with whiskey and contentment and just a dash of wanting something wild to happen next.

Davis set down his shot glass and leaned back on the high table, his lip curled just slightly enough for it to seem natural.

"Well," I asked, "what's it going to be?"

"Well, Red," he said, and I swear he was drawing this whole thing out, speaking in slow motion. "The only thing I could think of was that you and I are finally going to finish that one-on-one, with no interruptions. And maybe, just maybe, I'll tell you everything you want to know. If that's how you want to spend the time."

The smile that spread across his face seemed sincere, and even though he was in full rock-star mode, I could see just a hint of the actual man in his eyes. Of the boy he had been when this all began.

Of all the things he could have said, none could have taken me more by surprise than this. The shock was almost enough to sober me up.

"Well, as a wise old sage once told me, you have to accept the consequences for your actions." I glanced in Vince's direction to find him staring at me in that direct way he did, and for a second our eyes locked and I thought about saying no.

But then he not only looked away, he walked away.

"When?" I asked, squaring my shoulders at what felt like Vince's rejection.

Davis picked up the bottle of whiskey and took two steps toward me. "No time like the present."

It was only when he slung his arm over my shoulders that I felt the potential of being in over my head. But I shook it off.

Davis seemed willing and open to sharing his Golden Tiger stories with me. I had, in the past twenty-four hours, somehow earned his respect, enough that he was letting the curtain part for me to step through. He was dropping his act even for a little while. Was I going to get to talk to the actual man, not the rock star?

I didn't know if it was possible to have your brain turned on, or your confidence, but that's what this felt like. And it didn't waver. But as I caught sight of Vince, alone by the bar, looking as lost as I always felt when he turned me away from the party, it did make it all slow down for just a second as a question rose in my mind.

Was this what I really wanted? The adult me, not the girl I had been. What was I really chasing here?

But I shook it off, because, for the first time, I felt like I was actually with the band.

Chapter Thirty

I stopped by my room to grab my camera bag, Davis waiting as patiently as Davis waited for anything in the hall. I was quick, because I didn't want him to get distracted and wander off. Luckily, he seemed as focused on this as I was.

"Make yourself at home," Davis said, pointing to the sitting area that contained a couch and two chairs. "I'll make us some drinks."

This presented a dilemma: where to sit. On the one hand, Davis seemed to be taking this seriously, no overt or sexual innuendo as we came up to his suite. Which meant I should take it seriously and sit in the chair. A professional distance. But on the other hand, sitting on the couch upped the intimacy of the interview.

I was still standing and trying to decide which angle was best when Davis brushed past me to the couch and sat down. He patted the spot next to him.

"Why are you still standing?" he asked.

Decision made. I sat on the couch, though not quite as close as he had patted. And found, surprisingly, as I lifted my camera, that the close-up suited the angle I was looking for.

"Going for a before and after sort of thing?" he asked, with his signature smirk. The sexy, put-on charm was back in full force. Was he using it as a shield? "No one's ever asked for that before."

His inuendo hung in the air like the cocky overture it was. I lowered my camera. I'd all but talked myself out of wanting Davis since our almost kiss in his dressing room. The shine on his rock-star appeal had dimmed a bit once I realized it was all such a game to him. He was still sexy as hell, but I'd regulated myself to spectator once I'd gotten a glimpse behind the facade, but now here we were. What if I just went with it? Maybe seeing how this played out would give me some insight as to just why Davis acted the way he did. It was a way to let my long-held fantasy play out at the very least.

The flirting, the innuendo, that part I could do in a heartbeat.

I could check the box, reverse the choice. See where it led. That's why I started this whole thing after all. Up until now he'd been all snarl and no sex. If I went along with it, maybe he'd blink first. And if he didn't, well. I'd worry about that if it came.

I swallowed. Hard.

"Well, then I guess there's a first time for everything." I slid off the couch, snapping from different angles as Davis drank from his whiskey. I turned the lamp on and pulled a scarf off the pile next to it and threw it over the top. I could do this.

"Speaking of which, why don't you tell me about your first time?" I kept taking pictures. Photos of Davis talking about Davis? Gold, I was sure.

He laughed, deeply, almost husky, "My first time? For real?"

I returned his throaty laugh. "I mean your first time, once you were famous. Is that how you knew you'd made it? The women lined up outside the bus?"

He was playing with his hair like a teenage girl. I knelt beside him to get the profile shot.

"Yes, and no. Girls will always go crazy for the lead singer of a rock band. Even back when I was a skinny, pimple-faced nobody. As soon as I got up on stage, the cool girls, the ones who made fun of me in junior high for having high water jeans, suddenly were screaming my name and passing me notes with their phone numbers written on them."

He took a long drink then set his glass down in front of him.

"I'd be lying if I said that wasn't thrilling. I was nobody in my hometown, less than actually. But on stage, suddenly I became some sort of sex symbol. It blew my mind."

This Davis, the one he didn't let anyone see? He was so authentic.

"But it turned into something else after a while. Sure, my image was as this sexy rocker with a beautiful woman on each arm, but it never felt like it would last. Like at some point everyone would wake up and realize I was still that same skinny, dorky kid and they'd all have a good laugh about it and move on."

I sat down on the table in front of him, between his knees. The look on his face as he confessed this, I just hoped it translated to film. That I could do the story justice if he'd let me retell it the way he was telling me. Using these pictures.

"So, it became a game to me. But not like everyone thinks. I wasn't sleeping with as many women as I could *because* I could. I was *propositioning* as many women as I could because I was trying to find the one who would turn me down. Because she's out there, the sixteen-year-old boy in me knows it for certain."

He took my camera out of my hand and set it on the table beside me. I was frozen by the story and the thought that Davis Scott, the gold standard as the sexiest man I had ever known, didn't think of himself that way. For all his flashiness and ego, he was actually pretty insecure. Which made my realization even trickier.

What I wanted was for him to keep talking, sharing. That was the intimacy I wanted out of this. Not a roll in the sheets, but that was what he was angling for. He was setting it up that I could be the woman he feared. The one who said no. Could I do that to him? I knew from years of watching that as soon as he slept with a woman, he lost all respect for her. I needed him to keep talking to me so I could do my job. But if I turned him down, it could crush his ego.

But then he pulled pack and gave me my out.

"I'm so glad you and Vince gave up on whatever that was." He tucked the hair behind my ear and leaned forward and so did I.

After all these years, I was kissing Davis Scott. And he was good at it, obviously. He had loads of practice. But instead of fireworks and desire and all of that, I felt nothing. And all I could think was how much I wished this was Vince instead.

Vince. These months on the road, even when he ran hot and cold, it was Vince who'd made me feel like I was a part of something, not this song and dance flirtation with Davis.

I thought of him as Davis and I had made our grand exit, standing alone by the bar, a look of what on his face? Sadness? Disgust? Disappointment? I realized that I cared which one it was.

And I wanted to be the one to take that look off his face.

I pulled away from Davis. "The truth is, the thing with me and Vince, well, I'm not really sure if it is over." And though I was using it as an excuse here, I knew deep down it wasn't.

Even if I didn't know what was going on between Vince and me, I could admit that something was.

Now Davis was the one who pulled back. "Whoa. Hold up."

I bit my lip to try and look more like I was the kind of woman who could play coy with a rock star. I wasn't being coy, but the vulnerability that Davis was showing made me feel like outright turning him down was not an option. Especially since he was trusting me with his story.

"It's sort of unresolved, I guess you could say."

Now he retreated to his space on the couch. "What does unresolved mean?"

I shrugged and slid to my own corner, thankful for the distance as it helped me clear my head.

"Well, it's sort of cat and mouse with us, I think it always has been." Was this true? In the clearing of my head, had a truth I'd always known slipped out?

"So, currently, are you the cat or the mouse?" Davis asked, his tone shifting but not to one of annoyance or rejection, more of an interest in what I was saying.

"I think I'd be the mouse, but honestly, I'm not one hundred percent sure I even know anymore." This was true, since I'd really just come to accept that something was actually going on between us, and I had no idea if Vince thought so too.

The look on Davis's face changed slightly to serious. He pointed at me. "I think you're the cat. Vince is the mouse."

"Why do you think that?" Was I really getting relationship advice from Davis Scott? In all the scenarios I'd played out in my head for this one-on-one, getting romantic advice about Vince was not one of them.

"He's running scared. Making himself scarce all the time. I knew there was something brewing with that dude." He smiled slyly. "Though you leaving that party with me probably has him kicking himself. So, you're welcome."

Impossible. Jealousy was not an emotion that occupied even a pinky of Vince Caparelli. In my experience, he felt nothing but disappointment in me for my choices when it came to Davis. And that wasn't something I wanted to talk about because I'd been conditioned most of my life to feel as though I was a disappointment if I didn't follow the script.

"I guess this isn't exactly the night you had planned," I said, reaching for the glass of whiskey he'd poured for me.

"Not exactly." He laughed. "But it isn't all bad. I like you, Red. You're a straight shooter. And you're loyal. Those are two things I value above all else. Vince better pull his head out of his ass and realize it too. That dude is always in his own way."

I didn't know how to respond to that, so I was happy when my phone buzzed so I had something to shift my attention to.

Marissa.

I can't stand it. How's it going?

Not as anticipated. Then I had an idea.

"Mind if my friend Marissa comes up?" I asked Davis.

"The more the merrier, right?" he replied, his sexy smile taking place of the earnest look he'd had only minutes ago.

I texted her the invite and the room number, and then because I still had a few minutes, and for the most part Davis was being fairly honest, I took a risk.

"What is it with you and Vince?" I asked.

He nodded. "Vince has done more for me than any person on the planet. So as far as I'm concerned, he is my family. I'd never do anything against him. Even if he can be a stubborn jackass."

"That's pretty much what he told me about you, too."

"Loyalty is something that you can't take for granted, especially in this business."

"And it all comes from growing up together, this blood

oath loyalty you all talk about?"

Here, he paused and glanced down at his hands before he answered. "More or less."

I was about to follow up on that vague answer when there was a knock at the door, and Davis in one fluid motion jumped over the back of the couch to answer it. Happy, apparently, to get away from me and my questions.

"You didn't tell me your friend Marissa was the absolute stunner from the party." Davis growled, rock star back in full effect.

"That she is," I replied, winking in her direction.

"And what is the lovely lady drinking?"

"Margarita or white wine?" she asked hopefully.

"Let me check the fridge, doll." He winked and headed off toward the kitchen.

Marissa, wide-eyed and cheeks flushed, rushed to me. "What is going on?"

I shrugged. "Change in plans."

"What the hell does that mean?"

"Oddly, I think it means that I care more about getting this book right than sleeping with Davis Scott."

"I can appreciate your dedication, but seriously?"

"Seriously. It's enough for me to know I *could* have slept with him, I guess."

"Not me. I couldn't walk away from that."

Davis walked back into the room at that exact moment.

"Good news, doll. Plenty of white wine in the fridge." He held up both a glass and a bottle, which he'd put into an ice bucket. A surprisingly thoughtful detail.

As he set it on the bar and started to pour, he hummed to himself and I leaned into Marissa and whispered.

"I think you're going to get the chance." She pulled back, eyes wide. I shrugged. "At least one of us will get the whole rock and roll fantasy. But only if I take off. You fine with that?"

She paused, then smiled, then nodded.

"I'm going to call it a night," I said and Davis barely acknowledged me as he handed Marissa her glass of wine. Which she took with a nervous giggle. "I'll leave you to it, then," I said. It was a bit crass, but it wasn't like either of them was paying attention.

Which was fine by me. I grabbed my purse and let myself out, already thinking about how I was going to structure the story, caption the photos.

I couldn't help wondering just what it was that Vince had done for Davis that warranted the sort of loyalty that stopped a player like Davis dead in his tracks.

Chapter Thirty-One

Whether I wanted the play-by-play of her night with Davis from Marissa was irrelevant. Because she gave it to me anyway. Every last sexy, sultry detail.

So detailed, I felt like I needed to take a shower when she was done.

And it didn't stop there, because after the first concert in Vegas, she spent the night with him again. And proceeded to spill all the details of that encounter to me as I drove her to the airport.

"And here I thought I was coming to Vegas to lend you moral support." She had this ridiculously dreamy look on her face. "Did I tell you what he said to me when I left this morning?"

She had. Twice. But I shook my head.

"He told me these twenty-four hours had changed him in some way. I had changed him."

I didn't have the heart to tell her that he'd said the exact same thing to vending machine Mandy in Kansas City.

"He's smooth, that's for sure."

She sighed. "Listen, I'm not naive. I know exactly who Davis is, but still. To have him say that to me, well, I'm going to just cling to this little fantasy for a while. So, I'd appreciate it if you'd just play along."

"Totally. I'm here for you," I said, rubbing my lips together to keep from smiling. "And you never know, he let you post that picture of the two of you. He's never done that before." This was true—usually Davis lived by a strict no photo policy. Not to mention the back to back nights together. The Davis I'd come to know was strictly one and done. So, maybe she had changed him somehow?

"He did," she practically cooed. "Do you want to see it again? I wonder how many likes it's gotten?"

"You sound so hip with your lingo! Likes!" I laughed and glanced at her phone that she was shoving in my face. I didn't need to see the picture, I'd taken it. Davis had his arm slung across her shoulder, wearing his signature half smile as his chin turned toward Marissa, whose flushed cheeks made her look sultry, sexy. It was the sort of photo any woman would die to have.

"It has over one hundred likes!" she exclaimed, clutching the phone to her chest. "Not all of us have the willpower to kick a rock god out of our bed."

I pulled into the passenger drop-off lane. "That's me, the queen of willpower!" I put the car in park.

"The legend of this is only going to grow and you're just going to have to deal with it."

I laughed. "I'll swear to any and everything you say. Thanks for coming out on the road to surprise me."

"I think I should be the one thanking you. And apologizing."

I raised an eyebrow.

"For accusing you of only wanting to relive your past. And saying you were being irresponsible for wanting to throw away your life to sleep with a rock star. Ultimate pot/ kettle situation there."

"You had no way of knowing." I was laughing now, and so was she.

"Still, I can see the perks." She smiled wickedly and pulled me into a hug.

She opened the door and jumped out. It was like Chicago all over again, except this time I wasn't terrified to see her go.

I rolled down her window as she closed her door and she leaned in for a final goodbye.

"FYI, the rules still apply. When you finally do sleep with Vince, I want the same amount of gory details I just gave you." She stuck out her tongue and disappeared into the crowd.

"UGH!" I shouted after her.

Vince had gone from barely acknowledging me to ignoring my presence altogether after I'd left the bar with Davis, even though Davis and Marissa were clearly hooking up. He didn't want to hear my side of the story. The one where I'd said no to Davis because I wanted it to be him.

It was fine. I'd had years of practice denying my feelings in my marriage. I could do it with Vince, too. After all, my feelings for him didn't matter if he didn't feel the same. It was just some silly post-divorce crush. Or so I told myself.

I needed to focus on the book anyway.

After my one-on-ones with Rex and Davis, things were starting to take shape a little more. I was meeting with Tony as soon as I got back and then tomorrow with Alex. Staying in one place for the week gave me the time and access I needed.

And I had managed to sketch out a rough vision for the book. Which was good, since I had no idea just when Harrison was going to materialize and demand it. The thought of it made me run cold and then hot. Terrified and then exhilarated. I guess this was what following your passions really meant.

I turned up the music and sped back to the hotel, windows down, the desert winds whipping my hair. I felt light and, oddly, young. Or maybe just good about myself for the first time in a really long time.

I swung my car into the valet line at the hotel and smiled at the young man who opened the door for me. "Thanks!"

"You're welcome, miss!"

Miss? Not ma'am? Huh. He was probably just being kind for a bigger tip but I didn't care. Like anytime I was carded at the liquor store. You take what you can get.

I winked as I stepped around him and headed into the hotel. I had just enough time to run a brush through my hair and grab my camera before I sat down with Tony. I breezed through the lobby and up the elevator to my floor, digging my key out as it zoomed upward. I barely looked up when it stopped, and the doors opened.

Which is why I didn't see the man I ran directly into.

I mean square into his chest. Like vaudeville, and then I dropped my purse, and everything spilled out, covering the hallway with my worldly possessions.

"Oh my God. I am so sorry," I said, kneeling down and scrambling to scrape everything back in my bag. Including the tiny bottle of whiskey that Marissa had stuck in there as a joke. I had almost everything before I realized he hadn't even tried to help.

Which was fine, but yet. What an ass.

I stood up and squared my shoulders a bit and looked him in the eye. "Next time I'll try harder to watch where I'm going." My voice was cool because I wasn't sorry in the least. I turned on my heel and walked down the hall, stopping in front of my door to wave the key and unlock it.

"Ms. Cavett?"

I turned to see he was walking toward me.

"Umm, yes?"

"Great, glad I was able to track you down."

"Well, I don't know if you tracked me down so much as I ran you down," I said, trying to add some levity. He didn't crack a smile.

"Whatever the case, I need to speak with you."

"And you are?"

"Harrison Wentworth. From the label."

"Nice to finally meet you, Mr. Wentworth." I knew who he was without him explaining. I was just caught off guard. I'd thought our meeting would at least be arranged and semi-formal. This seemed like an ambush.

"Perhaps we could talk in your room?"

My mind raced a bit. This guy was clearly an asshole, and I didn't really want to invite a stranger who presented as such into my room, alone.

"I'm sorry, but I'm not inclined to just invite a man I've never seen before into my empty hotel room."

He raised an eyebrow. "Is that so? Well, then, there goes my first assumption as to how you conned your way into getting a job that you are in no way qualified for."

My mouth flew open, but not in shock. What I felt was red hot anger.

"How dare you imply I slept with anyone to get this job."

He shrugged—obviously he was used to people being furious at him. "Pardon the assumption, but why else would that half-washed-up stage manager go to bat for a woman no one has ever heard of instead of the photographer I carefully screened and hired?"

"Well, I know a thing or two about this band. Like he does. More than a someone who only sees them through dollar signs."

He laughed. "Ah, so what are you, an old groupie? That makes sense, too. I guess."

I couldn't form the words to protest or agree, and he took

this as some sort of sign that he should just keep going.

"Either way, I only went along with it to get my hands on the shots from opening night and now that I have those in my possession we won't be needing you. As I said, the label has a very firm idea of what this book should look like, which is why I hired who I did."

I went cold. "What do you mean you have my photos?" I'd sent them along as he asked when I'd signed the contract, but they were still mine.

He smiled. "You sent them to me, or have you forgotten? And apparently you didn't read the fine print of that contract you signed. Anything sent to the label via official channels becomes property of the label."

He was right.

"So, that's it? You're not even going to look at my proposal? You're just going to fire me?"

"Firing is such a negative word. But no, I won't be needing to see whatever it is you've come up with. I did a little digging and your background as a children's portrait taker isn't really the look we're going for. You're done. You can check with Vince as to whatever you're owed money-wise and the arrangements for leaving the tour. He handles all the intricacies of that."

Not only fired, but I was going to have to meet with Vince? I sank back against the door, defeated, willing myself not to give this sanctimonious asshole the thrill of seeing me cry.

I squared my shoulders. "Well, I appreciate you coming to tell me in person."

His phone rang, and he held up a finger as if I was now supposed to hold on, midway through my firing, while he took a call. Which, I have to say, I appreciated because my grief was once again replaced by anger.

"Woodsworth. Yes. Yes. I took care of it. No. There

won't be any problems. No, no severance. Okay, fine. I'll see you backstage tonight."

He ended the call. At least he was a dick to everyone.

"Again, thanks for coming to let me go face-to-face." I turned and opened the door to my room, craving being alone so I could fall apart. I should have known this whole thing was too good to be true.

"I'll just need any photos you've taken, your notes," he said, sticking his foot in to stop the closing door.

I yanked it back open.

"Excuse me?"

He was looking at his phone, and he glanced up. "Any notes you might have taken during your 'interviews.'" He mimed air quotes with his free hand when he said this last part. "And the photos you took, I'm sure you have them on a flash drive or something? I don't need you taking the materials you took under contract and trying to publish your own book, now do I?" He smirked.

"All of that is mine. I took those pictures. Why would I just hand it all over to you?"

He sighed dramatically. "Well, again, if you'd read the contract, any materials created in service to fulfilling the deal belong to the band, which means the label, which means me."

"Hmmm, well. I think that I'm going to pass on that one." I put my hand on my hip.

"You really don't want to get into this with me. Like I said, any problems you have you can take up with Vince. I'd hate to have to fire him, too. You know, for pushing you on me in the first place." He tilted his head.

Fire Vince?

No matter what was going on between me and Vince, I couldn't be the reason he lost his job. Golden Tiger, this tour, and the band were his whole life. He'd told me as much over and over again. It didn't matter how much I needed this, how much I wanted this.

Flashes of those perfect photos scrolled in my mind like a slideshow. That feeling I'd gotten backstage, framing the perfect shot. I'd felt alive, confident. Myself for the first time in ages. But even if the thought of walking away, of not finishing the book and actually turning over my work, made me physically ill, I wasn't going to win either way.

And I couldn't take Vince down with me.

Without saying a word, I went to retrieve what he was asking for.

Harrison followed, stopping just inside, holding the door open by standing in front of it. I crossed the room and handed the flash drives and my notes to him.

"Thank you. For seeing the writing on the wall," he said. "I can see why Vince was so enamored. You're fiery." He snickered and then turned and let the door close as he walked away.

I slid down with my back to the door. Too numb to cry, too mad to throw anything.

This was inevitable. I'd let myself believe that this whole charade could work, that I was actually qualified enough to pull it off.

I'd been kidding myself.

In my pocket my phone vibrated, and I pulled it out to see a text from Tony.

Where you at? I'm jacked for our chat. You standing me up or what? Everyone wants to hear from the drummer!

That was what finally broke me. Through tear-filled eyes I replied.

Sorry. I just got fired.

It was totally unprofessional, but it was all my heart. Maybe that was my problem. I'd never actually been a professional anything. Just a wannabe second-tier groupie after all.

I shut my phone off before I could see Tony's response, then pulled myself up from the floor and lay down on my bed and cried as the sun set and the lights of the strip came on.

I had no idea what I was supposed to do now.

Chapter Thirty-Two

I lay there for hours. Alternating between rage and disbelief. Both accompanied by tears. My cheeks were sticky, and my eyes burned. I'd never wanted anything as much as I wanted to produce this book. I'd believed I could do a damn good job of it. Now I wouldn't get the chance.

Then there was a small window of delirium when I was upset I had passed up the chance to sleep with Davis since I wasn't going to be needing his respect anytime soon. Nor Vince's. Hell, Vince was probably thrilled I'd been shown the door. That made me cry again.

I was a mess, to say the least.

The cherry on top came in the form of a text from Sam, my realtor. Somehow, in the chaos that was my life, I'd forgotten today was the closing on my house.

I was officially homeless—right when I needed somewhere to go. And I had to figure out what the hell I was going to do with all my worldly possessions, or at least the ones Jack hadn't taken in the divorce.

What had I done? Why hadn't I listened to Marissa

when this whole thing started? I'd thrown away a perfectly sustainable boring life for some sort of far-fetched adventure. And now I had nothing.

I rolled over and tapped out a thank-you to Sam. She'd done her job and done it well. I couldn't blame her. And at least I'd have the proceeds from the sale to survive on until I figured out what and where I was going next. That was the only good thing I could think of in this entire mess.

I thought about calling Marissa, but I couldn't make myself do it. I was too embarrassed. In my entire life I'd never felt so pathetic, and talking about it to anyone would make the whole thing more real. Even my best friend, who I knew would be empathetic. Hell, she'd probably even have a litany of reasons why this was for the best. That would only make it worse.

Instead, I burrowed under my covers and cried. Again.

A pounding on my door invaded my pity cave. I lay there and hoped whoever it was would give up and go away. I didn't want to see anyone, and I was so overwhelmed with relief when it stopped, I started crying. Facing anyone at all just felt humiliating.

Then the pounding started again. Louder, heavier. And there was yelling. Which, in all the times on this tour someone had pounded on my hotel room door, had yet to happen.

"Campbell, open the damn door."

Vince.

Had Harrison lied to me? Had he fired Vince anyway? I stood and found my bearings in the dark room and went to see what other destruction I'd caused. The thing was, it wasn't exactly an easy thing to do to come face-to-face with Vince after all the weirdness that had been going on between us. Was he here to rub it in my face that if only I'd done it his way maybe I'd still have my job?

Had he been behind getting me fired? In cahoots with

Harrison? That gave me pause, because surely not. But what did I really know about anything? I laid my hand on the handle, took a deep breath, and opened the door.

As it turned out, no amount of mulling would have prepared me for the Vince who greeted me.

"Jesus, Campbell, what the hell?" His gray eyes bore right through mine, the laugh lines I'd grown to look for were gone, and instead there was a crease of concern between his eyebrows. He shook his head and stormed past me into my room.

The rage came like someone had flicked a switch. I let the door fall closed with a bang.

"What the hell, *me*? What the hell *you*!"

I didn't anticipate we would be thrown into complete darkness when the door closed. I fumbled around to find the lamp switch, which took a bit of the show out of my bluster.

By the time I found it, I was a little sheepish, but still mad.

Apparently, so was Vince.

"Me? That's rich, Campbell. Or should I call you Red now?"

Red? Was he here because of Davis? Maybe he didn't even know I'd been fired. Well, two could play at that game, and I was suddenly itching for a fight.

"Are you kidding me? That's why you're pissed off? Because the band took up the dumb nickname you gave me? Or is it because I left the bar with Davis?"

His face turned bright red, and I wasn't sure if it was from anger or embarrassment.

"There's quite a lot for me to be angry about, actually. But we can start with your little one-on-one with Davis. Imagine my surprise when he tells me not to worry about him interfering between us, since you and I apparently have something going on. Cat and mouse, is that what you called it?"

I trembled with rage. Of all the things for him to show up at my door and be pissed off about.

"So, you're mad because I implied we had something going on? So sorry to have embarrassed you by tying us together, of all the horrible things. Which I did, by the way, to let Davis save face when I turned him down." I paused to let that land before I continued. "Which you'd have known days ago except that, for reasons unknown, you completely stopped talking to me!"

God, it felt good to unload all of this. Even though Vince looked like his head was going to explode he was so mad.

"Right now, though, I really don't care why you're mad," I continued. "I have bigger problems, in case you haven't heard."

"Oh, I've heard," he said, with a sarcasm that was completely unwarranted.

I glared at him. Speechless.

"I was backstage, cornered by Davis who was going on and on about how I should get my shit together or I was going to blow it with the one woman on the planet who gets both rock and roll and me. Then Tony shows up and tells me you canceled your one-on-one with him because you'd been fired. So, he's pissed off at me because he thinks I did it. My head is fucking spinning because they're all suddenly team Campbell, which is confusing as hell. But wait, because how could it get any worse? Fucking Harrison is backstage in his slick suit, acting like he's somehow king of the kingdom."

He glared, like this was all my fault. It was enraging.

"How about you get over yourself?" I said. "I know this might be hard for you to understand, but this isn't about you."

"Isn't about me? It's all about me! How are you not seeing that?" He took one step forward as he roared.

The anger in his voice made me take a step back. I'd

never seen this level of emotion from Vince, even if his anger was just meeting my own.

Seeing my reaction, he shook his head, turned away, and put his hands on the table under the window. Grabbing the edge to settle himself down, he stared down the strip.

But I couldn't let things settle until I'd said my piece. "Fan-fucking-tastic, Vince. You convince me I'm good enough to take this job, when I had zero experience. Then you show up here pissed off at me when I get fired?" I worked to keep my voice even.

"Is that even a question?" He spun around and for the first time I noticed my notebooks sitting on the table. The ones I'd given to Harrison just hours earlier.

Everything inside me froze.

"Why do you have those?" I asked, pointing.

He turned and picked one of them up. "You mean the photos you took for the book that I hired you to put together? The ones you just handed over to Harrison?"

"Obviously, Vince. What else would I be talking about." I put my hands on my hips.

He took a deep breath and raised his gaze to look me in the eye. His voice was softer when he said, "I want to know why you gave them up so easily. Why didn't you call me when he showed up here and—"

"Fired me? That's what happened; it wasn't like I had any say in the matter. I don't know, Vince, maybe because I knew deep down this was the inevitable conclusion to this scam I was trying to pull off? Or maybe because he threatened to fire you, too!"

He burst out laughing. And my rage returned in full force.

"Go ahead and laugh at me. I guess that's what I get for trying to look out for you!"

"I'm not laughing at you. I'm laughing at the absolute

balls on Harrison to think he could possibly fire me." He turned and picked up the flash drives and held them out. "Or you, for that matter."

I froze. "What do you mean?"

He stepped toward me. "I mean he isn't firing you."

"Why not? How?" This made no sense at all.

"Well, for one, I'm the one who signed your contract, not him. So, legally, he can't fire you. And two, I told him he wouldn't find anyone better than you. Which he had a hard time arguing with since he had the pictures you took that prove it."

"You said that?"

He nodded.

"And he agreed, just like that?" I was shaking. Why was I shaking?

"Well, I had to let him save face a little. He wants to see a sample layout by the time we get to L.A., not the rough draft he took from you, but something a bit more structured, he said."

I threw myself into his arms, but this time it wasn't just from shock. I'd been fighting my own battles my entire life. Even when I was married, if I had any sort of dustup, Jack was quick to point out how I could have caused it. Why I was ultimately the one at fault. I couldn't think of one time he'd ever stuck up for me.

Never in my life had anyone gone to bat for me like this.

"Thank you," I said, my face buried into his shoulder muffling my words, so I pulled my head back. "You won't be sorry. I can do this, Vince. It is going to be one hell of a good book. I promise."

His eyes softened from their usual piercing stare to something else. He tucked my hair behind my ear, his fingers lingering there, before his thumb stroked the trail left from the tears I'd been crying.

"I'm sorry. I shouldn't have been such an ass. But, seeing you...you'd been crying, and you looked so broken. It was enraging that he did that to you. That I let him do that to you."

His hand went to my chin, and then he leaned down slightly and kissed me.

Chapter Thirty-Three

Of all the things that could have happened, I was least prepared for this—yet it seemed so inevitable. This anger turning on itself and ending up at this moment. Like it was where we'd been heading all along.

I didn't stop him, even when he pulled back, his eyes asking me for permission to keep going. I nodded and then let him pull me closer. Kiss me deeper.

That spark between us finally caught. All that chemistry I'd tried so hard to muster up with Davis was plentiful, palpable with Vince. Davis had been like whiskey and unresolved teenage angst, and something wild. Vince was like having been somewhere you'd never been before, yet it was coming home.

The normal ease and comfort I felt in his presence was replaced with an urgency that pumped through my veins. I pulled at his shirt, tugging it over his head and then tossing it on the floor. I was not at all surprised to see a tattoo on his chest. An intricate *G* and *T* wound around each other. I stepped forward and traced it with my fingers.

"I always forget that's there. I've had it so long. It looked better when I was younger, I can tell you that."

"Didn't we all?" I kissed it and then lifted my face to him. "But then again, those younger roads led us here."

He shook his head. "The things you say, Red. You have no idea what they do to me." And then he leaned down to kiss me again, urgent, wanting.

I pulled him backward toward the bed, dropping the rest of our clothes as we went until we tumbled into the mess of blankets and sheets where earlier I had lain, broken-hearted and weeping. His lips on mine, like if we separated he couldn't breathe. I knew, because I felt it, too. His hands skimming my skin like he wanted to touch every inch of me. And every touch of his fingers took me to a new level of wanting. Until want was replaced with need, and then finally that need was replaced with Vince, all of him.

Afterward, I barely could remember any of that as I laid my head on his chest.

I'd never experienced anything that could live up to what had just happened with Vince. How he'd known what I'd needed, where to touch me. *How* to touch me. Like we'd done this a thousand times, but with the thrill of it being the first. My lips felt puffy and bruised because through it all, he'd kissed me. Kissed me like that connection was the air he needed. And maybe it was.

After all, oxygen is the main component for fire. And what had happened between us was pure combustion.

"Vince—" But he put his finger to my lips.

"No, don't say anything. Just let it settle a bit." He kissed my forehead and pulled me closer.

We lay like that for I don't know how long before he spoke again, his voice soft. "You said that night on the roof that you stayed married all those years because it was easy."

I shifted and propped my head up on my hand so I could

look at him. "Yes."

"Well, that's why I"—his eyes darted from my face to my hair. His hand reached out and he let his fingers tangle in it—"that's why I keep my distance from most people. Stay out of the fray, it's easier to just not get connected."

The vulnerability on his face tore at my heart. I leaned forward and grazed his lips with mine. And then when I pulled back, unsure what to do with all I was feeling, I resorted to a bit of teasing.

"So what, you're some sort of lone wolf instead of a Golden Tiger?"

He laughed softly. "Nice turn of phrase, Red, as usual. You know exactly how to put into words what's stuck in my head." He reached out and pulled me to him, kissing me lightly before nestling me back where I'd been with my head on his chest.

I sighed, not feeling any need at all to ask for more from him. I was drifting off, but I could have sworn he added, "It sort of scares the hell out of me." But I was too far gone to be sure.

I fell asleep feeling more content than I think I ever have in my life.

But when the sun from the open curtains woke me the next morning, I was alone.

Vince was gone. The only sign that he'd ever been there were my notebooks, piled on the table.

Gone. Not a note, not a text, not a call. Nothing.

Was this his idea of letting it settle? Did he regret sleeping with me? Was he going to Davis me? That gave me a pit in my stomach. But I didn't have time to dwell. Not if I was going to get the sample pages to Harrison by the time the band arrived in L.A. in just four days.

I grabbed for the hotel phone on the bedside table and called room service for a pot of coffee, then went to the bathroom to splash some water on my face. I threw my hair up in a ponytail, grabbed my notebooks, flash drives, and laptop, and settled back down in bed, propping the pillows up as I tried to formulate a plan on how I was going to take all that I had collected and create something out of it.

It began and ended with the music, the songs. How they were created. How they were played. What it meant to the band, to the fans. So that seemed like the place to start.

I picked up my notebook from the first tour, the one I'd transcribed the lyrics into. Back then, it was liner notes on tiny cassettes. But I'd made my own with annotations as to who I thought wrote what and my interpretations of every line.

It seemed a little over the top in retrospect, but now it was the most valuable resource I had. Years of listening had numbed me to the meanings behind these songs. Now, they were wrapped up in golden memories, and regrets, which made them tainted in a way. The notebooks were a chance to look at them almost as an anthropologist would. With clear eyes and heart.

What did the band intend them to mean before I'd let my life experiences put my own personal meaning to them?

Back then, my time with the band had been limited to attempts to crash their parties or make my way on the bus. I'd never really spoken to any of them. But now I'd spent time with them, heard their stories.

The albums told those, too.

Then it hit me. The missing piece that could tie it all together. I would lay the book out by song, each chapter a different song title complete with the story of how it was written and the meaning behind it. The photos of the guys, both portrait and casual, set at angles like a scrapbook. I'd include anecdotes of it being played on stage. The book itself would be like an album, with liner notes. Maybe even some photos with blurred edges of my copies of the lyrics. And I'd use my old pictures too.

It was brilliant, if I did say so myself. And it also gave me somewhere to start, to give order to the copious number of photos and stories I had from both then and now.

Hours later, my back and hand cramped from bending over and scribbling in a whole new notebook, I was a woman possessed. It was like a giant jigsaw puzzle, but I couldn't get it to fit together. At first, I'd tried going through the songs and seeing what stories fit where. But then I'd reversed it, read the stories and looked for lyrics. Still, they didn't match up. Other than the typical teenage-boy-in-a-Midwest-town bend of some of them. How was that possible? All the stories they'd told me in their interviews. Not to mention the hundreds more I'd sat through at post parties, in bars, or just hanging out in hotel rooms.

Maybe I was looking too closely? Or maybe my brain was fried.

I stood, stretching out my sore back and shaking my fingers. The sun had risen and set, and I'd never left my room. My stomach grumbled, reminding me I hadn't eaten all day either. Room service seemed in order.

I went through a brief debate on the health benefits of ordering a salad versus the mental benefit of a cheeseburger and fries.

Cheeseburger and fries won. It seemed much more rock and roll and I needed to get deeper into that headspace. Plus, the fries had been amazing the night Marissa had used them to cure my hangover. I needed to call her and bring her up to speed on what was going on: my firing, rehiring, and those *details* she'd made me promise to give her.

I leaned my head against the window, still warm even though the sun had set. I closed my eyes and played the scene from the night before in my head. Even in my own retelling, it read like something out of one of those *True Confessions* magazines my mom always bought at the grocery store. It was a story that needed to be told if for no other reason than to cement it in my memory.

I reached for my phone to see there was a text.

From Vince.

Just one word.

Sorry.

Chapter Thirty-Four

Sorry?

I felt sweaty.

Sorry?

About what?

Leaving? Sleeping with me?

That he'd saved my job?

Vince was always a man of few words, but this? This was an all-time record. One word that could have so many different meanings.

My finger itched to hit reply, but I hesitated. Replying to the text opened me up to another level of anxiety. What if he didn't reply? I'd stew on it, and I didn't need the distraction. And what if he did answer? What could be worse than this single word?

Don't ask questions you don't want the answer to—it was the one lesson from my marriage that still rang true.

"Damn you, Vince," I muttered out loud to the empty room.

I needed a distraction from this distraction. I thumbed

through my music and pulled up the album that always did the trick, the under-loved third album from Golden Tiger. The very one that Vince had teased me for listening to.

I hit shuffle, turned up the volume, and sank down into the chair in the corner.

Whiskey never tasted as smooth
As the sunset cast shadows on her face turned away.
Reflecting red on the glass in her hand, curtained by
hair that looked like fire caught.
Like the words in my throat.
If she only knew, if she only knew.
But instead, I sipped my whiskey and enjoyed the view.
Mountains behind, but they couldn't compare.
A night I'd stolen, as her savior.
But I couldn't complain.
If she only knew. If she only knew.
But instead I sipped my whiskey and enjoyed the view.

Wait. How had I never heard that before?

Mountains behind, but they couldn't compare.

I scrambled for my notebooks. Flipping until I found what I was looking for—the night Vince and I got trapped on that roof outside of Denver.

The sunset that night, according to my notes, had been brilliant and red.

Alpenglow. Not the actual sunset, but the reflection of it. It couldn't be a coincidence.

I grabbed my notebook from this tour, turning the pages so quickly I risked tearing them out. I hadn't sat down with Vince for an interview, but I'd jotted notes on the stories he told me these weeks we'd spent together. I found the one I was looking for and then grabbed for my phone and switched the song, back to one from the first album. Then I grabbed my notebook from twenty years ago that had the lyrics.

Blood Brothers
Friendship born on a dusty playground
They'd kick dust in my eye, but never yours.
I don't have much to bring to this table
But that didn't matter to you
Blood Brothers tried and true

It matched the story Vince had told me about Davis saving him from playground bullies and then taking him home. I sat back. What was I reading?

I scrambled to come up with another option, that Davis could have written it. But Davis wasn't the one who had been saved, it had been Vince.

Was I delirious or was this what I had spent my entire day looking for?

A connection from story to song, except none of these connections were from the band. They were all from Vince.

My heart thudded. I grabbed for a pen and scribbled the connection down and then went back to the original lyric notebook. It seemed the easiest way to go about this was to read the lyrics and then try to make the connection to Vince. Either to prove or disprove my theory.

I cued up each song as I read the lyrics, reminding myself of years ago when I used to unfold the liner notes from my cassette and read them over and over as I rewound the songs until I knew them by heart. But this time I had a whole different mission, and I didn't know if I wanted to be right. But with every song it became clearer and clearer that I wasn't wrong.

Once I knew what I was listening for, it was so obvious. There was a Vince story for every single one of them. A quick Google search showed he wasn't listed as even a contributor on the albums. It made no sense.

If Vince wrote these songs, why didn't they give him credit for it?

Then I remembered something else. That first night in the hall, Vince had told me that he left the tour right after I did. If he wrote their songs, had he also *stopped* writing them? Is that why Golden Tiger disappeared? It seemed impossible but apparently so possible.

I needed answers. There was only one person who could and would give them to me. But he was currently on stage for the third sold-out show of this Vegas residency. I checked the clock on my bedside table. It was only ten. Even if they had started on time, which they never did, I could just get to the show before it was over.

I threw on clothes, not even bothering to shower. I kept my hair in its ponytail, and the mascara that had run under my eyes was close enough to a smoky eye. My appearance was the last thing I was worried about.

If I didn't get there before the show ended, I ran the risk the band would disappear into another party scene and I'd have to wait until tomorrow to get to the bottom of this. And I didn't have time to spend drumming up more conspiracy theories. Harrison had given me only four days to come up with something. And this was the something I needed.

I grabbed my notebook, my "proof," and raced out the door.

By the time I got there, they were just starting the finale. "Hearts Afire."

I waited for Davis in his dressing room, feeling the encore in my chest as it kept time with my own racing heartbeat. If Davis played it straight with me, this could change everything.

The crowd roared and I knew it was over. I paced like I was in a cage, waiting for what seemed like hours for him to come back, and then finally the door opened. I don't know if it was the shock of finding me there or the look on my face, but it froze him in his tracks.

"Red, what are you doing here?"

I stepped forward, holding out my notes connecting Vince to every Golden Tiger song.

"Davis, I need you to be straight with me." I handed him the notebook. "Did Vince write Golden Tiger's songs?"

He looked at the mess of words in front of him, then back up at me. He blinked and his rock star mask fell.

"Yes, he did," he said in a voice that bore no resemblance to the man I'd known my whole life, more like a skinny kid who practiced his guitar in his grandma's garage.

"Look, I can't talk about this here." He closed the door behind him. "Not with Harrison here and Vince AWOL.'

I stopped. "What do you mean, Vince is AWOL?" I thought briefly of the text I'd never responded to, and my breath caught.

Davis shrugged. "I don't know. He just called and said he had something he had to take care of, so he was taking off."

I leaned against the arm of the couch. "Did he say when he was coming back?"

Or *if* he was coming back? The rest I finished in my head, not wanting to raise the possibility that somehow, sleeping with me had driven Vince away from the tour.

Davis nodded. "Said he'd see me in L.A." He handed me back the notebook. "Meet me back at the hotel."

As relieved as I was to hear that Vince planned to rejoin the tour, I wasn't sure I wanted to let Davis out of my sight.

"I'll wait. We can go together."

Davis shook his head. "Nah, Red. I need a minute."

What could I do but take him at his word that he'd show? "The bar?" I said, retreating to the door.

He nodded. "Try to find a booth in the corner, out of sight if you can."

I smiled. "Yeah, I'm a bit of a mess, I can see why you'd rather not be seen with me."

He shook his head. "You know that has nothing to do it with it."

I did. And so I left.

This was big. Davis Scott dropping his act big. I was about to find out the hows and whys of everything, and I wasn't so sure I was ready for any of it.

And where the hell was Vince?

At the next red light, I pulled out my phone, looked at his text, and considered my options.

Ignore?

Reply?

What would I even say? Do I let on that I know the truth?

The light changed to green and I powered it off. What was the point of sending a text until I really knew the whole truth?

Or at least that's what I told myself as I pulled up in front of the hotel. I made my way to the lobby bar, happy to find it relatively quiet and a small booth in the dark back corner empty.

Perfect. No one would think to find Davis Scott here.

The waitress came and I ordered a bottle and a bucket of ice. Two glasses. And then I waited, for the drinks and for Davis. A continuous narrative in my head. I had been right. Me. I'd uncovered something that no one else in the years of covering this band had figured out. Just by listening to the music.

Well, that and by getting to know Vince. Sure, it had been in pieces, small moments, and stories. Looking back at the whole of it, how he'd doled out his story to me and how all along he'd trusted me with those parts of him that maybe no one other than Davis knew. My heart ached that he'd run as much as it swelled that he'd shared that part of himself.

I'd spent my whole life thinking Vince didn't believe I

was worthy, only to find out that instead he thought that of himself. And now he was gone, and I was going to have to force Davis to give me the missing pieces.

Though one piece that finally made sense was why Vince had been pushing his vanilla version of the book on me from the start. He hadn't wanted me to figure out this part of his story.

I checked my watch. Maybe I'd been a fool to think Davis would show. But I had to hope I wasn't. I needed an answer to the one question I couldn't for the life of me figure out: why?

The drinks came before Davis, and I poured one to sip while I waited. My nerves were fraying, my ice mostly melted when he appeared at my table. I had to do a double take, and even then, it wasn't until he slid across from me and spoke that I knew for sure it was him.

Not a stitch of makeup, his jet-black hair tucked under a cap. He was wearing an old Cubs T-shirt and a pair of jeans.

He couldn't look less like a rock star, or more attractive, if he tried.

"I figured if you were going to go au naturel I should too," he said sheepishly to my wide-eyed, open-mouthed reaction. He reached for a glass, not bothering with the ice, and filled it halfway with whiskey.

"I wouldn't know it was you, if I didn't know it was you."

"That's sort of the point," he said, smiling ever so slightly.

"The point of wearing the makeup or of not wearing it?" I said without a thought. And then I pinched my lips together as I watched the reaction on his face.

He lifted his glass to take a drink before raising one finger to acknowledge my question. "You're really good at this, you know that?"

I opened my mouth to protest, but he cut me off.

"Really. Here I thought you, of all people, would put together a love letter to the band, but you're going after it.

Digging out the hard shit." His voice was somehow awash in both admiration and bitterness.

I didn't know how to respond to that because I wasn't sure if it was a compliment or resentment. But I had to say something. "I can't blame you. I did ask about Rex and the French teacher."

This earned me a chuckle but nothing more. We sat in silence as he drained the drink and then reached for the bottle again. Around us, the bar hummed with quiet conversations. We could be anywhere. It certainly didn't seem like Vegas to me right now. No pounding music or flashing lights, no crowd noise or really crowds at all. Just small groups of people sitting together. I wondered how many of them were sharing secrets. Because that's what I was doing with Davis, or rather he was doing with me.

I wished I had my camera. I pulled out my phone and raised an eyebrow to ask if it was okay. Davis nodded slightly. And I snapped a few, changing my angle, taking a few through the whiskey bottle. Blurring the edges of him, then it. Until I felt I had enough and put it away.

"So," I said, calling an end to the silent stalemate, "where should we start?"

"The smart-ass answer is the beginning."

"I think we're well past the smart-ass answer, aren't we?"

He set his glass down and leaned forward on the table. "Fine, Red. What do you want to know?"

"I want to know why, mostly."

"Why what? Why none of us wrote any of the songs that made us the biggest rock band in the world?"

I shook my head. "No, I want to know why it's a secret that Vince did."

"I guess it would look like that from the outside. But let me say this right off, I never intended for that to be the way it turned out."

I pulled out my notebook and started to take notes, hesitated and then said, "Do you mind?"

He sighed. "I know I should say I do, that you shouldn't put this in the damn book, but I've wanted this story off my chest for a long-ass time." He gave the slightest nod and then continued.

"So, back when we started, it was just me and Vince, hanging out playing guitars in my basement. Mine was a used one, bought it at a garage sale. But Vince, he had his dad's guitar. Sob story as they always are, Dad left long before Vince could hold his own dick to piss." He stopped there and smiled slyly. "Sorry, I forget that you aren't one of the guys sometimes."

"I'll take it as a compliment. I know all of this. Your story—how you and your pals played around and then as a joke entered a talent contest, which you won so then started playing local gigs, added Tony. But what's interesting is that there's never been any mention of Vince, even anecdotally. You wouldn't even know he grew up in the same town you did if you read anything about Golden Tiger. The first time he told me you were friends growing up, I was floored."

"Well, some of that you're going to have to ask Vince. But I think you already know the biggest reason." He pointed toward his own makeup-less face.

I nodded. "I get that. Vince told me he never wanted to be a part of the show, the spectacle. But he's clearly always been a part of the band. So why cut him out of the story altogether?"

"To start with, the Vince you know is not the Vince I grew up with."

I raised an eyebrow.

"He was shy. Zero self-confidence, negative actually. Never said boo to anyone. He was always at my house when we were kids and my mom used to call him the mouse. Because he'd barely speak, and when he did it was so quiet, like barely above a whisper. How he looks out for me now? It was the opposite when we were kids. It was me looking out for him."

Sometimes the quietest voice has the most to say. I won't be the one begging, but baby I think you should stay.

The lyric popped into my head immediately, and I jotted it down as yet another connection. Davis glanced at the paper and smiled.

"Some real gems in there. The ones that hit the closest are all from something Vince doesn't want to talk about or remember."

That made sense, I guessed. But still.

"So, you're saying Vince didn't want anyone to know he wrote the songs, because he was shy? Or because they were too personal for him?"

"Yes, and yes," Davis said, downing his drink and then filling the glass again. I held mine up for more, too. I was glad I'd asked for a bottle, the last thing I needed was a waitress busting in when Davis was getting to the good parts.

"It's all part of that fucked-up childhood stuff, you know?"

I did know, more than I cared to admit.

"His mom wasn't awful, but she was way more concerned with finding another man, then another, each worse than the last. I mean it's the exact story you'd think. Vince wrote a lot of early stuff about that, used it to make some epic songs that'll break your fucking heart. Listen close to those early ones, that first album. That love I'm singing about is Vince's mom. But he didn't want anyone to know, because he thought it'd hurt her even more if she knew how he actually felt."

I swallowed. That was awful. At least my shitty parents had just ignored me. "No one is more loyal than Vince."

"That was part of it, but it was also because he thought they were all shit. Like I said, no self-confidence at all."

"But they weren't shit. Obviously, they went platinum…"

"Double platinum!" Davis broke in. "They were fucking brilliant and I told him so, back in high school, and when we were playing clubs."

I leaned back. Davis was on a roll now, and he didn't need me to keep prompting him to tell the story.

"I almost had him convinced to let me at least give him a shout-out when we were playing, but then record producers started showing up and really taking a look at us. And here's the part that I'm not proud of."

I nodded, hoping that was enough encouragement.

"By that time, I was already building up this image. I was drinking hard, and other things, too. Because that's what I thought rock stars did. And my ego? It was buying into all of it. The girls screaming at me, throwing themselves at me, which was just blowing my fucking mind. I told you what a punk I was growing up. As much as it scared Vince, I ate that shit up."

He shook his head, like he wanted to shake the memories loose, but the smile on his face was enough to tell me they weren't all bad ones.

"Then we started playing bigger places, and the crowds were singing along to songs I used to play in my basement and Rex's grandma's garage. By the time we signed with the label, we had a huge following. And it wasn't like we were trying to keep it a secret that we hadn't written the songs. We just hadn't mentioned it through the whole process." He leaned back in the booth, adjusted his baseball cap. "When we recorded the album, we talked about it. I mean at that point, the songs were huge, he didn't have to worry about them not being good enough. But the label really liked the idea that we'd written our own songs. This idea that the four of us from the shitty, poor part of Chicago came together and wrote these gut-wrenching and rocking tunes. Harrison kept gushing about how badass it was that the stories were ours.

And they were ours, technically."

I felt the knot in my throat. "But seen through Vince's eyes."

He nodded. "Vince was fine with it and we were all so wrapped up in signing and hitting the big time that we didn't think the whole thing through. We were kids really, and way more interested in being rock stars than in writing songs. It seemed to be the perfect solution."

"And Harrison, the label. They never knew?"

He shook his head. "Everyone got what they wanted."

"Except you got famous, and Vince got what?"

Davis flinched back, like I'd slapped him. "What he always wanted, to write music."

"He essentially built you into the biggest rock band of a generation and got no credit. No one outside of the tour even knows who he is. And then what, he just stopped and walked away?"

Davis shrugged. "You'd have to ask him. That part of the story isn't mine to tell. One thing that never changed with Vince is his loyalty. I mean, look what he did for you."

I stopped and put my pen down. "What do you mean, what he did for me?"

"You don't know? He threatened to quit the tour if Harrison fired you. And you might remember what a Golden Tiger tour looks like without Vince."

I did. Without Vince the whole thing had fallen apart twenty years ago. Harrison wouldn't have wanted that to happen.

So why had Vince walked away, then and again now? Were they connected?

He'd looked out for me, like he always had with Davis. Threatened to quit his job to save mine. Even if he'd pulled a disappearing act, I had to believe that meant something. Had to.

Chapter Thirty-Five

My chat with Davis had left me buzzed and emotionally exhausted. I desperately wanted to try and make some sense of the story as I now knew it, but when I'd reached my room, I just felt numb. I dropped my clothes in a line from the door to my bed and pulled my well-worn Golden Tiger T-shirt over my head. I climbed under the covers, hoping sleep would give pause to the constant stream of questions going through my head.

But there was one that I couldn't let go of, not now that I knew most of the story. I grabbed my phone and fired off a response to Vince.

For what?

I flipped off the light and let myself fall down into the hazy tunnel of sleep that too much whiskey always brought.

...

I woke up with the sun in my eyes. I'd forgotten to close the curtains. No deep dark room until noon today. Which was good. I had too much to do to sleep the day away.

There was no reply text from Vince. I flipped to my email and was shocked to see one from Harrison. I sat up, as somehow that felt a more professional way to read it, ignoring my bedhead and that I was still in my nightshirt.

Ms. Cavett,

Per my conversation with Vince Caparelli, I have adjusted my position to keep you on as tour photographer and creator of the contracted book, pending approval of sample pages from you in three days' time. You can deliver them to my office in Los Angeles when the band finishes up this leg of the tour here. The address is below. At that time, we can discuss your future in this role.

Warmest Regards,
Harrison

Vince was right, Harrison was a grade-A asshole. And a condescending one at that.

Los Angeles. I tried to remember the shows there. What club had the band played? Where had I stayed? Any bit of it, but my mind was blank.

My mouth went dry. I didn't remember L.A. because I hadn't gone to L.A. Vegas had been the end of the road for me as a Golden Tiger groupie wannabe.

Vegas is where I'd met Jack, which in and of itself was an unbelievable part of our story. Vegas and all it represents was the complete opposite of Jack's core principles. But it was where we met nonetheless. He'd been there for a conference, and not happy about it. I'd met him at his welcome reception. I'd snuck in for the free food and drinks so I was trying to be inconspicuous and out of the crowd.

If I'm being honest, I was emotionally strung out, tired of being broke and needy and rejected. Jack, who always did as he was supposed to, was only there because it was a mandatory meet and greet. I thought he was busting me for crashing, so I'd flirted my ass off to try and charm him from kicking me out. Or at least from making a scene about it. He always said he'd fallen for me on sight.

At the time, it had seemed so romantic. A whirlwind. He'd showered more attention my way than I'd felt in my lifetime. I'd always thought of myself as without need of that sort of thing, but that couldn't have been further from the truth. I became so addicted to it that I forgot everything else. And when he suggested I quit following the tour and instead follow him home to Iowa, I'd done so willingly. And whether it was the stability, or the attention, or the fact that I wasn't sleeping in my car anymore, when he proposed six months later, I accepted.

Everything I'd never thought I wanted all in one package.

I'd like to think there had been a lingering small voice in my head telling me to slow down, but that came later. Now I realized I'd given up everything I liked about myself for that marriage, allowed Jack to redefine everything about me. I'd gambled and I lost. It was some poetic shit that Vegas would be the place I got to make the choice again.

I stood and went to the window and looked out over the strip.

My mind cleared and I knew one thing for certain.

Not only was I going to make it to Los Angeles this time, but I also wasn't going to let anyone else decide what was right for me, besides me.

Including whatever was going on with Vince.

No matter what he was sorry about. Nothing could matter as much as me telling the story that needed to be told. My way. And I couldn't do that in this hotel room.

I showered and packed up my things methodically. In my mind I was already on some two-lane highway headed west, so I was not at all pleased to run into Davis in the lobby, still sporting his clean face and toned-down appearance.

"Still trying to fly under the radar, I see," I said as he approached.

He nodded, a stiff smile on his face. "Actually, I haven't been to bed yet."

The sunglasses on his face hid his eyes, so I couldn't be sure if he was being honest.

"Well, you know the saying, what happens in Vegas." I craned my neck, looking for my car. The last thing I wanted was to have Davis pour his heart out with regret over what he'd told me last night.

"I never believed in that bullshit." He turned and looked in my direction. "What you find out about yourself in Vegas should be how you fucking live every day after that."

"Meaning?"

"Meaning, put the story in your book. Use the photos of me from last night. It deserves to be told, no matter the fallout."

I think I nodded, but I can't be sure. At that exact moment, the overly flirtatious parking attendant squealed to a stop in front of me.

"Okay," I said, to myself and to Davis. "I'll see you in L.A."

I let the attendant put my bags into the trunk and slid into the driver's seat of my car, itching to hit the road.

I didn't need Davis's permission, but it was nice to get it.

As I drove down the highway, I knew the whole picture was way too cliché: woman driving off to take a stand, reclaiming her life. The wind in my hair screamed independence, but it also screamed in my ears. An hour into it, I'd had enough symbolism and put the windows back up.

And I called Marissa. She'd kill me if I delayed the details I promised any longer.

"So…" I said when she picked up.

"OH MY GOD!" I pulled my phone back but not in time to avoid her scream vibrating through my eardrum. "IT HAPPENED!"

I stayed quiet and let her continue her enthusiastic freak-out, not at all surprised that she knew just why I was calling. Waited, and bided my time. Because I knew what was coming next.

"I told you so! I knew it that first morning in his hotel suite—the chemistry was so thick, I had to excuse myself to get a breath of fresh air!"

I laughed, because what else could I do? I wasn't going to start out the story with the ending. The one that proved her wrong.

"Spill it. And I mean *all* of it."

"Well, it started when the record label fired me—"

"Wait, what? You got fired? And how does that have anything to do with sleeping with Vince?"

Exactly.

"Are you going to let me tell the story, or are you going to keep interrupting me?"

"Fine. You're the professional storyteller now. Tell it your way!"

With the compliment, a warmth of pride spread through me.

"That I am, and you better watch yourself, or your little Vegas fling will find its way into my book."

She gasped. "No way. Don't you know what happens in Vegas stays in Vegas?"

"Funny you should say that, apparently it doesn't."

"Wha—" she started, but I cut her off.

"Let me tell it!"

And so she shut up, and I did, dragging it out detail by detail. Just like she wanted, though the details I was providing weren't of the sexy-times variety. I wasn't quite ready to share those yet.

"He was just gone when you woke up?" She gasped.

Literally gasped. And I had two thoughts: my life had gone from boring to overtly sensational in the span of a month. And two, I was a damn good storyteller.

"Yep. Gone. Not even a note. Though I did get a text message hours later."

"What did it say? You're purposely drawing it out to drive me insane."

"Nope, just to get you to turn the page."

"Whatever. What did the text say?"

"Sorry."

"I said, what did the text say?" she practically yelled into the phone.

"I can hear you. That's what the text said, just one word, 'sorry.'"

"For what?"

"I have no idea."

"So that's it? That's the end?"

The road sign I passed as she said it read *Los Angeles 100 miles.*

"Actually, I think it's just the beginning."

"For you and Vince?"

"No, for me."

"You are really cryptic today. And let me tell you, it's making me insane. What are you talking about now?"

"The book, the story I'm going to tell. I had quite the nightcap with your boy-toy last night. A real deep emotional baring of the soul sort of thing."

"Davis? Did he ask about me? Wait, don't tell me. I'm going to let Vegas stay in Vegas. Unless, of course, he asked about me."

Ah, Marissa, forever the romantic.

"Actually, he was the one who told me *not* to let what happens in Vegas stay in Vegas. So, I wouldn't count him out just yet."

"PHTT! I don't believe that for one second." Her voice tilted like an old lady at a church picnic hearing gossip that both thrilled and horrified her. The kind that was hard to believe to be true. "He's the poster boy for that slogan."

"Shockingly not. He gave me the real story of Vince and the band. The one I'm going to tell and blow the socks right off that pompous ass of an executive."

"Do I want to hear it? Or do I want to read it when it comes out? I think I want to read it. Tell me again how a photo book is going to tell a story?"

"The pictures will tell the story, that and a few well-placed anecdotes. You'll see, if it ever gets published. If it doesn't, I'm going to need to couch surf while I figure out my next step. My house sold."

"You're welcome to couch surf with me for as long as you require, you know that. But you aren't going to need it. This thing is going to be a blockbuster. And people will be lining up begging for you to cover them next. The next great rock and roll biographer, that's what you'll be!"

I laughed. Everyone needs a Marissa in their life. "From your lips, my friend." It felt preordained when she said it like that.

Her follow-up, however, did not land the same. "But what about Vince?"

I took a deep breath. "I think that'll have to be up to him," I replied. I still had no idea where he was or why he'd left. But he'd offered himself up to save my job, so getting those pages seemed the least I could do. Even if the story I was going to tell was one he'd kept hidden for twenty years.

Chapter Thirty-Six

I'd purposely taken the two-lane highways to L.A. so that I could lose myself in the landscape without having to worry about the aggressive drivers on the freeway. As those yellow lines ticked by, the story I wanted to tell started to come together in my mind. Finding the roadside motel was purely a lucky coincidence. So reminiscent of that place in Colorado, I took it as a sign and pulled in and got a room.

I stayed for two days, doing nothing but laying out photos, writing their stories, and eating from the vending machine. And ignoring my phone. In fact, I'd turned it off as soon as I checked in. On the morning of the third day, the day my sample pages were due to Harrison, I looked them over one more time, packed up my car, and headed toward the city.

I felt an odd sense of calm *and* catastrophe. The pictures were outstanding. I'd managed to capture Davis as both a rock god and a kid from Chicago. And Rex and that guitar on the bed? Stripped down sex appeal. The action shots were good, but by far my favorite was the one at the after-party, when they'd all just been shooting the shit. And Vince, doing that first sound check in St. Louis. That was where I laid it all out.

It was good. After all, the stories came straight from the guys. But the overall visual narrative? It was far from the love letter I'd been hired to put out and instead a raw, honest truth about the music, the men, and a loyalty that they obeyed to each other and the band no matter the cost.

The possible fallout made my mouth go dry. I very well could have shot myself in the foot before I even took the first step on my new career path. But this was the story I was meant to tell. I was sure of that.

And since the only way to know was to turn it in, I powered up my phone and called Harrison, ignoring the beeps and buzzes of texts, calls, and voicemails that had come in while I'd been off the grid.

"Ms. Cavett, how can I help you?" His voice made my skin crawl. His tone dripped with condescension.

What an asshole.

"Harrison. I have the pages ready, per your deadline today. What time can we meet so I can give them to you?"

He snickered. Not chuckled or laughed, but actually villainously snickered.

"I must admit, I am surprised you hit the target. I assumed when my secretary told me who was calling, you'd be asking for an extension."

Secretary? Who used that word anymore?

"Nope, I have them ready to go. Just let me know what time." I kept my voice as even as possible.

I could hear him flip some papers. "Looks like I can see you at one."

Secretary and a paper calendar? Apparently, I was time-traveling back to *Mad Men* for my meeting.

"I'll be there," I replied and hung up before he told me to wear something that showed off my legs.

I punched the address for the tour's hotel into my GPS and I was off. If the ETA was right, I'd have enough time to make myself just a bit more presentable. Thank God I'd made Vince send me the master hotel list, otherwise I might have been forced to reach out to him, and I wasn't quite ready for that.

With a plan in my head, and my car on the road, I turned up the volume and let the music play me to Los Angeles. Eager to just listen and drive, willing a sense of calm and confidence that I really didn't feel at all. I pulled into the hotel in plenty of time. It was nice, upscale of course. All its flashiness made me miss my little roadside motel all the more. Even when the cute young valet opened my door and welcomed me with a "miss" and a wink.

Once I had my bags, I went to the front desk to find I was already checked in with a key waiting for me. Vince must have surfaced—or found someone else to do his job.

"Do you have a business center on site?" I asked the front desk attendant.

"We do. What can I help you with?"

I fished the flash drive with my chapters on it from the outside pocket of my bag.

"I just need to get this printed as soon as possible."

"Of course. I can take care of that for you." She held out her hand for the flash drive. I paused for one second. Printed pages seemed a bit too real. Once they were printed, they'd be seen. Once seen, they'd be judged.

I swallowed, pulled my shoulders back, and handed it over.

I crossed the marble floors of the grand lobby, its dark wood tables decorated with brass fixtures next to overstuffed velvet couches, and so many flower bouquets the huge room smelled like a garden. Old-school Hollywood glamour, in an almost romantic way.

The elevator doors were open when I reached them. I punched my floor and waited as they slowly pulled to a close, but then someone stuck a hand in. They opened again, just as slowly, and I found myself face-to-face with Vince.

And he didn't look at all happy. My whole body tensed.

He stepped on and punched his floor without acknowledging me. I went from tense to angry in a hot second. I wasn't experienced with sleeping around by any means, but still. Even an asshole says hello to the woman he banged in Vegas, right? I bit my tongue to keep from pointing that out.

So, imagine my surprise when the doors closed and he spun around, fire in his eyes.

"Campbell, where the hell have you been and why haven't you answered any of my messages?"

I blinked in response, stunned. Messages? But then I remembered the symphony of beeps and buzzes my phone had produced when I'd powered it on to call Harrison.

"Seriously, you can't just disappear out of thin air."

"*I* can't just disappear?" I laughed at the absolute absurdity. "You're kidding, right?"

"I had some things I needed to sort out." He was almost sheepish, his hands in his pockets, as he eyed the space on the floor in front of my feet like it was the most fascinating thing he'd ever seen.

Sort out? The most amazing sex of my life, which left me wanting more, had left him with things to sort out? I just stared at him.

The elevator doors opened at what was my floor, thank God, and I marched past him without saying a word.

"Hold up, just one damn minute," he said, following behind me. But I charged forward, searching the doors for my room number and sanctuary.

I'd never been so angry and humiliated in my life.

I found the door and slipped my key out of my pocket

to open it. "I don't have time for this right now, Vince"—I turned—"whatever this is." I waved my hands between the two of us, hoping he would back off, but it only seemed to encourage him. He pushed past me and into my hotel room.

"You haven't answered my question. Where have you been?"

I sighed. "Doing my job. I stayed at a motel outside the city so I could get the sample pages done. Without anyone barging into my hotel room and interrupting me with their opinions. Which is all that seems to happen in these fancy hotels you choose for the band."

"You can't turn them in, Campbell."

I spun around, ready to unleash. I was so damn tired of being told what I could and couldn't do. I had a lifetime of it, and I was done.

But then I saw the look on his face.

It wasn't demanding or angry. It was pleading, almost scared. And all the anger inside of me just deflated.

"Why?" I wasn't just talking about his edict, and I could only hope he got that.

He sat down in the chair by the windows. In keeping with the retro glam of the hotel, it was small, chintz, and it made him look bigger than he was. He leaned forward, elbows on his knees, his fingers tented.

"I talked to Davis. He said he spilled every last secret and told you to put it in the book. You can't do that."

I sank down on the edge of the bed across from him. He didn't get it. At all.

"Why not?"

He looked me directly in the eye. "Well, for starters, it isn't a story anyone wants to read."

I shook my head. "I disagree with that entirely. And I think you do, too."

"Then you think wrong. Listen, I know Davis, especially

when he's drinking. He gets melancholy, exaggerates. I can't guarantee what he told you is all true. You can't put lies in a biography."

I laid my hand on his. "The thing is, Vince, what he told me only backed up what I'd figured out on my own. You wrote every hit Golden Tiger ever had and never took credit. I talked to Davis to find out why, not if."

He hung his head, shook it from side to side a bit, in what I assumed was acceptance. I was wrong. When he looked up again, it wasn't sadness in his eyes. It was determination, and a hint of fear.

"Look," I continued. "I understand, to some degree, why you don't want this to be the story. And I understand now why you tried so hard to steer me in another direction. But I'm telling you, Vince, it's the story you hired me to tell."

He stood up so quickly.

"No, it isn't, that's for damn sure. I hired you to write the love letter to the band that every washed-up groupie wants to read. That's what you're qualified for, uniquely so, I'd say."

"Nice try." I felt eerily calm. "You're trying to pick a fight with me so I doubt myself, back off, and do it your way. But guess what? That isn't going to happen. And I think you know why."

He looked at me, and if the vulnerability he'd shown in my bed had tugged at my heartstrings, the look he had now nearly devastated me. "I have no fucking idea."

I stood and crossed the room to him. "Because you don't really want me to." I bore my eyes into his, like he would to me when he was trying to make me see a truth.

"Um, yes. I do. Why else would I have hired you, of all people, and given you the exact questions I wanted you to ask?"

"And then left me to my own devices? Reminisced? Told me stories that would lead me to figure it all out. You laid the breadcrumbs. I just followed them. Whether you want to admit it or not, you want your story told."

He walked toward the door but stopped before he got there. He turned and fixed those gray eyes right on me. "You don't know the whole story, Red. You just think you do, and I can't for the life of me figure out what's gotten a hold of you."

"The music, of course. Your music. It's always been about the music for me. And for you. Now that I know it's yours, I hear it differently." I stepped toward him wanting to grab his hand in mine. Squeeze it to reassure him that I meant what I was saying. But instead, I just said, "If I don't know the whole story, stay. Tell me."

His mouth fell open, like maybe he was going to do just that. But then as though he thought better of it, he gave me a sad smile, then turned to the door, and left.

Chapter Thirty-Seven

Watching Vince walk away, my heart cracked a bit. But for the first time in my life, I wasn't going to back down because someone else thought they knew better than me.

I sighed, straightened my shoulders, and my resolve. I didn't need Vince to tell me what I knew was true. But I did need to get to Harrison's office.

I took my time getting ready. Redoing my hair and makeup in a sleek but professional way. And when it came time to choose what I was going to wear, there was no other choice.

The red power suit. Its time had finally come.

I pulled on my ass-kicking boots and took one final look in the mirror. The woman who looked back at me was a far cry from the one who'd started this adventure; the skittish sadness was gone from her eyes. And in its place was determination.

I called down to check to see if my printing was ready. It was, and after a quick cab ride, I found myself at the Flame Records offices.

Framed platinum and gold records lined the walls, and still

photos from concerts and awards shows. Some of the biggest names in the business. I walked slowly down the hall, like I was at a museum, with a fleeting sense of being way out of my league. My familiarity with Davis and the rest of the guys had made me forget just who they were. How big they were.

My palms started to sweat. But before I had a chance to turn on my heel and make a run for it, the door to Harrison's office opened, and he emerged, a sneer on his face.

"Campbell! So good to see you! I just got off the phone with a very irate Vince telling me under no circumstances am I to see what you've brought for me."

A stomach clench, like a punch to the gut, joined my sweaty palms. I opened my mouth, not even sure what I could say to defend myself.

"So, to say I am interested is an understatement. Come on in." He winked, in his smarmy way, stepping aside so I could go in first. It felt like I was selling my soul to the devil, but I walked into his office.

I sat across from Harrison and watched his very botoxed face attempt expressions while he looked it over. It was a good distraction. But it didn't stop the battle with the voices inside my head.

Vince was right. Nobody will want this story.
I should have just stuck to what they wanted.
I blew it.

Harrison's eyes got as wide as they apparently could as he flipped the last page over onto his desk. Then he stared at me blankly.

"Sorry, but I'm having a hard time gauging your reaction," I said slowly.

He drew a deep breath and let it out, and still said nothing.

"Listen, Harrison. I am going to need you to speak." I was a little shocked by my own boldness, but enough was enough.

He cleared his throat. "That's the thing. I have no idea what to say."

This was very unexpected. And still managed to tell me very little. "Is that a good thing or a bad thing?"

He leaned back in his chair and put his feet up on the desk. "It's a thing. That's about all I can tell you, for now. Thanks for bringing it in."

I was being dismissed?

Um, no. Not without some idea of his thoughts.

"So that's it? What do you want me to do now?"

"There's a two-week break until the next leg after tonight's show. I guess go home."

Go home? I stood.

"Just so you know, Davis was the one who filled in the blanks for me. Davis is the one who wants this story told. It'd be good to remember that. It's going to get out, you might as well control how. And frankly, no one knows it, or has captured it like I have here."

And then I walked out of the office and directly into Vince.

"Vince…"

He shook his head, but I kept going.

"You convinced me I should take this job because you were sure my life's goal wasn't to take studio portraits. And you were right. No matter how this turns out, I want to thank you for seeing something in me I couldn't see in myself."

His face softened at this, but he still didn't say a word.

I lowered my voice. "I'd be a shitty friend if I didn't return the favor." I laid my hand on his arm. "It's time for you to stop hiding in the wings. That spotlight has your name written all over it—because you are one hell of a songwriter, probably the best damn one on the planet. Stop letting whatever is telling you that isn't true make your decisions for you. Sow what you reap."

Then I leaned up and kissed him on the cheek, turned, and left.

Harrison was right about one thing: I should go home. Marissa would help me through this. I'd leave today, even if it meant that once again I wouldn't get to see the show in Los Angeles.

Back at the hotel, I was crossing the lobby to the elevator when I thought I heard my name. I stopped and looked around.

Nothing.

I took another step forward and heard it again.

"Psst! Campbell!"

This time I looked in the direction I'd heard it, and immediately burst into laughter.

Rex was standing behind one of the big palm trees, hat and sunglasses on. He could not be more conspicuously trying to be inconspicuous. I crossed to him, and just as I reached him, he reached out, grabbed my arm, and pulled me behind the plant. But the adventure didn't end there. He opened a door I hadn't seen, and we found ourselves in what seemed to be a small private bar.

"Rex, what the hell?"

"My question exactly. Why don't we have a drink while you fill me in." He winked, in that mischievous way of his.

"I can't. I need to pack up and head home." To my embarrassment, tears pricked the corners of my eyes and I pursed my lips, hoping to keep them there.

He shook his head. "Okay, we'll have none of this." He waved his hand at my face in a vague recognition of my tears. "And the tour is never over when you're one of the band."

This made the tears actually fall.

That one statement made me feel even more torn about what I'd done. Was it a betrayal? Vince thought so, Davis didn't. I hadn't realized how much I wanted Harrison to come down on one side or the other. The crying intensified.

"Seriously. I won't have any of that. People come and go on the tour all the time. And if you're going to go, well, not before we have a drink and a toast." He turned and walked toward the bar where there was already a bottle of whiskey, a bucket of ice, and two glasses.

"Do you guys just have some sort of assistant who scurries around behind the scenes and sets out bottles of whiskey for you?" I asked.

"Nah, I just say I want whiskey three times and it magically appears." He snapped his fingers. "Just like that!"

What could I do but join him? Suddenly, I really needed a drink.

"To Golden Tiger," I said, holding my glass out to his. He clinked and then took his all at once.

"I'll miss this," I said, watching him do that shot like I'd seen him do so many times before.

"Then why leave? There's a whole lot of tour left." He stood beside me, leaning on the bar, shoving the stool out of his way.

I shook my head. "I need some perspective. And a plan, if this doesn't all work out. What's next for me out there in the real world?"

He pointed at my glass. "Take it from me, the real world isn't all it's cracked up to be. There's no melody for people like you and me. Out there it's just background noise."

"Doesn't that just blow your mind? People treat the music like something to fill their silences and nothing else."

"Right? It's insanity. It shouldn't be background. It should be front and center." He pointed at me. "That first night in Chicago, when you said that about the bridge, I knew you got it."

"Vince doesn't seem to think so. And I have no idea about Harrison. It could all be for nothing." I took a sip of the whiskey and knew right then and there that if nothing else, the taste of whiskey, cold over ice, would forever be cemented with the sounds and men of Golden Tiger. I almost started to cry all over again.

"Nah. Because no matter what, with you, it's all about the music. And that's what Golden Tiger is all about."

I sat with that, sipping my drink, mulling it over. There was truth to it, but I still had doubts Vince would ever see it that way.

"You don't know the story I told," I finally said.

He turned and faced the bar, putting both hands on either side of the spot where the whiskey bottle sat.

"I know enough, and I lived it. The way I see it, even if it is some big scandal, it's going to make people want to listen to our music again." He turned and nodded. "And that's all that has ever mattered to me." He paused and took a drink from his glass, finishing it and setting it down on the bar. "And to Vince."

"He doesn't seem to see it that way."

Rex shrugged. "Vince is a stubborn dude. Always has been. He'll come around. He just needs to get used to the idea that he deserves the attention that's about to come his way."

I laughed. The thought of Vince soaking up attention was comical.

"You should at least stay for the show tonight. Golden Tiger down on Sunset? It'll be a good one."

The L.A. show. The original one had been iconic. They'd shot the music video for "Damn, Damnation" there.

I remember seeing it for the first time after Jack and I were married and agreeing with him that it was debauchery, all the while ignoring the punch-in-the-gut of regret I felt that I hadn't been there.

"Fine. I'll stay. Not that I had much choice after this whiskey. Which I feel like was your plan all along."

"Busted," Rex said.

"But not backstage. Front row center, balcony. I want to see the whole scene."

"I can do that," he said, smiling and pouring himself another shot before moving on to fill mine. I slid my hand over the top to stop him. I didn't need it.

I was going to see Golden Tiger. And it still made me giddy.

Chapter Thirty-Eight

Hours later, I was in my seat when the lights went down and the base came up. Historic venue aside, this was the first time I'd hear the songs live since finding out Vince had written them. And it was with that in mind that I watched and listened. Trying to hear just what in those songs would make a kid so nervous that he wouldn't lay claim to them.

Four songs in and I was overwhelmed. It was stunning to realize how many of the early songs about wanting the love and attention of a woman weren't romantic at all. They were about his mom. Wanting her love.

And, well, that was just sad.

Not that you'd know it from the way the guys were performing. They were better than they'd ever been. Midway through, Davis stood in the middle of the stage, a spotlight on only him. I knew the set list, they were supposed to be launching into their breakout hit, "Always Your Needs," but instead he leaned back onto a stool that had magically appeared, took a drink from the water bottle at his feet.

"Me and the guys, well, playing again together, this is

just a dream come true for us. And to have the crowds, our fans, show up the way they have, it has been a real treat." He stopped here. Was he choking up? What was going on? Finally, he spoke again.

"Me, and my brothers, because that's what these dudes are to me—we have an old saying. We never go easy. We go all in or we don't go at all. We were gone for twenty years. But you all, you've made coming back a dream. Like we never left."

I could tell from the looks on the other guys' faces that they had no idea what Davis was talking about, or why he was even talking. Off to the side, where I knew Vince was standing, there was movement, a shadow. He had to be wondering where this was going too.

Rex glanced toward Vince's shadow and shrugged, then he turned and gave a slow nod toward Tony, who gave a barely audible click of his drumsticks, but it was enough to get Davis's attention.

"Anyway, that's all I wanted to say. Actually, needed to say. I hope you all take that message from the show." He shifted so he was facing the exact spot where Vince was standing before he spoke again. "You go all in or you don't go at all."

I sucked air into my lungs, wondering if, in the end, Davis would be the one to convince Vince that his story needed to be told. Davis, his brother. The one who gave voice to his words. The voice and the words that had always been there for me when I needed them. And this was no exception, because once Davis started singing again, nothing else mattered.

Except maybe the glimpse I caught of Vince, stepping barely onto the stage and looking toward the balcony. Where he had to know I was, because Vince knew every single thing that happened on this tour. What did it mean? Acknowledgment? Acceptance? Was it his olive branch or his goodbye? My heart pounded, but there was nothing I could do but listen as Davis sang Vince's words and hope that at some point, Vince would say them to me himself.

"Going forward without looking back, that's how I roll. But you know, I know you do, baby, the only thing I look back for is you."

. . .

I drove late into the night. Until the lines of the highway felt hypnotic and I had to pull over and sleep in my car. The thought of another hotel room or motel room made my mouth go dry. Whatever Vince was doing by stepping out onto that stage, he hadn't followed it by trying to contact me. Not after the show or in the hours since. The only message I'd gotten had been a goodbye-take-care-see-you-soon, from Davis.

It was sweet but ominous and it didn't make me feel better. At all. I'd pulled into Marissa's house exhausted in all ways possible: physically, emotionally, and intellectually. And like the true friend she was, she was ready for me.

Sweatpants, pizza, and beer.

Life on the road had been glamorous at times, but could anything really top that trifecta? Add in sitting on the floor of the living room using the coffee table like a dining table and there was no surpassing it.

I told her about my meeting with Harrison, about Rex making me stay for the show in L.A. that I'd missed the first time around. I talked about anything and everything except Vince. Which I'm sure she noticed but didn't point out.

I couldn't talk about him because while I was worried about the book, the emotions I felt for Vince I couldn't pull together. All I had thought about as I'd driven west was that I had literally screwed up everything in one fell swoop.

Harrison sending me home to wait for his decision had

made me question everything. I'd thrown away my chance to get my book published by diving too deep. And by doing that, I'd hurt Vince in a way that I wasn't sure he could forgive me for.

If I tried to talk about it, I knew I'd just cry, and I didn't want to ruin the homecoming celebration she'd laid out.

"So, now what?" she asked, when we'd consumed the pizza and climbed up on the couch, curled on opposite ends with a blanket thrown over us both.

"Now I wait and see if Harrison green-lights the book." I took a drink of my beer.

She nodded, but her eyes narrowed. "And if he doesn't? Will you come back here, for good?"

The thought of that panicked me even more. For good? Here? I hadn't considered it. I shook my head.

"Davis texted me earlier. He said that no matter what happens, I always have a home with the band."

Her eyes softened. "Aw, Davis the old softie. You're always welcome here, too."

"I know." I sighed. "I'm just not sure I fit here anymore." I glanced at her hoping what I was about to say landed softly. "It feels too small somehow."

She took a drink of her beer. "If we're being honest, that's what I was afraid of when I left you in Chicago. Even in that one day you had started shedding the Campbell I knew."

My stomach clenched, and I waited for her to continue, hoping that the rest of it sounded better than the opening. The look on my face must have told her to soften the blow.

"Not that that was a bad thing. Like I said then, it was so obvious that you'd let yourself become someone else. The person I knew as Campbell isn't the person you know as Campbell."

"If it makes you feel any better, I had hidden her so deep, I didn't know myself." This was the biggest truth I had learned on the road, and probably why being back in this town felt so surreal.

She smiled. "Selfishly, I want you to stay."

I took a drink of my beer, and then pointed the bottle at her. "Selfishly, you should want me to go. I mean without me reliving my glory days, you wouldn't have slept with Davis Scott."

"Excellent point." She took a drink from her bottle. "Are we purposely not talking about Vince? Because I'm down with that, if you need me to be."

The mention of his name made the tears threaten in the corners of my eyes. "I don't know if he can forgive me. For the book. Nothing is more important to Vince than loyalty. And I know he sees what I did with his story as betrayal of that."

"But you said it was Davis who told you, so how can it be betrayal?"

"Davis only confirmed what I figured out on my own." I took a drink. "And apparently it doesn't matter what Davis wants when it comes to this." I told her about Davis and his message on the stage in L.A. "He was clearly talking to Vince, and maybe it mended fences with them, but I haven't heard a peep." I set my beer down, suddenly exhausted.

"You will. Remember I was there, before any of this drama. I saw the way he looked at you." She pointed at me. "You know that night at the party in Vegas, when I was talking to him, he was constantly glancing your way, checking on you, making sure you were okay."

I opened my eyes. "Or making sure I wasn't getting close enough to anyone to learn his secret."

Marissa shook her head. "No, I called him on it, told him you were a big girl and he didn't need to keep tabs. And he just smiled, but the way he did told me everything I need to know. He'll come around, I know he will." She patted my leg and stood up.

I pulled the blanket up around me. I wanted to believe her, I really did. So as my heavy eyes fell closed, I held on to her certainty, because I had none.

. . .

I woke up the next day feeling the same way. And the next. On the third day, Marissa forced me to shower and come to her coffee shop.

"You have to at least get out. Who knows how long these things take?" she'd said in her mom voice.

"You might as well just agree," her daughter, Sasha, had said. "I know that tone, and there's no arguing with it."

So I didn't. I went to The Jitterbug café and set up my computer optimistically, thinking I'd do some work on the book. Get ahead for when it was approved. But looking through the photos and my notes just left me even more upset. This was worse than the last time I'd left the tour. I'd been a part of it, not just chasing after it.

To make matters worse, more than one patron looked down her nose at me. And I overheard an entire table discussing how I had some nerve showing my face after I'd broken poor Jack's heart.

I packed up my bag and found Marissa in the kitchen.

"I gave it my best, but I'm not quite ready for the public yet."

She put down the mixing bowl she'd been drying. "What do you mean?"

I sighed and waved in the general direction of the dining room. "They are all squarely team Jack. At least I know for sure that if I don't go back to the tour, I am not staying here."

She glanced out the small cutout window at the women gathered at the tables. "Leave it to Jack to get the old ladies on his side. You want me to say something?"

I shook my head. "Nah. You don't need them badmouthing you or this place. They aren't wrong. I did break his heart."

She shook her head and pulled me into a hug. "Well, he broke your spirit. So, he deserved it."

He had, but I'd put it back together, and now here I was right back where I started. Except minus a husband, a job, or a place to live.

And not a peep from Vince.

I knew, because I checked my text, email, and voicemail at least seventy-five times a day. It was hard to not wonder where I'd be if I'd just listened to him. Asked the bland questions he'd suggested. Would I still be with the band? Would he have stayed in my bed?

It was my own special purgatory. But it felt more like hell. I went back to getting off the couch as little as possible.

The day the tour resumed, I woke up to Marissa looming over me. "The farmer's market is today. We'll head down there after we shower."

"Or we could stay here and watch movies?" I suggested hopefully.

She shook her head. "Nope. Enough is enough. You have to go out sometime. No arguing. Off to the shower. And don't make me send you back because you don't look to my standards."

I did as I was told. Begrudgingly, because I knew better than to argue with her.

We emerged at the farmer's market an hour later, me in big dark glasses, hoping to not draw any attention, and Marissa looking like an Instagram model, complete with adorable hat and basket.

After an hour of looking at produce, I tugged her toward the artisan stands. Beautiful handcrafted leather and mixed metal jewelry. Exactly the sort of thing I would need to go with my tour wardrobe. I let my eyes take them all in until I spotted a bracelet that made me catch my breath. A hammered silver bangle with an inlay of imitation tiger fur. My first inclination was sadness—would I ever see the tour again? But as quickly as the sadness came, it was replaced with anger, and then something else.

Sheer will.

"How much for this bracelet?" I asked, picking it up and handing it to the artisan.

"That's one of my favorites," the artist replied. "Strong, but feisty. Forty dollars."

Strong but feisty.

Marissa squeezed my arm.

I liked that. I fished the money out of my wallet and paid her. Declining her offer of a bag, I slipped it onto my wrist. Buying it felt like a manifestation of what I wanted.

To be back on the tour. To see my friends. To write my book. For Vince to forgive me. I smiled at the thought and let myself believe that I could will it to be true.

Chapter Thirty-Nine

I spent a month holed up at Marissa's, barely going out unless she forced me. Beating myself up for what I'd done, to the band, to Vince, to myself. Harrison had called and told me they still didn't have a decision, so there was no need for me to rejoin the tour. So, it went on, the entire Eastern swing of it, without me.

It made me sick to my stomach, but I did it. I even went to the coffee shop on occasion.

And then, with no fanfare, a plane ticket arrived. And then an email saying my draft was approved. And then a text from Davis, of all people, demanding I get my ass to Chicago.

Back to where it all began.

Those words held even more meaning for me as I stood outside, gazing up at the club's marquee. This was where my new life had begun. All because I bought a ticket to a concert.

Part of me wanted to watch from the balcony, like I had the first show in Chicago. But in the end, I wasn't really given a choice. The band wanted me backstage, and without a doubt, what the band wanted, the band got.

I pulled out my backstage pass, threw the lanyard around my neck, and walked through the door like I owned the place. Not even bothering to glance at the gathering hordes waiting in line.

"Campbell! Campbell!"

It was more of a shriek than a greeting. I turned and followed the voice to an oh-so-familiar face.

April.

Standing in the will-call line.

I raised my hand to wave and kept moving toward the entrance, but she was waving me over frantically.

"April. Nice to see you," I said, and I found I actually meant it. April was as much a part of the history of this scene as anyone.

"Can you get us in? No one left any tickets." Her eyes cast down as she said it and then as she raised them, they paused on my pass.

"How'd you get that?"

I picked up the large plastic pass from where it hung around my neck and glanced at it, feeling a sense of pride. I'd earned this thing, more than anything else in my life, ever. "The label sent it to me. I'm with the band now. Official photographer, visual storyteller."

I stepped in front of her and held it up to the guy in the ticket window. "Get this woman however many tickets she needs, okay?"

He squinted at my credentials and then nodded. "All we have is balcony."

That seemed fitting.

I stepped aside. "Enjoy the show, April." And though she looked less than pleased at her seating assignment, she still uttered a thank-you.

Which was very satisfactory.

Not that I was going to lord it over her, my new position.

Hell, as far as I knew she already knew where the after-party was and would be glued to Vince's side all over again.

Vince.

I don't know what I had been more nervous about in the past month, the verdict on the book or what would happen when I saw him again. I hadn't heard one word from him. Which was hard. I'd worked through wishing that I'd done things his way with the book. And I even hoped that he'd come to see this as an opportunity, that I'd meant what I said at Harrison's office that it was time and he was more than deserving of stepping into the spotlight. But his silence told me he didn't agree. I'd gotten half of what I wanted from my new life on the road, my book deal. That was just going to have to be good enough.

Even if it made the edges of my heart ache at the thought that our love story was not going to get an emotional, power-ballad ending. I'd been a warm place to fall for Vince and nothing more.

But hey, that was rock and roll.

Backstage was chaos. I flashed my badge at the very same young man who had told me to scram the last time I was here.

"I'm official this time!" I quipped to his confused face. Obviously, all middle-aged women looked the same to him. He managed a smile as I covered my embarrassment by walking quickly by his post.

"You're the puker! From the last time they were here. The lost puker."

"You must have me confused with someone else!" I replied, picking up my pace. I had not puked! Even if I'd felt like I could. Sort of like I felt right now.

I followed the noise farther into the labyrinth of backstage.

Sure enough, the noise got louder, and I could pick out a few familiar voices above the din as I wound myself around the dark hallways, and then there I was smack in the middle once again.

I swallowed. It felt like an eternity since I'd seen them all and now, here they were, in the flesh. And here I was, at their invitation. I hung back and just watched. Lifted my camera and started snapping the moment, the smiling and slapping each other on the backs.

Man, I'd missed the entire pack of overgrown teenagers.

I lowered my camera and was greeted with hoots and hollers, but above it all a thunderous, "Red!"

The circle parted as Davis made his way to me and pulled me into a hug. The kind you give a long-lost friend, but Davis being Davis still held it just a beat too long and whispered breathily in my ear.

"Red, if you looked any hotter, you'd blot out the sun."

I turned my head and replied directly into his. "You know, if you channeled these cheesy pickup lines into actual lyrics, you might have a hit on your hands."

He pulled back and looked me in the eye, shaking his head and giving me his signature smirk. The whole thing warmed my heart.

Rex was next, already handing me a shot of whiskey.

"I hope you haven't stopped practicing your drinking."

I took the shot, slammed it, and handed it back to him. "Nah, someone told me once, you should never get out of practice."

"Okay boys, the crowd won't wait another second for your sorry asses."

The sound of his voice startled me apart from Rex, whose eyes shot to the source and then back in my direction.

Vince.

I swallowed hard. Obviously I knew I'd see him. So why

was I so unprepared for the actual moment? And while I wanted to be professional and say hello, instead I shrank against the wall, behind Rex, and hoped he didn't see me.

"The house is full. Those people out there paid for a show!" he yelled.

"Let's give them a damn show!" the band yelled back in what must be a pre-show ritual I had never witnessed but was quick to capture on film. That instinct, to grab my camera and start shooting, made me forget for a second all about hiding.

They all started hooting and jumping, like a high school basketball team taking the court. They piled out the door, and by the time they had all cleared the room, Vince was gone, too.

I willed myself to ignore the way my heart had thudded. How the air had sizzled around me when I saw him, in his black T-shirt and jeans. How even though it had been oh-so-brief, I'd seen those crinkles around his eyes, the big smile he gave to the guys as he rallied them. I took a deep breath and headed to my spot in the wings. I had a job to do, after all.

Actually, I headed to Vince's spot in the wings. I braced myself to see him again. Here was my opportunity to show him that I was fine with how things were and be professional. But he wasn't there.

It was my answer. Whatever Vince and I had shared, past and present, was truly over. The friendship, the camaraderie, even that one perfect night, gone like a match once it's struck. He clearly couldn't forgive me for what he saw as betrayal for telling his story. I was gutted, and mad.

And then I was neither.

Because the click of the drumsticks brought my attention to the stage and the music started and I let it all go. After all, this could be the very last time Golden Tiger ever played together. This was the finale of the reunion tour, and I refused to let one second of stubborn Vince drama steal this moment away from me. And it wasn't just the bass or the drums, it was the lyrics, the harmonies. They came back to me, like they always had, and filled me with emotions I had shoved down for twenty years. But, gleefully, no longer.

Instead, they were now a release. For all of it.

They moved through their set, from ballad to hard driving rock anthem, and I felt each and every one of them. Singing along, dancing, and even remembering to take some pictures now and again.

"Ladies and gentlemen, we want to thank you for coming out tonight, and on the whole tour," Davis said, sliding himself onto a stool that had appeared on the stage. This time the rest of the band didn't seem to panic like they had in L.A.

"It's a dream come true for us to play together again, for all of you."

The crowd erupted in screams, and very clearly women yelling their devotion and intentions toward Davis. Which brought a sexy sneer to his face. "I love you all, too." More screams, myself included.

In for a penny, in for a pound as they say.

But then Davis shifted slightly back on the stool, and my breath caught. Vince stood in the opposite wing of the stage, guitar in hand. I barely had time to process it, because Davis was waving him onto the stage.

"We have a special treat for you tonight. Vince Caparelli, the longtime fifth member of Golden Tiger. Most of you have never heard of him, but you should have. And you will."

I swallowed. Vince settled onto a stool that had appeared next to Davis, resting one foot on the rung as he reached and plugged his guitar into an amp. I watched as he took a deep breath and swallowed. Then he closed his eyes, his fingers danced over the guitar strings, a tune I'd never heard, but chords I was oh so familiar with.

When the intro was done, Davis lifted the mic to his

mouth and began to sing.

Whiskey and the setting sun.
Second chances are too good for a man like me.
Just like you.
But when life blew you back in my path,
I'd be a fool to let you get too far.

Then Vince came in, harmonizing in his deep husky voice.

If you have to walk away, I'd never beg.
But, Jesus, how much can one man take?
Rosy retrospection isn't always enough.
I'll get what I deserve, I just pray that this one time,
I deserve to be heard.

Vince shifted now, looking past Davis and right at me. That same intense gaze bore into me, and I met it and couldn't look away. What was happening? Was this happening? Vince was singing to me.

And the song, the words. Could he possibly mean them? About him, about us? Everything seemed to be slowing down, and though it was a song I had never once heard, I felt like I could sing along.

We stayed that way until the end, and the moment was broken by the thunderous applause of the crowd. Sheepishly, Vince stood and nodded his head in acknowledgment, then he took a step in my direction before Davis held out a hand to stop him.

Damn it, Davis!

"I am pretty damn stoked to announce that song will be part of a new album. Golden Tiger is headed back to the studio when we wrap up this tour."

It was a monumental announcement, but all I could

focus on was Vince pushing past and making his way across the stage to the wing, toward me. Ignoring the crowd's enthusiastic response.

"Vince…"

He put a finger to my lips to stop me, which if I'm being honest was a good move. I wasn't even sure what to say.

"Here's one thing Davis didn't tell you. The last bit of my story. All those songs, that damn third album you play on repeat? They're all about you."

He paused. His eyes leveled right at mine. And I met them, but my mind was spinning.

About me? I mean, yes. I had recognized our night in Denver from "Sunset on the Side." It had been my first clue that Vince was the genius behind those iconic songs. But all of them? Me?

The too skinny, insecure, wannabe hanger-on? It wasn't possible.

"The first time I laid eyes on you, something burned inside me, it was like I was looking at something I didn't know I needed." His eyes bore into me as he spoke. The words coming so fast, like if he didn't get it all out at once, it wouldn't come out at all. "It scared the absolute hell out of me, and I handled it all wrong. Then and now."

I swallowed. Because what I'd come to realize, what I'd chosen to forget, was that I'd felt the same way. Vince, then and now, was like coming home.

I laid my hand on his cheek, and his went to cover it.

"You were my muse." He cocked his head to the side, a smile on his face. "On that tour. It's why I turned you away from the tour bus and the parties. So maybe, just maybe, you'd hang with me. Just having you around, for the first time in my whole damn sorry life, I had hope."

He let his fingers fall from my mouth to my waist. Pausing, but if it was for me to reply, it wasn't about to happen. Because

I knew what happened next, what I'd done.

"When you left that tour, my well dried up."

"Vince. I didn't know." It was a shock. I'd started this whole thing because I wondered what would have happened if I had made just one choice differently. And it turned out it was a choice I didn't even know I could have made.

All these wasted years. My eyes burned.

"How could you? I couldn't tell you. But with you gone, there was no point. So, I left, too. Abandoned my brothers, because I couldn't give them anything to play. They had to hire some songwriter to try and put together another album. And we all know how that went."

Another missing piece of the puzzle. Why the last album had been so horrid. I shook my head. I'd been searching for the story of what happened to Golden Tiger with no idea that I'd been a part of their collapse. I couldn't get my head around it.

"I hadn't written a damn thing in twenty years. God knows I tried. But it was all shit. I agreed to come on this tour hoping something would get me going again. Then lo and behold, you show back up, and I couldn't get my hand to keep up with the songs that came pouring out. That's why I left, in Vegas. I had to get it all out. But then you found out the rest, and I panicked. You knowing about me, about the music, when I'd just started writing again. I was terrified. I should have told you. I should have thanked you."

I smiled, softly. "Vince, you gave me my life back. I'm the one who should be thanking you."

His head was shaking back and forth. And I suddenly became very aware that on the stage, the band was not playing, instead they were all staring at us off stage, and the crowd, who couldn't see us, was starting to get restless.

Vince was oblivious, which was something in and of itself.

He slid his hands to my cheeks, as if to make sure I heard

what he said next. "I didn't give you shit. You took it. Like you should have all along. And you showed me it was time for me to do the same."

He rested his forehead on mine.

On stage I heard Davis whistle. And then lean into the mic. "My man, my brother. Finally." The crowd went insane and for a moment I feared Davis was going to wreck this whole thing and pull us out on stage and ruin the moment. But thankfully, Davis being Davis, he instead drew the attention back to himself.

"All right, enough with the mushy love stuff. You all came here to rock!"

And as the band finally started up their last number, the least romantic, guitar-blazing song they had, blasted as a backdrop to the most romantic moment of my life.

But it didn't matter. I lifted my chin to look Vince directly in the eye and found the familiar crinkle of the lines there as he smiled. Then, without hesitation, I kissed him.

Rock and roll fantasy complete.

From Publishers Weekly:

A starred review for Campbell Cavett's bombshell book on the Golden Tiger Reunion: Golden Tiger Uncaged

Cavett, an unknown in this space, breaks the mold in her photo essay book on the Golden Tiger reunion tour. Not only that, but she also introduces the rock and roll world to Vince Caparelli, stage manager, and apparently the man behind the band's biggest hits. This is a must-have for any true Tiger fan or rock and roll lover in general. Her photos, both action and portrait, are stunning peeks into the men who plastered the walls of our youth. She is a talent we should all be keeping an eye on for years to come.

From Rolling Stone:

Golden Tiger to release new album. Tour planned to promote it.

Fresh off their sold-out smash success reunion tour, Golden Tiger is poised to take back their place as the must-see tour of the summer. The new album, Flame to the Moth, is the first to give longtime stage manager, Vince Caparelli, the title of songwriter. And while he may step onto the stage from time to time on tour, don't expect him to become the permanent fifth member of the band.

"The spotlight isn't really my thing. So, while I'm happy to be making music with the guys, I'd rather leave the glory and all that goes with it to them," said Caparelli when we reached him by phone.

The album itself is a masterpiece of power ballads and beat-driven anthems, a throwback to their earlier work, most similar to their third album. Which is no coincidence, according to Caparelli.

"This album is inspired by my wife, Campbell Cavett. It's about comebacks and second chances and never being too old to bet on yourself."

Cavett is the creative force behind the best-selling book that both documented the reunion tour and introduced the world to Vince's talent. She is set to join her husband and the band on this tour as well to document it, though the angle for this is more of a behind-the-scenes vantage point.

"My vision has always been to show the average fan just what happens to make the songs they love come to life. That's the goal with this book," Campbell said. "I'm thrilled that the label and the band are having me along for this new tour. I am really looking forward to showing the workings of the operation. How a show like this is put on, all the love and work that goes into it."

When asked how she feels about being the inspiration for the songs on the album, Cavett demurred. "Vince has a real knack for capturing emotion in his songs. I hope my pictures can do the same for others."

As to the rest of the band's feelings about this new power couple dominating the story around the album and tour, they don't seem to mind one bit.

"Campbell, she's the real thing. What she does with that camera is like what Rex does with his guitar, pure magic," said longtime drummer, Tony Stephens.

"Happy to have Red join the tour. And for the world to

know that Vince is a genius when it comes to songwriting. But mostly I'm just happy to be playing together again. That's all it's ever about for me, getting to play music with my boys. We're all really just one big happy family," was the comment from Rex himself.

"Anything that makes the music come alive, that's what I'm about. And the ladies, I'm all about them, too," was the not-unexpected comment from lead singer, Davis Scott.

The album drops June first, and the tour kicks off at Wrigley Field two weeks later. Catch them if you can. A Golden Tiger show never disappoints.

Acknowledgments

Writing a book is hard. You start with the idea, and you build to your inevitable conclusion. But in the middle, you struggle, and you question, and you are sure none of it will come together in any way that is compelling or makes sense. But if you're lucky, like me, you have a whole host of people surrounding you to help you through the rough bits.

First, I'd like to thank all the women in my critique circles. My OG writing group of Shelley Shepard Gray, Heather Webber, Cathy Liggett and Hilda Knepp. Nothing is more fun than a writing retreat with you, and I would be nowhere without you. I am lucky to have you to challenge me, listen to me, and cheer me on. Jennifer Shirk, man, without you and those lockdown, virtual write-ins I'm not sure this book would have gotten finished. I can never thank you enough for all your hand holding and question answering. You are the stuff of legends, my friend. Kali White Van Baale, thank you for finally being the in-person critique partner I had been searching for since I moved to Iowa. You are always ready, willing, and more than able to lend a fine-tuned eye, or a kick in the pants when I need it. I am forever grateful to you!

Huge thanks to my agent, Jessica Faust for always pushing me to be better and think bigger. And for doing all you can to get this book we both love into the hands of readers.

And my editor, Stacy Cantor Abrams thank you for making this story the absolute best it could be. Through maybe the craziest year of your life, you took this diamond in the rough of a story and turned it into a gem. I appreciate it more than I can say. And to the whole team at Entangled, I cannot express enough gratitude for the work you have done on and for this book.

To my family, and my framily. My husband, kids, sister, brother and bestie thanks for being hands down my biggest cheerleaders and support. Thanks for listening to my never-ending stories about everything. Without you, none of what I do is possible. I love you all, oodles!

And finally, to Jenny O'Shea, who will never say no to any reunion tour ever, who are we seeing next?

About the Author

Julie Stone writes Rom-Coms with a more mature heroine, because Happily-Ever-Afters shouldn't have an expiration date. She grew up watching John Hughes movies, pegging her jeans, and avidly reading everything Judy Blume and Sweet Valley High. A native small-town Iowan, and graduate of the University of Iowa, she happily settled back in her home state over a decade ago. Always a fan of big hair and an even bigger fan of Eighties music, she is currently working her way through a bucket list of reunion tours. Follow her on twitter and Instagram to join in on the fun!

Discover more romances...

APRIL MAY FALL
a Mommy Wars novel by Christina Hovland

April Davis is a social influencer with a reputation for showing moms how to stay calm and collected through yoga—but behind the scenes, she's barely holding it all together. Then a live video of the "always calm" April, while she's most definitely not, goes viral...and her calm jumps ship quicker than her kids running from their vegetables. She's going to need a boatload of margaritas just to find her way back to herself again.

NOT SEEKING MR. RIGHT
a novel by Natasha Moore

Dumped by her wedding date, Ginny gives the guests some real gossip when a cute, younger man serving champagne flirts with her. But the incredible one-night stand gives her more than great memories. A few weeks later she's holding a positive pregnancy test. Lakeside is way too small for Josh's big dreams. When he gets a job offer he can't refuse, will Ginny follow a guy half her age across the country?

THE WEDDING CRASHER AND THE COWBOY
a One Week, Cowboy novel by Robin Bielman

Kennedy Martin is in for the longest week of her life. When her ex calls and expresses second thoughts about his upcoming wedding, Kennedy has no other choice than to crash the wedding and make him see that he's found the right woman for him. However, she ends up crashing into Maverick Owens, her old college nemesis. Now, through a week of wedding activities, Kennedy's stuck with Maverick...even though he looks way too sexy in his cowboy hat.

Made in the USA
Middletown, DE
06 February 2022